CRISS CROSS
Niallus J. Toner

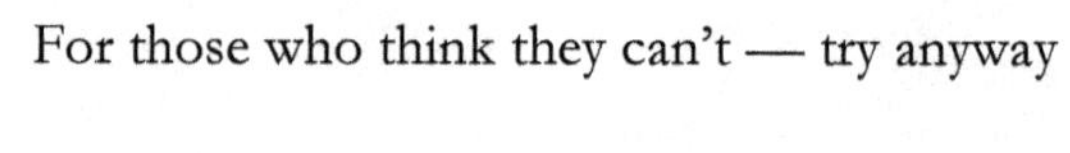

For those who think they can't — try anyway

ACKNOWLEDGEMENTS

Many thanks to my wife, Joan, for her patience and encouragement as I took this *Criss Cross* journey. I am especially grateful to my friends Barbara and John, who offered honest criticism, which allowed the characters to tell their story.

Published by The Fews Publishing

ISBN: 979-8-9951573-0-4

CHAPTER 1

The Prisoner

The prisoner awoke in a screaming sweat. Was it a dream—or his new existence? He surveyed the room: whitewashed walls, sour antiseptic smell—unfamiliar. The dull, pulsing pain in the back of his head yanked him to the here and now. Gallagher remembered his transfer from the cell to the hospital wing. The sterile scent of disinfectant was oddly comforting after years of cruelty, blood, and grime. He had temporarily escaped the prison's constant din—the clanging of metal and the shouting of men—but he would have exchanged this new quiet for that old noise if it meant silencing the throbbing pulse behind his eyes.

He pressed his palms against his temples, trying to crush the pressure from the outside in, but the rhythm just hammered on. He stared at the ceiling and waited for the room to stop tilting.

The door swung open. A man in a white coat stepped in, clipboard in hand. His gaze was neutral, his movements rigid. Gallagher pegged him as the prison doctor—a man whose clipped tones and stiff posture spoke of a soul long since cauterized by the system. He didn't look at Gallagher's face; he looked only at the chart.

"Your tests are back," the man said. His voice was flat—a mechanic reporting a broken part. "It's brain cancer." Gallagher offered no response. He didn't blink. He simply watched the man, his own face a mask of indifference that had served him well in darker places than this.

Without another word, the doctor turned and left. The heavy click of the lock echoed through the silence, a sound as final as the pronouncement itself.

Gallagher's blood ran cold. A tremor began in his hand, spreading quickly through his body, a silent scream building in his chest. For a long moment, he stared trancelike at the ceiling. The words hung in the air—somber. He lay still, wondering what would come next.

The last few years had been a whirlwind: from the oppressive heat of rainforests to the stench of overcrowded Colombian prisons. It was ironic that the thought of returning to semifamiliar surroundings had once brought him a measure of hope.

The trial was a farce. Witnesses had either died or claimed no memory of the incident in 1984. The English prison was tolerable compared to Colombia.

He swallowed hard in utter shock. A leaden weight pressed behind his eyes, a thick, dull ache that felt as if some cruel hand was squeezing his skull from the inside. He had thought that it may have been a tension headache or at worst a migraine, but cancer?

He had experienced tension from several sources recently. The extradition from Colombia, that was unexpected. He had thought that after six years in the hellhole in Bogotá he would be free to return to Ireland, or somewhere neutral. The British authorities had long memories and longer reach. They waited— never relented in their pursuit and had negotiated his extradition upon his release.

Most of the prisoners were too young to remember the conflict or ambush, and those who did were indifferent to it. Gallagher had become accepted by most of the prisoners as he had brought stability and ended bullying. The prison guards had come to respect his leadership; this news was going to change everything.

He lay wondering. He didn't have long to wait.

The heavy lock turned twice with a metallic clang. Bruce McIntosh filled the doorway—broad shouldered, close-cropped rust-steel hair, boots polished to satisfy a sergeant major. The keys didn't rattle; they sat heavy in a gnarled palm—a landscape of rope-burned ridges and thick calluses earned from years of service. His hands held the unnatural stillness of a man used to waiting behind a trigger, his thumb clamped over the brass to keep them silent. "Brendan." he said, voice throaty, the glens still rolling in the vowels. "Sorry for the news. It's a hard one." Gallagher gave a dry smile. "Aye. The Reaper, Bruce, he keeps his appointments. I've used up my quota." McIntosh swallowed. Something tightened along his jaw; he chewed once on the inside of his cheek and set a plastic cup within reach, straightening the blanket with one hand. "You've seen your share," he said. Not pity—just the blunt truths, measured out— no fancy wrapping, just like he did everything.

Gallagher's gaze stayed firm. Whatever twisted in his gut, he wasn't letting his guard down.

McIntosh nodded slow—rubbed his chin. "If you need the priest, I'll see to it. Five minutes."

He tapped his ring once against the bed frame—an old habit, then turned leaving Gallagher with his thoughts.

The British authorities had been secretive about Gallagher's arrival at the prison, but McIntosh had no problem with his new inmate. Some of the prisoners had responded unfavorably to the Irish rebel but before long Gallagher's behavior and his willingness to defend the underdog found favor.

The turning point came the day he stopped a beating. He found a trembling young lad crying behind a laundry bin. He was shaking, blood oozing from the corner of his bashed lip. Gallagher pulled him out, then turned on the attacker with fists like bricks. No warning, no words—just two savage blows, one to the gut, one to the jaw. The bully dropped like a sack of dirty laundry moaning and retching.

The other prisoners backed away in stunned silence, their eyes wide and glued to the crumpled form on the ground— then to the Irishman's inflexible eyes. Gallagher, his chest burning, stood over the bully, fists still clenched, his gaze hard and determined.

He didn't wait for him to get up—turned and walked away— tighthe thumping in his chest the only sound in the sudden quiet.

The bully lay in a heap—groaning. No one helped him up. Word spread.

The thumping in his head didn't stop until Gallagher reached his cell. The adrenaline from the fight began to cool, but the burning in his chest didn't fade—it climbed. The pulsation in his ribs moved upward, settling behind his eyes until it became that same rhythmic hammer he'd felt before.

He sat on his bunk and waited for the world to stop gyrating. The prison was quiet, but it wasn't the relief he wanted. The only thing he could hear was the steady, heavy pulse in his skull that refused to let him rest. Something from before this room had followed him in.

He set his jaw in stubborn determination—he had been in tough spots before and survived. This was just another hurdle, but the nagging pain told him otherwise.

The door opened with a loud clank as two powerfully built guards with blank faces of men lacking any semblance of pity, pushed a medical gurney into the room. Gallagher forced himself upright, determined to show no weakness. "Ready for your journey, general?" sneered the younger one, his voice contemptuous. Gallagher ignored the gibe and lay down on the stretcher. "Let's try and keep you comfy" said the older guard as he laid a pillow under the patient's head and strapped him in.

Within minutes they had exited the ward and into a large courtyard.

Gallagher could hear the familiar whirl of the blades of the helicopter before he saw his latest transportation, a Lynx. His mind drifted to the hundreds of unsuccessful attempts he had made to shoot one down. A powerful calm settled upon him, a quiet acceptance that the revolutionary days were gone.

No more insurrections. No more rebellions. No more causes to die for. The earlier injection began to kick in as he slowly drifted into a stupor.

The Lynx lifted into the grey dawn, its steady thrum drifting Gallagher toward uneasy sleep. In his haze, he dreamt of foggy alleyways and hurried plans, slipping through shadows as MI5 closed in. The rain in London fell like a river breaking its banks, sheets of water obscuring the city's ragged edges. The fugitive stood at the docks with a duffel bag slung over his shoulder, the salt-laced wind tugging at his jacket. Behind him lay a cause that had shaped him, bruised him, betrayed him, and denied him. Before him, a commuter boat waited to carry him away to another cause, another revolution.

After the failed mission in England the leadership had denied the movements involvement and made it clear that Gallagher was no longer welcome in its ranks. No word of acknowledgment, no support. The men in the small group he'd led—fought beside had evaporated into the London fog. It was not the leaving that saddened him, but the manner of it.

Gallagher had spent his boyhood in Derry's sectarian divided streets, where he learned to fight playground bullies and stand up for those who couldn't. This fierce instinct had drawn him into trade union meetings as a teenager, where he witnessed the exploitation of working men   by indifferent bosses.

The IRA had seemed a natural extension of that cause, a fight against tyranny in uniform. But like so many wars, this one had turned in on itself.

As the ferry pulled away, he didn't turn back—a figure on the deck, a solitary silhouette against the sinking sun. The only passenger carrying nothing but a battered bag and a history too heavy for a man his age, hoping that his new chapter would have a more favorable ending.

CHAPTER 2
The Cage

Bogotá's air hit him like a soggy, clammy towel. Thick, soupy heat and diesel fumes gripped his lungs the moment he stepped off the bus. The city's pandemonium was everywhere—a wild chorus of honking cars, hollering vendors, and spluttering motorbikes. Gallagher fumbled through his pockets for the note, his fingers slick with dampness.

He'd been sent the name of a contact—a former Irish labor organizer named Kerrigan. Kerrigan was a man who had blended into this dubious environment, trading his old socialist ideals for a shady life overseeing protection for wealthy landowners.

Kerrigan's words felt like a gentle touch, carefully chosen to disguise the truth. He painted a picture of the M.A.S. as a shield—a buttress of fairness protecting peasants who he insisted, had pleaded for their help against the guerrillas. He spoke of families huddled in fear, their homes threatened, their crops destroyed, and how the M.A.S. had stepped in—their presence a promise of safety in a land ravaged by conflict. He had assured Gallagher that the paramilitary group had been formed to protect the peasants against the guerrillas. They were a shield for the innocent.

He greeted Gallagher with a handshake like a vice and a smirk that made Gallagher's skin crawl. "Welcome to the new frontier, Paddy." Gallagher stiffened but ignored the slight. His stomach pulsed. He felt he was tightrope walking a treacherous gorge—was it too late? He convinced himself to believe the description his contact had given him. His heart rate increased, but he believed it might be

Kerrigan's obnoxious personality. Still, it paid well and promised purpose—or at least, the illusion of it.

Kerrigan assigned him to a squad, assuring him that once he had become familiar with the terrain, he would have his own squad.

Something curled in Gallagher's gut when Kerrigan assigned him to a "squad." The word sounded more like a hit team than a defense unit. The first raid made him question everything.

The village was called San Miguel—scarcely more than a scattering of huts with corrugated iron roofs. M.A.S. rolled in with jeeps squealing and machine guns at the ready. Men were dragged from their homes and lined up in the dust. A young man was pulled from the line. No questions were asked. The leader of the squad yelled accusations in the prisoner's face, giving no time for an answer. Without a shred of evidence, the man was executed in front of his wife and children. His crime? Owning a radio.

Gallagher watched in horror. He had seen this scene play out before, thousands of miles away. Later, back at the compound, when he voiced his anger, a commander named Vargas sneered. "You think this is your war, gringo? This is survival. These bastards would slit your throat for a kilo of rice."

Gallagher spoke to Kerrigan. The big Irishman clapped his hands and guffawed. "Don't let these vermin fool you, Paddy. We intend to crush the bugs, every damned one of them." It was a refrain he would hear often, each repetition whittling away at his belief that he was fighting for the people. But which people?

The faces of the victims began to haunt his sleep: a girl with a bloodied doll, an old man clubbed to death for refusing to give up his land. Their eyes held the same shattered look he'd seen in the families on that terrible Sunday in his native home.

After such a raid, Gallagher sat alone at the edge of the camp, despondent. His brow wrinkled, a heavy sigh escaping his lips as the weight of his choice engulfed him—a decision he knew, with mounting certainty, he would forever rue. Poor planning—not investigating Kerrigan before he had walked into this quagmire.

The breaking point came six months later at a village called La Piedra. Gallagher knew there were no fighters there—only poor farmers too stubborn to abandon the land their forefathers had farmed for centuries. That night, under the cover of darkness, he slipped away from the camp. He reached La Piedra before dawn, rousing the elders.

When the M.A.S. arrived, they found a deserted village and makeshift defenses. In the brief firefight that followed, Gallagher defended the huts as if they were his own home in the Bogside. Many of his targets were men he had once called comrades. By nightfall it was over. The village smoldered, but the people had escaped into the hills.

His betrayal did not go unnoticed. M.A.S. patrols combed the jungle searching for him. Weeks later, one of his former M.A.S. members—a young fighter named Sandoval, whom he'd once saved in a skirmish—found him huddled in a ravine, bleeding from a bullet graze. "I should kill you," Sandoval spat, but his hand shook. "You betrayed us." Gallagher looked up, unafraid. "I betrayed murderers. You are young, my friend. You will come to believe me some day. I hope for you it is not too late." The young squad member glared at Gallagher, turned and disappeared into the jungle.

Gallagher moved furtively under the cover of night clouds, breathing lightly as he slouched unnoticed from village to village. The peasants weren't farmers any more. They worked coca fields under the eyes of armed men, their harvests weighed and loaded into government trucks while they were left with barely enough to live.

Gallagher's arrival brought them more than tactics—it gave them a reason to push back. He taught them how to buttress their land, carve escape routes through the hills and use the terrain to their advantage. Concealed paths were improvised, food and weapons buried, first-aid shelters camouflaged. To them, he was a phantom. They called him

Fantasma—the ghost—appearing without warning and gone by dawn, leaving only stories of his exploits. In the end, it wasn't M.A.S. that captured him.

His luck ran out in Santa Lucía.

Gallagher had moved to a small village named Santa Lucía and learned that M.A.S. had searched for him and burned most of the village in reprisal for the villagers being unable—or unwilling— to give any information of his whereabouts. Feeling both guilty and obligated, he delayed leaving. This punishment on his behalf grated on him—causing Gallagher to stay longer than usual in the village.

One of the villagers unwittingly divulged his presence to the guerrillas, and days later the village woke to the sound of jeep engines roaring and sputtering—tires spraying sand, gunfire and barking dogs as six jeeps screeched into the sleeping settlement. Gallagher sprawled for his M-16—too late. His wrist stung as a heavy boot stomped. Because of his earlier involvement with M.A.S., he expected a bullet and a shallow grave. But these were pragmatic men.

A foreign mercenary was a valuable asset. They'd find a use for him. They hustled him into a jeep, lined four young men along a ditch and riddled them with bullets. The ghastly sight and traumatic experience would remain with Gallagher for the rest of his life.

His prison was a bamboo cage deep in the jungle, guarded by men scarcely older than boys. The air was thick with mosquitoes, and sickness was a constant companion. The food was watery gruel, the water drawn from streams that ran brown in the rainy season. There was a boy named Tomás, no older than twelve, who brought him books scavenged from deserted schools—faded pamphlets of Marx and Guevara, dog-eared copies of Gabriel García Márquez. Gallagher read them all, hunger for understanding filling the void where old convictions had died. One of García Márquez's quotes had stuck with him. His grandfather, whom he called Papaleo, had said, "You can't imagine how much a dead man weighs." Gallagher read and reread the line. Too well he knew there was no greater burden than to have killed a man.

Six years passed in that cage, marked by scratches on a bamboo pole. Then, as suddenly as a torrential downpour he was traded. A new President in Colombia, seeking to ease international pressure, negotiated the release of foreign prisoners. The prisoner Gallagher was handcuffed, shackled, with ankles bound, marched through the Colombian jungle, relentless rain driving him onward as he navigated thick jungle terrain in extreme heat, hollowed by hunger. A shift hit like a tripwire, sudden and jarring. At the end of the harrowing march, he was handed over to government forces.

He had assumed his starvation was over, but the British were waiting. Processed as a terrorist, he was sent back to the Kesh prison in Belfast, only to find himself a pariah. The IRA command viewed him as a "political embarrassment." Old comrades refused to visit. He was a relic of a war they were trying to dress in suits and ties.

New factions viewed him as a relic—lesson learned. The British authorities later transferred him to Durham Prison— what they called "for his protection," a polite way of saying he was a man without a country.

When the seizures started, they were mild at first. Then came the transfer to a prison hospital as they increased. A possible tumor, they said. Inoperable. Three months, maybe less.

Now, lying in the pitiless bed as autumn light leaked through barred windows, Gallagher chased ghosts. He spoke to the ceiling, to faces only he could see—to the girl with the doll, to Tomás with his battered books.

Did any of it matter? Gallagher waited in edgy anticipation. The carefree confidence he once had was diminished by the undefeatable enemy attacking his body. Any sign of courage now was strictly bravado.

He wondered where he was and what was in store for him. The Brit had said he was back in Belfast—but why? There were none of the usual protests or negotiations to return this prisoner. He was no longer part of any republican faction. Many of his former comrades would consider him a deserter of the struggle. His thoughts felt wrapped in fog, every memory muddled and jumbled, yet somehow it was the past that always forced itself to the surface—clearer than the room around him.

CHAPTER 3

The Transfer

The damp chill was a sharp needle compared to the heavy, humid blanket of Bogotá. Gallagher felt the transition not in his mind, but in his lungs. The air in the Belfast ward was thin and carried the biting scent of industrial bleach—a cold, sterile greeting that told him he was home, even if home was just another set of locked doors.

The door opened, and two men in white coats entered. Their mannerisms contrasted with the military personnel. They weren't soldiers or guards—their quiet movements lacked the rigid discipline Gallagher had come to expect. They showed professional etiquette as they lifted him from the cot and placed him on a gurney. Gallagher maintained his composure, but the unbidden wince as they shifted him told the real story.

The wheels of the gurney rattled over rough floors as they rolled him through a dark tunnel and a maze of cold corridors. They finally reached a small, sterile room equipped with two threatening monitoring devices that pulsed with an ominous, mechanical rhythm. The hospital smell hit him first—a familiar scent of disinfectant. Another prison cell.

The orderlies showed a surprising touch of humanity as they gently laid him on the bed. Gallagher groaned; the movement sent sparks through his skull. He felt the prick of a needle in his arm. "What was that?" he managed.

"Just something to help you relax," the orderly replied kindly. "It's been a difficult few hours."

He had no idea how long he'd been out when the clatter of utensils on the metal tray at his bedside woke him. He turned toward the sound. For a moment, he wondered—was it an angel? Was he dead? The pain assured him otherwise. He squinted at the figure of a beautiful young woman in a nurse's uniform. He coughed quietly to get her attention. "Oh, you're awake, Mr. Gallagher," she smiled.

Several wisecracks came to mind, but he decided to stay silent. It had been a long time since he'd seen a woman—let alone one so pretty. "My name is McCracken," she offered.

Gallagher couldn't help but smile. "You're amused?"

"No, no," he hastened. "It's just the name—I'm sure not Joy?"

She recognized the humor. "No—happens to be Henrietta," she said coyly.

Gallagher choked with laughter and coughed until Nurse Henrietta McCracken brought him a cup of water, supporting his head gently until he could swallow. He lay back, gesturing his thanks. The nurse busied herself preparing a syringe and gave him another shot. As he drifted off, his last recollection was the irony of Henrietta McCracken—and he wondered what the backstory was. Henrietta McCracken—a name with enough history to fill a book.

The relief was short-lived. He was awakened by the familiar pain in the back of his head. The click of the door sharpened his reflexes. He instinctively closed his eyes and waited. Years of caution had made it automatic. He strained to listen—the footsteps were heavy, rhythmic, the sound of authority. A large man.

As he squinted through failing eyes, he made out a police uniform. He felt the man's glare like a physical weight. Is this it? Will this assassin outdo the cancer? The thought wasn't entirely unwelcome; a bullet might be cleaner than the excruciating slowburn of the tumor. He waited and thought of God. It was too late to ask for forgiveness or clemency. It had been too many years since he'd spoken to Jesus or Mary; it would be hypocritical to start now.

The minutes dragged like hours. The pain began to control his emotions. He wanted to cry—just to end it all. He could feel the cop's breath, smell the cigarettes and stale beer. Then came the voice, filled with pure, unadulterated venom. "I hope you suffer for a long time, you bastard."

"You bastard," the man repeated, louder, as he stomped toward the door. Gallagher groaned. He hadn't the strength or desire to answer. He turned away and hoped Nurse McCracken would rescue him. Instead, the door swung open with a whoosh of talcum powder and medication—but it wasn't McCracken. An older, sharper nurse stared the officer down.

"Aren't you supposed to be standing outside the room?" she said, emphasizing "outside." The cop turned and left without a word.

Gallagher lay exhausted, his emotions tangled. Escaping death felt natural enough, but it might only have delayed the inevitable. He looked around the sterile, impersonal room. Functional—vital sign monitors on one side, a tray stand on the other. The clock on the wall ran silently. With his failing eyesight, he strained to read the time. Two-thirty-five? Seven ten? He guessed morning—seven ten made sense. Changing of the guard, perhaps. The heavy cop just starting his shift. That meant the day nurse would be on soon—and with luck, morphine. He wondered how long he'd have to wait.

He waited—time uncertain. "Okay, young man, let's get you more comfortable," a voice said. The nurse pulled his weak body up and propped two pillows behind his head. She poured a glass of juice. "Can you handle this?"

"Thank you, yes. I can manage. I promise not to spill it." "Good boy," she said casually.

He studied her—no-nonsense, sharp-edged, treating everyone the same. "Young man" wasn't mockery; it was control. He didn't take it personally. In fact, "young man" was almost welcome. He watched as she adjusted the monitors. "What's your name?" he asked, forcing friendliness.

"Nurse Moffett," was all she said. He realized the conversation was over. He moaned and hoped she was preparing a shot. From the corner of his eye, he saw her holding a syringe. He wasn't sure how long it had been since the last one. "What time is it?" he asked finally.

"It's not time yet," she said—words she'd spoken too often. "It's seven o'clock. I'll be back in an hour."

Seven A.M. or P.M.—did it matter? Nurse Moffett didn't allow appeals. The door clicked open again. No heavy boots this time. No patter of soft steps, either. She was beside the bed, arranging medications on the table. Gallagher coughed, and she turned. "Good morning, Mr. Gallagher. I hope you had a good night."

She was pretty—about thirty, he guessed. "Yes, thanks," he lied. He watched impatiently, fingers twitching in anticipation of the oblivion as she filled a syringe with a blue liquid and slid the needle

painlessly into his arm. He knew that within thirty minutes, the pain would ease. "Thank you, nurse.
What's your name?"

She was already at the door when she turned with a smile. "I told you yesterday—I'm Nurse McCracken."

And she was gone. The twitching in his fingers moved up his arm. He closed his eyes, craving oblivion. No relief came. With a terrifying jolt, he realized his memory loss. Was he losing his mind? He had no memory of seeing the young nurse before. What was happening inside his head now—the threads of his life were fraying, snapping one by one.

The door opened again. Nurse McCracken returned. "I forgot to mention—your clergyman will be here tomorrow morning."

Struggling to control the pain, Gallagher grunted. "My clergyman? Believe me—" he inhaled, "—I don't have a clergyman."

"I'm sorry—your priest," the nurse replied.
The pain was winning. He didn't insist he had neither priest nor clergyman. He simply nodded, thinking McCracken might well be Presbyterian. "And one other thing," she added.
"The doctor will come and chat with you in the morning."

Her news distracted him. A priest and a doctor? Who— and why? He knew death was creeping closer, but who had called a priest? He'd long ago cut ties with religion. His old comrades had disowned him. His family was gone. Who would bother to send a priest? Then it dawned on him. He wasn't in a prison hospital anymore—this was a hospital, perhaps even a hospice. A place where priests came fishing for souls on their deathbed.

Morning came in dull gray light. Gallagher's eyes hurt. Nurse McCracken was back, carrying a cup of water and her usual smile. "You've a visitor," she chirped.

"A visitor?" Gallagher frowned.

A tall, clean-shaven man in a priest's collar stepped in. Midforties, a condescending gleam in his eye. Gallagher stared through the blur. His gut tensed. The priest's patronizing smile rubbed him the wrong way. "I'm Father Taylor," he said aloofly. "How are you feeling, son?"

"Like shite," Gallagher muttered.

The priest gave a half-smile. "You're lucky to be alive."
"People keep telling me that," Gallagher replied coldly.

Taylor pressed on with strained small talk about family and where he was from. Gallagher rearranged the knives and forks on his tray, giving little away. "Donegal," he said at last.

"Good people up there," the priest nodded.
Gallagher turned toward the window, silent. They sat in uneasy quiet until the priest finally stood, glared, and left.

At the nurses' station, he muttered to McCracken that she might want to find another chaplain. Moments later, McCracken poked her head in, her mischievous smile softening the room. "You gave that man a hard time?"

"He's a priest," Gallagher rasped. "Comes with the territory."

She laughed—a light, easy sound that made him think, just for a moment, of better days. Of a girl he'd known long ago. A memory that felt real, even if he couldn't remember her name

CHAPTER 4

The Confirmation

Gallagher lay in a stupor that dulled the edges of the world. The monitor's steady beep held him in the room, a tether to reality that grew thinner with every pulse. Every so often the line between memory and present blurred. At times he was clear-cut, speaking with purpose; the next, he wasn't sure if the words and thoughts belonged to now or to some half-remembered dream.

The morphine had taken control. He had gradually passed into a fleeing, confused blankness. He was buffeted from place to place. In the haze, he was an altar boy in his native Derry only to be thrust centuries back, a warrior general fighting on the banks of the Blackwater River, as he led his men in the Battle of Benburb in 1646. His dream was a chaotic mess, hurling him from childhood simplicity through guerrilla skirmishes and severe sleep deprivation.

Then, slowly, the noise abated. He forced his eyes open, clutching at the here and now. The ceiling above him was blank, steady, real. He lay still, breathing hard, waiting for the world to stop spinning.

Dr. Collins knocked gently before entering. Mid-fifties pale-faced, eyes weary from years of suffering. There was kindness in him, a quiet steadiness Gallagher welcomed. No idle chit-chat— straight to the point.

"Mr. Gallagher… I'm afraid the recent scans confirm what we suspected. It's a malignant glioblastoma—a tumor deep in the temporal lobe."

He let the words settle. Gallagher felt them more than heard them—like a stone pressing into his chest.

"It's aggressive," Collins continued. "Fast-growing. Without intervention… months, perhaps a year at most." Silence.

Only the clock answered.

"We can consider options. Surgery—though risky given the location. Radiotherapy might slow progression. It wouldn't be easy, but it could buy you time."

Gallagher exhaled, leaned forward until his hands found his knees. "And what the hell would I do with that time, Doctor? Fade away in a hospital bed while the world eats itself alive outside my window?"

The doctor nodded. "It's your decision. But without treatment, symptoms will worsen—headaches, confusion, seizures. It won't be a gentle road."

"I was never one for the gentle road. I've walked the road less traveled so far—why change course now?"

"I understand," Collins said, accepting the answer. "If you change your mind, my door's open. Tell the nurse."

"You're a good man, Doctor. But I'll die on my own terms."

After he left, Gallagher drifted again. The colorless scent clung to him like a shroud. A searing pain—hot, piercing— spread through his chest. He gripped the bed frame until his knuckles whitened against the cold metal. "End it now," he choked. "It's too much." Silence answered.

Then—soft hands, a gentle voice. Nurse McCracken.

"We need to get you freshened up for your visitor."

Visitor? The word felt foreign. He had forgotten entirely. The nurse shaved him with patient care, brushed his hair, and stepped back with a small smile.

"Now you look handsome and ready."

The pain eased. The hum of the room softened.

The door opened again. Nurse McCracken returned, this time followed by a man in civilian clothes—tall, athletic-looking, balding, with a face that still held a trace of youth despite the years. The man came close, leaning into the light so Gallagher could see him clearly. The priest's face was creased with sadness as he came close.

"Don't you recognize me, Brendan?"

Gallagher flinched. The sound of his forename was like a ghost calling from the fog. He squinted, his failing eyes searching the blurred outline of the man's face.

"The altar boy… Gasworks…" he whispered, then drifted again.

O'Kane watched him, guilt settling like dust in an ignored house. His childhood protector reduced to frailty and chaos. He had spent his life in the sanctuary of the Church, while the man before him had been out in the storm.

O'Kane reached out, hesitant, and finally held Gallagher's hand. The skin felt like dry parchment over bone.

"I should have stayed in touch," O'Kane whispered, his voice cracking. He realized now that while he had been praying for souls in the abstract, the soul that had once saved his own had been suffering in the dark.

He whispered a short prayer—not the aloof, polished Latin of Father Taylor, but a desperate, quiet plea—then stepped out, promising Nurse McCracken he would return. He walked down the corridor, the "Mannerly" priest finally forced to face the man he had left behind.

CHAPTER 5

The Divided Path

The past came flooding back to a glen in Donegal. It was a chilly early spring morning as Gallagher and his comrades sat tired and wet, eating breakfast after a night running demanding drills— training and maneuvers in the nearby mountains. All eight of them hunched on the damp grass, steam from their mugs rising into the pale air. They ached, but the newly arrived rocket launchers had them enthusiastic; victory felt close enough to taste. Most were convinced that victory was close at hand.

The conversation was lively as each man discussed his future.

"So, what do you think we'll all do when the country is free?" one asked, his eyes bright with hope.

"Politics for me," another said— "already half in with the party men."

One swore he'd keep soldiering. Others spoke of going home, picking up the lives they'd dropped. Gallagher warmed his hands over the stove, keeping his thoughts to himself— quiet.   Rain drifted in, and the group shifted under their jackets.

"And what are your plans, Brendan?" one finally pressed.

Gallagher turned, slow and deliberate. "Well, I'll tell you... I'll be surprised if they don't screw it all up. But if this ends, I'll just go and find another war. There's always plenty of revolutions going on."

The words hit them like a physical blow. A silence spread through the glen. Someone cleared his throat; another studied his mud-caked boots. No one knew what to say and if they did, no one was prepared to question Brendan Gallagher. He wasn't fighting for a seat in a new parliament; he was fighting because the fight was the only thing that made him feel alive.

The glen faded.

He floated to the grey streets of London on a cold, wet afternoon. He and two comrades were pinned down for two hours in a flat at the corner of Wharton Street and Lloyd Square. The air was thick with the smell of cordite and old wallpaper. One of his team had been shot as he tried to escape through the back yard. Gallagher felt the guilt like a lead weight. He had led them into a dead end. They had blown up a pub frequented by soldiers, and the retreat had turned into a bloodbath. Two police officers were down. But now disaster.

His men had trusted him as their leader and protector.

There was no easy escape. Gallagher looked at his two remaining men—young, terrified, looking to him for a miracle. Gallagher had gone over multiple options, but none seemed workable. He made his choice. He would claim he had forced them at gunpoint to let him inside the flat, taking the full weight of the ambush onto his own shoulders to save them from a life sentence.

As he stepped from the building with his arms raised, he shouted into the sirens, "I'm here! I'm here!"

The dream broke. Nurse McCracken pressed her hands on his shoulders, steadying him. Panic seeped from Gallagher's every pore; he shivered, a clammy chill consuming him.

The nurse wiped his brow with a warm towel recognizing the night sweat. "Good morning. That was a nasty dream. It's time for your shot."

Gallagher breathed rapidly — heart pounding. He was exhausted but relieved. He wondered what the time was, knowing it was irrelevant. The nurse released the contents of the syringe painlessly into his arm with compassionate and professional care. He lay waiting for the relief, hoping there would be no repeat of the earlier nightmare.

The relief came quickly. No dreams—just a shot.

When he awoke, sunlight filled the room. A tray had been placed beside him by a silent young aide with an ashen face. Gallagher watched him go, feeling helpless, purposeless. A heroic death in some imagined battle would have been preferable to this slow humiliation.

"How are you feeling Mr. Gallagher?" It was nurse McCracken. "Did you sleep well?" When confronted with such warmth Gallagher was forced to respond in kind. "Glad to see you today," he answered, still not being sure of the time, but glad he remembered her.

"Come, let's try and get some food into you," she coaxed, as she struggled to raise him up.

He tried—for her sake.

"Oh—before I forget," she added. "You're having a visitor today."

"A visitor? For me?"

"Yes. Your old school friend. Father O'Kane", she said.

"He said you nodded off yesterday and he wanted to come back."
O'Kane? Gallagher searched his memory. A blank ache throbbed at the
back of his skull.

"When did you get your last medication?" she asked softly,
preparing the syringe. Gallagher didn't answer, The answer was right
there, a flickering shape just behind the fog—beyond his reach.

The needle's bite felt sharp, an icy sting in his arm Then came
the heavy rush, a wave of liquid lead that started in his arm and
surged toward his throat. The nurse's face softened, stretching into a
pale, featureless shape before the dark pulled him under. Within
seconds, he drifted into oblivion.

The bright light startled him as he came to. A man stood over him.

"Hello, Brendan. How are you?"

The voice was gentle. Civilian clothes, not clerical.
Gallagher blinked, focusing his eyes.

"It's been a long time. Don't you recognize me?" "No,"
Gallagher rasped. "Who are you?"

"It's Liam O'Kane."
The name struck him like lightning. He remembered the altar
boy. A sad smile flickered across his face.

"Yes… Liam. I see you now. Where did all the curls go?"

O'Kane laughed. "Long gone Brendan. Long gone."

"You're not here to convert an incorrigible, are you?" Gallagher
managed.

"No. I'm here to thank a great friend."

"For what?"

"For rescuing me from a beating by the school bully—

Maxwell."

"Maxwell," Gallagher muttered, the name tasting like bile. "God's gift to the schoolyard."

"Aye. Strange how paths cross again," O'Kane murmured.

"Do you ever think of the hereafter, Brendan?" the priest asked quietly.

Gallagher laughed weakly. "I'm a believer in living in the now—whatever that is. Yesterday's gone. Tomorrow? We'll deal with it when it comes."

"You clerics have no idea. People live in Sodom and Gomorrah every day."

He sank back into the pillow.

O'Kane leaned forward. "Brendan… you still have a say in one thing. How you go out. Not them—you."

"Out? There is no out. They shot my father without a word. Broke my mother's heart. You think I've any illusions left?"

"I've seen good men left without a voice at the end," O'Kane whispered. "You don't have to be one of them."

Gallagher coughed, half-laughing. "I've already told them. No treatment. Just morphine. No property to give away. No last famous quotes. Incinerate me and scatter my ashes anywhere. Who gives a damn?"

"I do, Brendan… I do."

Gallagher drifted again, this time to the last day of his and O'Kane's childhood.

They had met by chance on a dull afternoon. O'Kane spoke shyly of attending St Patrick's College in Armagh.

"You're going to be a priest?" Gallagher asked.

"Well… maybe someday," O'Kane muttered, his voice almost apologetic.

Gallagher laughed. "When we were serving Mass, I thought I heard a calling too—but it must've been for you."

O'Kane whispered sensitively, "Many are called, but few are chosen."

They parted ways. Two boys. Two paths.

That night, Gallagher lay awake thinking of the eleven-plus. His stomach twisted.

His failure had been a great disappointment to his parents, and he realized it would be the end of his friendship with Liam.

CHAPTER 6

Echoes

The air felt fresh as O'Kane exited the hospital. His mind was in chaos. Nurse McCracken had prepared him for the visit. He was ready, or so he thought. He knew that Gallagher was ill, extremely ill, next to death, but he was not prepared for the image. He had administered to dying patients before, but the shock of seeing his boyhood protector was excruciating. He had only seen Gallagher once from their school day years. They were both in their early twenties. O'Kane was a recently ordained priest, and he assumed his friend Gallagher was a trade union organizer. Gallagher, ever the leader, was handsome, fit-looking, and friendly. Their meeting was by chance. There was no blame game as to why either had forsaken their earlier contact. Within minutes, the years had dissipated. The priest and the trade unionist were no longer; just two boys chitchatting, laughing, remembering old times. The meeting was brief; the parting was without ceremony—no promises.

Gallagher had always shown great confidence, but the more O'Kane became acquainted with him, the more he learned their similarities. Gallagher had come across as being nonchalant, but as they chatted on their way from school, he was to learn that his new friend had a soft side, with the same fears and insecurities of most boys of pre-teen years. They were both religious, without being "holy Joes." They, with other boys, had long discussions about Heaven and Hell. When conversations came up about Confession, it always finished in controversy. Some suggested it was unfair for priests to hear about sins, while others thought it was boring having to tell the same stories each time. They planned that each boy would admit to a new sin at their next Confession. O'Kane had listened in silence, with no comment, about the pros and cons. Gallagher always enjoyed the debate, playing the part of the contrarian.

The eleven-plus had brought a change to O'Kane's life. Summer flashed by, and the day of departure came too quickly. Gallagher was starting his first week in the trade school while O'Kane was embarking on the first leg of his journey to priesthood. They vowed to remain friends. Although St. Patrick's College in Armagh was less than an hour's drive away, it was another world. That first day was a new experience. After the initial friendly greeting tour, his family said their goodbyes and were gone. Young O'Kane stood vacant as the sound of the black Ford faded into the distance, the echo of its tires on the gravel marking the exact moment his roots were severed. He watched the car disappear, feeling the boy inside him shrink as the shadow of the seminary walls grew long. The gate clicked shut—a metallic finality that reminded him that in the priest's life, even the closest ties were only temporary.

But there was worse in store. There was a complete transformation in the attitude of the school Dean. Gone were the welcoming smiles—replaced by a stern list of dos and don'ts. It seemed to the young postulant that the don'ts far outnumbered the do's.

The somber stipulations complete, the Dean led the way to the dining room. The speed with which the stern priest walked and the cassock's swishing sound unsettled O'Kane and added to his anxiety. The dining room hushed to the arrival of the Dean. Father Moran ignored everyone and brought O'Kane to a tablse at the end of the long dining room. Moran pointed to the one empty seat and left to take his position at a table at the head of the room. O'Kane could feel the glare of the boys at the table. Everyone jumped to their feet when Dean Moran stood. O'Kane bowed his head as grace was being chanted. He was so confused that the words failed to come. He was jolted to his senses by the loud stomps of several feet and scraping chairs as the boys rushed to wolf their midday meal.

O'Kane sat sheepishly and reached for a piece of bread. Halfway through the buttering, a boy across the table leaned forward.

"How's your mother off for jam?"

The question splashed like a rock in his tea. O'Kane froze, knife in hand, searching the boy's face for clues. The boys nearby were already grinning, their eyes bright with expectation. Laughter rippled down the long table, though not cruelly—just enough to make O'Kane's face blush. Was this an inside joke? A test? He shuffled his feet smiling self-consciously, unable to solve the riddle. Only later did he learn that O'Reilly's odd turn of phrase was just his way of breaking the ice.

Over time, the rhythm of St. Patrick's became familiar. The days were not without their dark moments—an occasional priest's sharp tongue could feel like a lash—but most were cordial enough. Some of the harsher ones made O'Kane wonder what had led them to the priesthood at all. It was an unkind thought; one he'd have to own up to in Confession— though certainly not to one of the sharpies.

Lessons rolled along without much strain, apart from Latin. He could still parrot off the Mass responses he'd learned as a boy, those strange tongue-twisters that had once felt like a secret. But now, with the language slipping out of the liturgy, he found himself wondering why it still mattered so much.

He stayed well clear of the playing fields. Father Murphy, who ran the sports program, had long since stopped trying to coax him into football boots. O'Kane's loyalties lay with the library—its dust, its solemn monastic silence, the way the afternoon light sliced across the rows of books like a benediction.
It was all inexplicably comforting.

Four years passed in a blink. The train rides home became part of the routine, and the faces of his childhood friends slowly drifted into memory. Gallagher was already working—he never seemed to be around. Others had gone off to special schools— diverse jobs. Even the few girls he remembered seemed changed somehow, their shapes altered, their presence different. When the thought lingered too long, he pushed it away quickly, as if afraid someone might have seen him and talked about it. By the time his bags were packed for All Hallows in

Dublin, Armagh had grown comfortable—predictable even. The day boys who had once felt like strangers were now part of a small, easy world. Even the sharpy priests seemed softer with familiarity. But it was time to start another chapter, to leave the close-knit warmth for something more glum, lonelier, and unknown. Few from his circle were joining the priesthood, and fewer still were heading his way.

The move to All Hallows was a quiet disruption—just enough to remind him that in the priest's life, even friendships could only be temporary.

The rain had eased. His mother had stopped her fussing— more somber now as she constantly brushed nonexistent flecks from his shoulder. The guard's whistle cut the air—O'Kane's eyes skimmed the faces on the platform. It was in hope more than expectation. His mother's grip felt—a breath—a gentle push. "Go on," she whispered.

The guard waved. He kissed his mother on the cheek and climbed aboard. He found a window seat and with a slow inhale watched Derry drift away. The train hummed along by vacant lots and depressing backyards until it left the city behind. His mood changed with the weather as the sun came out. The fields green and his thoughts fresher. The boy had stepped back inside him. Liam's mind drifted even further back, past the seminary walls and the train rides, to the very first time

Gallagher had truly seen him

Gallagher had been his hero, and someone he wanted to make friends with. After school was out, he had intended to run and thank Gallagher, but when the opportunity arose, he froze. Gallagher was laughing as he walked surrounded by a group of other boys. O'Kane knew them all, but he was intimidated as he was not part of the in-group. He recalled how he continued tagging along on the fringe of the group in the hope that Gallagher might recognize him. He was flabbergasted one day when Gallagher turned to him and said:

"Have you ever thought of becoming an altar boy?"

The question startled him. How did Gallagher know? He had wanted to become an altar boy but lacked the courage to ask the priest. He realized Gallagher was staring, waiting for an answer.

"Well," he stuttered, "I have wanted to."

Gallagher laughed. "So? What's stopping you? I'll sign you up and let you know when the next practice is for rookies. See you tomorrow."

They had reached O'Kane's street, but he was oblivious. The excitement of not only being acknowledged by his idol, but now being part of his brotherhood, made the bashful boy brim with confidence. Liam O'Kane—an altar boy with Brendan Gallagher. The idea filled him with pride.

Father Donaghy was glad to see the new recruit to the altar boy brotherhood. He had always felt the young O'Kane showed potential. Liam took to his new role as a badge of honor and watched and learned from the experienced Gallagher. He became spellbound with the immediacy of being in the sanctuary during religious ceremonies and soon became a leader in his own right.

Being part of an in-group was satisfying, but the group had many members—including Maxwell. Because he was a fellow member of the school's sports team, Maxwell remained within the group. He seemed to have turned out to be less physically aggressive; in fact, he had become overly friendly to O'Kane. Although it was not a welcome approach, O'Kane continued to be intimidated by the mere presence of the bully.

CHAPTER 7

The Embers

When his childhood friend departed, Gallagher felt exhausted and was overcome with deep loneliness, sadness, and self-pity. Tears dampened his pillow—something he would never show to the world. The years had raced by years of war, violence, and recklessness. Sure, he had been surrounded by comrades, close friends, but more and more he had drifted from his core beliefs and principles.

He had cried himself asleep, and when he awoke, he felt strangely rejuvenated. His many years of imprisonment and solitary confinement had not broken him, so why allow a weakness now? He decided it was the reminder of his youth that had triggered the wave of self-pity. He was determined to be self-disciplined.

The door opened, and a young, perfectly groomed policeman entered.

"Is everything OK? I heard you call out," he asked.

Gallagher strained to focus before he could see the young man. He looked more suitable for a job as a clerk or schoolteacher. Gallagher smiled through the pain. Not guerrilla warfare material.

"No, just a bad dream," he gasped. He pushed himself upward, forcing a smile to hide his pain. "Are you guarding me from escape or attack?" he teased.

The young cop smiled compassionately. "It's hard to say." Gallagher tilted his eyes, squinting. "What are the letters on your collar?"

Determined to remain polite, the cop answered, "PSNI—

Police Service of Northern Ireland."

"Oh, right… a kind of prissy name, don't you think? Not like the RUC. Royal Ulster Constabulary… Now that was a bold, aggressive name."

The young man was aware that the patient was teasing and took no offense. As he left the room, Gallagher called after him, "Thanks for checking in."

The banter with the young cop was a distraction. The rookie was a mannerly young man. Gallagher had seen and experienced his fair share of the other type in several countries.

His mind was clearer. He thought about the morning visit with the priest, and his attention traveled back to his childhood and his young friend, Liam O'Kane. Life had completed a circle. They had met through violence, when Gallagher was the savior. Now fate, through the twisted quirks of life, had reversed the roles. O'Kane had found his defender and was now attempting to shield the sinner from his just deserts.

He shifted on the pillow, following the faint cracks in the plaster overhead. Strange how the mind wandered when the body weakened. A man could bury things for decades, but lying still like this, the past rose up whether he wanted it to or not. Maybe that was why O'Kane had come—why their roads had crossed again. Some debts waited patiently.

But confess? He sniffed. Sure, he would freely acknowledge past questionable actions, but not as a form of repentance.

His mind returned to his last confession. The confessional was cold and dank, with the tang of stale snuff from an earlier wrongdoer still hanging in the air. The priest's voice was muffled— fading. His eyes had become heavy, and he drifted off to sleep.

47

CHAPTER 8

The Burden

O'Kane's shoulders sagged, each step back to the rectory burdened by an invisible weight. The years dissolved into a distant haze, but as the mist of forgotten memories cleared, the Derry schoolyard materialized—a stark witness to Maxwell's heavy fist. Then, with a jarring shift, the image switched—the graveyard. His thoughts drifted to Aisling. His hand tightened instinctively around his rosary beads, gripping them like an anchor. The familiar shape steadied him, yet the conflicting thoughts of Maxwell and Aisling churned within him—a bitter cocktail of irritation and guilt.

He sat gazing into the open fireplace. In the glowing embers he could see the vision of young boys cavorting through the burning logs. He leaned closer, trying to identify the faces, but they were all a distortion—ghosts of a past he had buried too deeply.

He searched, willing one face to emerge. "Father O'Kane."

He turned sharply, annoyance flaring. Mrs. Reid stood in the doorway, hands folded.

"Your dinner, Father—it's ready."

"Ok. Ok," he muttered, waving her off as he turned back to the embers. The cavorting boys had vanished. He stared at the fire, willing them back, but the flames had settled into their ordinary glow.

Eventually, reluctantly, he rose and went to the dining room, where his favorite meal awaited him—Mrs. Reid's secret recipe of steak and kidney pie with mashed potatoes. Even the aroma, usually comforting, had lost its appeal. He picked through it with his fork before excusing himself. Mrs. Reid was quietly distressed; the pastor, watching from the corner of his eye, concluded that the hospital visit had been deeply upsetting.

O'Kane was startled by the chime of the grandfather clock standing guard at the foot of the stairs. Midnight. He had yet to read the Divine Office.

Back in his room, he knelt and tried to pray, but his mind kept dragging him back to the gaunt face of his long-ago protector and hero. The memory had been buried for decades— now it crashed through him like a cloudburst. He saw the Derry schoolyard, Maxwell's fist raised, and the young Gallagher stepping between them. A moment that had shaped his life, though he had not realized it then.

He reached for his breviary and forced his eyes to the page. "Teach me good judgement and knowledge, for I have believed thy commandments." The words refused to take hold. Forgotten thoughts flooded his mind—being bullied by Maxwell, rescued by Gallagher, the strange comfort of knowing someone had stood up for him. And later: the relief he'd felt when he heard of Maxwell's death. A shameful relief. The guilt had never left him.

He knew he should seek God's forgiveness, but the words caught in his throat. It felt hypocritical. The Scripture from Matthew pressed on him: "For if you forgive other people when they sin against you, your heavenly Father will also forgive you." Easy to read. Hard to live.

He laid the breviary on the nightstand and sat back. His rosary beads slipped into his palm again—his instinctive refuge. He clutched them tightly, as though they might hold the answer he could not form in prayer.

He closed his eyes, whispering a few uncertain words. They felt foreign, as though they no longer belonged to him. Was he losing his faith—or merely exhausted from carrying it alone?

He opened his eyes. The weight remained. But there had to be something more—he had to believe that.

He stood slowly, as though making a choice he did not fully understand. His thoughts drifted toward Aisling Maxwell. No. Not there. That path led nowhere good. Brendan Gallagher— another trap of memory. But he knew one thing with sudden clarity:

He would have to visit the patient again.

CHAPTER 9

Maxwell in London

Bob Maxwell disappeared from Derry in the late 1960s, which wasn't unusual for a Catholic youth at the time. He'd been a good student, finishing his education with the Christian
Brothers, and had applied—unsuccessfully—for a job in the
Civil Service. Gallagher heard rumors he'd joined the police in   London. He reckoned it was the perfect job for a bully like Maxwell and thought no more of it.

In London, Maxwell found work through Derry contacts on a building site. The work was tough, but he was fit for it, and the pay was decent. Still, he had no plans to spend his days on scaffolding.

The city felt bigger than he'd imagined—gray skies sagging over rows of soot-streaked terraces, buses hissing at corners, the air thick with diesel and fried food. It was impersonal and indifferent, which suited him fine.

One evening, as he sat at a bar with a pint, he flicked through a discarded newspaper. An advert caught his eye:
"JOIN THE POLICE FORCE—SERVE YOUR
COMMUNITY. A REWARDING CAREER FOR YOUNG MEN OF
GOOD CHARACTER." It promised steady pay, a uniform, and a future.

The next day, during his lunch break, he walked into a local police station and filled out the application. Weeks later, a letter summoned him to an interview at New Scotland Yard. The day the letter arrived, Maxwell grabbed it from the post with the other pieces of junk mail. Private & Confidential. He tore it open, hands shaking. His eyes scanned the page until he saw it: Invitation to Interview.

After vetting and basic training at Hendon, Constable Maxwell was posted to Walthamstow Police Station on Forest Road. He was on his way.

When the Troubles came, Maxwell decided a return to his native city wouldn't be wise. He settled into London life— intelligent, observant, and ambitious enough to draw the attention of his superiors. Before long, he knew his patch well and had stopped or arrested several troublemakers. His name soon surfaced as a potential Special Branch candidate.

He rented a flat above an old Victorian house on Forest Road. The owners, an elderly couple, lived downstairs—the husband, exArmy and discreet; the wife, a self-styled Miss Marple who was a constant source of local gossip.

On his nights off, Maxwell often went dancing at the   Galtymore Ballroom in Cricklewood. Nearly an hour away by Tube, it offered the advantage of anonymity. It was there he first noticed the red-haired girl— always surrounded, always smiling.

Two weeks passed before he finally asked her to dance. She accepted with the grace of someone who had already noticed him.

"I needn't be asking you if you're from Ireland," he said.
"Only where?"
"Aye," she smiled. "I'm from Mayo." "Oh, Mayo, God help us," he teased.

She ignored the jab and returned serve. "And yourself?" "Derry," he said, as though it were a title.

"Hmm. The Maiden City. I'm sure they're all disappointed you've left."

The band stopped, and tradition separated them—men to one side, women to the other. Maxwell tried for another dance, but she was whisked away before he could reach her.

Two more weekends passed before they met again. This time he moved quickly.

"I didn't get to introduce myself. I'm Bob Maxwell, and you?" "Aisling Walsh," she said.

"Well, Aisling Walsh, can I buy you a drink?"

She declined alcohol but accepted a lemonade. They talked— she was a nurse at Central Middlesex Hospital; he worked in Walthamstow, though he avoided saying police.

Nearly two months into seeing each other, her curiosity finally outweighed her caution. One evening, she drained half her lemonade and asked, "You've mentioned the building business, but your hands don't show heavy work. What are you digging for?"

Maxwell swallowed hard. He knew this day would come. "I'm not digging, Aisling. I couldn't get work in Derry—I'm just a beat cop."

Several thoughts flashed through her mind. She'd need time to digest that. For now, she let it pass with a laugh. "And there I was thinking you might be a building tycoon."

Aisling accepted Maxwell's explanation for why he had come to London and joined the police force. She had finished up in London for lack of work at home also. They were compatible, and he could be funny at times.

For his part, Maxwell liked that she didn't drink; her good looks and her job as a nurse raised his standing among his police friends.

After seeing each other exclusively for ten months, they became engaged and planned to marry six months later.

Through a police contact, Maxwell heard a piece of news that caught him off guard: a priest from Derry had been transferred to St. Francis Parish in Stratford. Someone from his past, perhaps? He was always wary of anyone who might carry tales back home.

Curiosity and caution tugged at him. He decided to check it out himself, saying nothing to Aisling for now.

At the rectory, the housekeeper told him the new curate was out. "Name of Fr. Liam O'Kane." O'Kane? Really—could it be? He wanted to laugh but restrained himself, thanked the woman, and declined to leave a message. He'd call back.

As he stepped onto the street, a strange sense of satisfaction and relief settled over him. If it was O'Kane—and he was fairly sure it was—there was no concern about the weakling. In fact, it was a stroke of good fortune.

Aisling would like this, no doubt. She'd be impressed. It wouldn't hurt for her to see him in the light of someone who had a priest for a boyhood friend—a touch of respectability to offset some of her doubts.

His mind drifted back to schooldays in Derry: the bookish wimp with a face too soft for rough housing games. Maxwell had never cared for him. He'd pretended to—had to, really. Gallagher had taken a liking to O'Kane and made himself the boy's bodyguard. With Gallagher, you didn't make enemies you didn't need to.

Still, he'd always looked down on O'Kane. Considered him weak, soft. Even now, the memory stirred little more than indifference— perhaps a trace of smugness. Yet here he was, a priest in London. Life had a way of tying knots you didn't expect.

Maxwell smiled to himself. He'd call back. How could this be turned to his advancement—for Aisling, and maybe in ways he hadn't yet worked out?

He walked away, scheming. He hadn't gone far before the plan struck him. "Perfect," he shouted aloud. Ignoring the stares from passersby, he hurried his step.

He decided he'd have O'Kane perform the wedding. The plan would work for now—there must be other pluses.

That night, when he told Aisling, she was delighted. "Did you ask him? Do you know he'll do it?" she asked.

"Of course he'll do it. Aren't we old friends?" he lied.
She was excited as they sat down to make the wedding plans. Aisling had already asked her friend Margaret to be bridesmaid. Her parents and brother had been alerted to expect an announcement.

The wedding would be a small one. Few friends could come from Mayo, and there was never mention of anyone from Derry. Bob had told her his parents were dead and that he was an only child. He'd ask one of his police chums to be groomsman.

CHAPTER 10

The Reckoning

Gallagher glided awake to the soft clink of glass and the faint sterile sting of the hospital room. A slow, crushing pressure throbbed behind his temples, spreading like mist through the inside of his skull. He lay still, breathing shallowly as he waited for the wave to pass.

The lunch tray sat untouched on the table beside him. He couldn't remember falling asleep—only the gentle hand of Nurse McCracken leaning over him and the warm weight of morphine settling into his veins.

"You missed your lunch," she whispered. "Will I warm the soup for you?"

He nodded. Even turning his head sent a dull ache spiraling behind his eyes. She lifted the bowl, and the faint smell of chicken broth stirred something faintly comforting—his grandmother ladling soup on cold Derry mornings. Her cure for every ailment. But even memory had its limits. Nothing cured this.

The first spoonful soothed his throat, but the warmth carried him somewhere else—somewhere he had spent years avoiding. A flicker of gunfire. A corridor thick with sweat and fear. Bodies crammed together in filthy cells. Maxwell's face— bloodied, contorted—crying out.

Gallagher jolted, breath catching in his throat. The sudden movement brought a sharp spike of pain at the base of his skull.

"Easy now," Nurse McCracken murmured, her hand resting gently on his arm. "You're safe." Safe. A lie, but a kind one.

When she stepped away, the room grew still again. A wall clock ticked lazily, each second dragging as if mocking him. The morphine was diminishing. The pressure behind his eyes returned, more insistent this time. Gallagher exhaled slowly, waiting for the ache to settle, but the room seemed to tilt slightly.

He let his eyes close. Darkness rushed in—merciful at first, then crowded with images he could no longer keep at bay.

Two hours later, the familiar ritual returned—the syringe, the steady voice, the careful hand. Warmth seeped into his veins again, gently blunting the jagged edges. He surrendered to it, drifting.

And in the drifting, he was back in Derry.

He saw himself laughing with friends whose faces he couldn't quite place—boys perched on street corners, shouting insults at one another, kicking tins along pavement still wet with the morning's rain. He remembered the gaunt men who drifted in and out of the neighborhood: unemployed, hollow-eyed men who appeared rarely and spoke little. His mother had called them "internment men"—though he'd barely understood what the word meant.

That August morning changed everything.

He remembered the early civil rights marches, the rising tension, the street fights that swept through Bogside like summer storms. Gallagher had kept his distance from it all. He was a trade union man—fighting for jobs, for wages, for dignity. He believed in protest, not violence. He believed one could suffer with dignity and still resist humiliation.

But the dawn raids shattered that.

He read about neighbors dragged from beds, beaten, tortured, branded subversives when many had never lifted a hand. The newspaper reports were worse than the rumors. The truth was unmistakable. It aroused something deep and sharp inside him—a fury he had never felt before.

It was time for action.

But joining the struggle was easier said than done. He had no direct link to the IRA. He knew none of the tortured men personally. His school friends were rumored to have joined, but he had no proof.

He only knew he had to do something.

He thought of one man—Pat Woods, one of the gaunt "internment men" his mother had spoken of. Gallagher found himself standing at the door of Woods's house, heart hammering like a boy caught stealing bread.

Woods's wife answered. Gallagher recognized her from his altar boy days, a quiet woman who rarely missed Mass.

Mrs. Woods stood in the doorway, a thin, weary figure with prematurely greying hair that clung to her temples in unwashed wisps. Her torn cardigan hung loosely from frail shoulders, and there was a neglected look about her—as if life had taken more from her than she ever had to spare. Gallagher felt a pang of pity; she had once been a tidy, constant communicant, but hardship had carved its own story across her face.

Her hesitation told him she understood exactly why he had come. She finally admitted him.

The hallway struck him first, the bare floorboards, the water stained walls. Poverty worn lean.

A few moments later Woods shuffled out fumbling with the belt of a raincoat that was two sizes too big for his scrawny body.

"How can I help you?" he rasped—the voice raw from cigarettes and lack of nourishment.

Gallagher swallowed. "I… was wondering how to join the IRA."

Woods stared, eyes rimmed red. "How would I know that?"

"I'm sorry," Gallagher muttered, ashamed of his own naïve boldness. He turned to leave.

He had taken two steps when Woods spoke again. "Aren't you that trade union fella?"

"Yes," Gallagher said, hope flickering.
But Woods shook his head and closed the door.

Two days later, outside the shirt factory in Gortnaghey, a broad-shouldered young man with a shock of black, curly hair approached him.

"You Gallagher?" the man asked.

"I am." Gallagher's fists tightened instinctively.
The man smiled faintly, sensing the tension. "You were talking to Patsy Woods?" Gallagher nodded.

Within the hour he was sworn in.

The early years came back in fragments—exhilaration, pride, the righteous certainty that he was defending his people. He didn't always take orders well, but he understood the need for discipline. With time he became a natural leader—calm, decisive, fearless.

But somewhere along the way, the cause had shifted. Unity was no longer his driving force. Retaliation was. Protecting his community mattered more than ideology. The leadership saw the change. They saw the insubordination. They saw the charisma that made him dangerous.

Their solution was simple: transfer him to England. Let him lead a small unit abroad where he could do less political damage but plenty of operational work.

Gallagher accepted. He welcomed the chance to impose more pain on the enemy. He became meticulous—obsessed with detail, with security, with precision. His men admired him. They trusted him. They felt safe with him, even when he no longer felt safe with himself.

He lived for the thrill and feared the cost. Each operation brought both. Everything worked—until the day it didn't. The first burst of gunfire caught him off guard. Glass shattered. A metallic scream tore through the air. He rolled instinctively, too late. Pain exploded behind his eyes—a blinding, white-hot burst—and then darkness swallowed him whole.

When he opened his eyes, the hospital room returned in flickers. The ceiling lights smeared into streaks of white. He tried to move, but his limbs were sluggish, tangled in cables. He fell hard, the impact sending a violent shock through his skull. Not pain— more a sickening surge of pressure, as if something inside was swelling outward.

Nurse McCracken rushed to him, calling for the orderly. Gallagher struggled in panic, caught between nightmare and waking.

"Shush… it's all right," she said softly.

After what felt like an age, he stilled. His breathing eased. The nightmare receded.

"Let's clean you up," the nurse said. "Father O'Kane is coming back to see you."

Gallagher stared at her, bewildered.

"Who… who is O'Kane?" he whispered. The nurse looked away, her chin quivering. There was something unbearably tragic about him in that moment—a man who had been feared, admired, followed, condemned… now lost inside his own dying mind.

Gallagher lay back, breathing shallowly, trying—and failing— to remember the name that had once meant everything.

Chapter 11

The Wedding Prep

A hunt for a house had been in progress since the time of their engagement. Maxwell said it had to be local for his job. They planned the search days around his days off. He was surprised when Aisling suggested taking notes of the pros and cons of each house. He hadn't seen this organized side of her before and was impressed.

Walthamstow Village was first on the list. Aisling liked the oldstyle cottages and Victorian terraces. Maxwell agreed; he liked the confined streets of the old villages—far more upscale than the dismal streets of Derry. East of Walthamstow Central was next, more working-class, but there were several decentsized terraced houses. Aisling liked the comfortable look inside," I can see us being very happy, Bob, "I love the comfy feeling." But Maxwell wasn't sold. He had something more imposing in mind. "We can do better than this. Besides, there's too many nosey people who might know me in the area. I don't want any snoops around."

Highams Park was their third search. They knew it was a bit of a stretch for their budget, but Maxwell might reach for it if he wanted to impress. It had a suburban feel—more semidetached houses near Epping Forest. Maxwell could picture himself mowing the front lawn. Aisling liked that there were good schools.

Lower Chingford, further northeast, was the last on the list. It was more open, with bigger residences. This was where Maxwell wanted to be.

"Chingford's a bit of a reach. But a man has to think ahead. If things go well, we might be needing a driveway before long," he said.

"Yes, dear. Let's wait and see," Aisling cautioned.

The decision that followed was difficult, but Highams Park won out. Both seemed happy with the choice.

The wedding day was approaching, and Maxwell had still not returned to speak with Fr. O'Kane. He had lied when Aisling asked him about it. Finally, he resolved that he would have to visit—or at least make a phone call to the rectory. A face-to-face meeting seemed best. So, the following Saturday, he arrived at the rectory in the early afternoon, guessing that confessions would have finished by noon.

To his surprise, the doorbell was answered by Fr. O'Kane himself. Maxwell was taken aback; he hadn't anticipated that. He was unsure how he should address the slim, tall man before him. "Hello," he said respectfully.

O'Kane frowned as a sudden rush of fear gripped him. He hesitated before recovering from the shock. "Bob?" he said, in disbelief.

Maxwell shifted uneasily on the doorstep. "Hello," he repeated, his voice curt.

O'Kane froze, a pulse of recognition tightening in his chest. The face was older, heavier, but unmistakable.

Maxwell forced a grin. "It's been a long time, Liam… Father."

An awkward pause stretched between them, thick and bitter.

"I didn't expect you," O'Kane managed.

"I need a word," Maxwell said, tone sharp—the old command in his voice.

O'Kane stepped aside. "Come in."

The front room was calm and quiet, carrying the scent of candle wax and old books. Maxwell sat without being asked. O'Kane remained standing, thumbing his rosary beads.

"I'm getting married next month," Maxwell said, getting straight to it. "I want you to perform the service."

O'Kane's stomach tightened. The years between them meant nothing in this room. The old fear he had long buried gurgled to the surface and lingered at the edges of his mind.

"Are you and your future bride regular churchgoers?" he asked.

Maxwell jumped in. "Aisling is—she's from Mayo. I haven't been in a while."

"I'm not in the habit of marrying men who haven't darkened a church door in years," O'Kane said, testing the ground.

Maxwell's eyes became callous, "It's not about you; it's not about me. It's for Aisling. She wants a church wedding. I told her I knew a man—a priest."

O'Kane hesitated, then drew a careful breath. "Very well. But it's church practice to meet with the bride and groom beforehand—to explain the meaning of the sacrament and its obligations."

Maxwell held his gaze, a flicker of irritation crossing his face.

"It's part of the rites," O'Kane added, steady now—a priest speaking.

Another lengthy pause. Then Maxwell relented with a tight nod. "Fine. We'll come."

"I'll expect you both next week," O'Kane said.

A small steadiness settled in O'Kane's chest as Maxwell gave a curt nod. It wasn't victory—not anywhere near it—but it was the first time he'd spoken to the man without shrinking inside. Just holding the line felt like something. A quiet thing, almost nothing… yet enough to remind him that he was no longer the boy Maxwell once bullied.

Maxwell stood, adjusting his tie. "See you."

He left without another word, the door clicking shut behind him. O'Kane stood in the gloom, feeling the familiar pressure at his temples. He wasn't sure if what he'd just done was defiance or surrender—perhaps a little of both.

The small parish office was tidy but worn, the faint scent of incense lingering in the air. A well-thumbed Bible rested on the desk beside a notebook marked with names and dates of marriages past. O'Kane sat behind the desk, posture upright, the years of priesthood giving him a calm confidence he'd lacked as a boy.

At precisely half-past seven, the front doorbell rang. Father O'Kane's shoulders tensed as he heard the housekeeper shuffle to answer it. A soft tap came at the office door moments later.

"Come in," he called, clearing his throat.

Aisling entered first, her face lighting up with a polite, beaming smile. She was striking, her auburn hair glimmering in the early evening light—poised, with an air of quiet confidence that made O'Kane wonder what she truly saw in the man behind her.

Maxwell followed, his presence heavy in the small room, eyes sweeping the space like a man casing a back alley.

"Father O'Kane," Aisling said warmly, extending her hand. "Thank you for meeting with us."

"Of course," O'Kane replied, standing as he took her hand, his eyes catching the sparkle of blue in hers. He gestured to the two chairs opposite his desk.

Maxwell dropped into his seat without a word, face expressionless.

"I thought it important we meet," O'Kane began, folding his hands. "The Church teaches that matrimony isn't simply a ceremony but a sacred covenant. It binds two souls together in faith, love, and duty."

His eyes lingered on Maxwell.

Aisling nodded attentively, while Maxwell leaned back, his expression hovering between boredom and irritation.

"I'll need to ask you both a few questions, in accordance with Church law," O'Kane continued, eyes flicking briefly to Maxwell, "and explain the vows you'll be making—not just to one another, but before God."

"Of course," Aisling said warmly. "I think that's lovely."

Maxwell gave a tight smile and rolled his eyes, as if he'd heard this talk before.

O'Kane opened his notebook. "First—are you both free to marry? No prior vows, impediments, or obligations?" "No," Aisling said.

"No," Maxwell answered, staring out the window.

"Do you both intend to enter this marriage freely and without coercion?"

"Yes," Aisling replied.

Maxwell smirked faintly. "I wouldn't be here otherwise, would I?"

O'Kane ignored the discourtesy. He pressed on, speaking more to Aisling now, though the words were for both.

"You understand that marriage, in the eyes of the Church, is a lifelong commitment—a sacrament that cannot be broken." Aisling nodded. "We do." Maxwell remained silent.

"I'll need you both at Mass this Sunday," O'Kane said, voice firm—uncompromising.

Maxwell's jaw clenched, but he said nothing. It was clear he resented being told what to do by this weakling—and yet, here in this quiet office, something in the schoolyard dynamic had shifted.

"Of course, Father," Aisling said gently, touching Maxwell's arm.

He glanced at her hand, then gave a stiff nod of submission.

"Then we'll leave it there for tonight," O'Kane said, closing the notebook. "Thank you both for coming."

Aisling rose with another smile. Maxwell followed but lingered a moment as she stepped into the corridor.

He turned back to O'Kane. "Don't push your luck, Liam," he said softly. "By the way, do you know anything about your buddy Gallagher? He joined the IRA."

O'Kane met his gaze—steady now. "I'm not the boy you remember, Bob. And neither are you."

For the first time, something unreadable passed across Maxwell's face. Then he gave a half-smile and walked out, the door closing firmly behind him.

O'Kane let out a breath he hadn't realized he was holding. The ghosts didn't leave—but they had retreated a step, for now.

As the couple walked away, Aisling was beaming in delight as she held Maxwell's arm. Maxwell was silent. The wimp avoided the Gallagher question… he never could hide a thing. The Yard has been sniffing around asking about me… maybe the right word dropped might help. An Irish priest hears plenty… Aisling's gleeful voice interrupted.

"Isn't Father so nice?"

"Yes, very nice," he replied.

CHAPTER 12

The Ceremony

The marriage passed without drama. The church had more parishioners than the wedding party. Aisling had her parents, brother, and bridesmaid while Maxwell had no one but his groomsman. Fr. O'Kane, for Aisling's sake, had kept a very positive attitude during the service.

O'Kane's voice did not waver as he spoke of fidelity and sacrifice. If any memory stirred beneath the words, it did not reach his face. He mentioned his school days in his homily and indicated that he and Maxwell shared many times together, choosing his words carefully so Aisling would hear them as praise rather than caution.

Aisling's mother was especially pleased that her daughter had married such an upstanding man—a young man from Ireland who had recently been promoted to sergeant, no less. He spoke of Aisling's gentleness, her strength of character, her devotion to her work, and how such qualities were the foundations of any good home. He ended with a quiet reflection on companionship—the sort that lasted not because life was easy, but because two people chose, again and again, to steady each other. It was gentle, crafted with Aisling in mind, and if Maxwell shifted slightly in his seat, no one commented on it.

After the service, the group went on to a restaurant, and that was where things began to slide. Aisling's brother Declan gave a speech, his voice growing louder with each toast until finally he could no longer hold his tongue.

"There's something wrong with a Derry man—and a Catholic at that—leaving Derry to join the English police at a time like this."   His voice rose, his resentment plain.

Maxwell's groomsman leaned in. "Max, want me to call a few blokes and teach Paddy a lesson?"

Maxwell shook his head. "Leave it. It's the booze giving him courage. He'll be back on a plane tonight."

Aisling's parents, desperate to avoid upsetting their daughter, hurried Declan out to a waiting taxi for the airport. Aisling, unaware of the row, was only sorry to see her family leave so suddenly. Declan, still fuming, hugged her stiffly.

"If you've any trouble with that bastard, let me know—I'll fix it."

Their mother was distraught. "Don't mind him, love. You know what our Declan's like after a few drinks."

But nothing could spoil Aisling's day. She was radiant—thrilled to be married, moving into their new home, stepping into her new life.

The celebrations went on longer than she'd hoped. Several of Maxwell's police friends had joined in. She sat quietly, fidgeting with the lace sleeves of her dress, a dull headache pressing at her temples. Her family had gone hours before; she'd been waiting for Bob to finish his "last pint" ever since.

The music had died, replaced by bawdy jokes and patriotic songs. Aisling's patience wore thin. She touched his sleeve gently. "Bob, love… it's getting late. Maybe we should head home?"

His mates snickered. Maxwell turned to her, eyes glassy, cheeks flushed.

"What's the rush, Aish? Not like it's a work night—well, maybe more for me!"

The table erupted in laughter.

Aisling's cheeks reddened. "Don't talk like that," she said quietly.

Maxwell's grin faltered. "Aish, it's a joke. Can't you culchie girls take a bit of craic?"

One of the older officers looked away. Aisling stood.

"I'll be outside," she said evenly, and left.

A hush followed. Maxwell forced a smile that wouldn't come.

"Ah, shite," he muttered, and stumbled after her.

She had only gone a few yards when he caught up. "Aish, I'm sorry. I made an ass of myself. I'll make it up to you—I promise."   She looked at him. She knew she would forgive him. "Alright… but you were mean."

They hugged, hailed a cab, and went home. The makeup was easy.

The next morning, Maxwell tried to hide the pounding in his head. It wasn't only the drink. It was something heavier—a dull, steady ache that no amount of sleep could shift. He splashed cold water on his face, staring into the mirror at a man he barely recognized.

Aisling's voice floated from the bedroom. "You alright in there, love?"

He pressed his fingertips to his temples. The pounding in his head was so fierce he could hear it.

He forced a smile at his reflection, though it felt crooked. "Grand," he said. But even to himself, his voice sounded hollow.

CHAPTER 13

The Honeymoon

The London Victoria to Brighton line has been running since the 1840s, and by the 1970s, it was a well-trodden route for holidaymakers, honeymooners, and day-trippers alike. The journey was going to take about an hour and a quarter, so Maxwell bought a newspaper and asked Aisling if she wanted a magazine. She declined, saying she wanted to enjoy the scenery.

They grabbed a couple of sandwiches and took their seats on the British Rail Mk1 carriage. The train chugged along through Clapham Junction then went down through East Croydon, Gatwick, Haywards Heath, and on to Brighton. Aisling sat wideeyed at the organized chaos of the maze of platforms at Clapham Junction. Maxwell, pretending not to be impressed, informed her that it was the busiest rail intersection in the world; it was something he had read in a newspaper article recently.

The train emerged from the gray drizzle into East Croydon, and the new office towers seemed to burst from the ground, glittering like futuristic glass lookouts. Aisling pressed her nose against the window, her breath fogging the pane as she gazed in amazement at the steel pylons. "Is this a new town?" she whispered, her voice full of a wide-eyed wonder.

Across from her, Maxwell's newspaper trembled with the slight, involuntary clench of his jaw. He lowered his newspaper an inch, his gaze barely clearing the top edge. "No. The new Whitgift Centre." He muttered the information with the quiet boredom of a local tour guide, not bothering to add that he'd seen the same billboards for months. He returned to his paper, leaving her to her own private, shining city. As the train pulled out of Croydon, there were more open spaces, fields, and tree lines. Aisling, sounding like an excited schoolgirl, whispered gleefully, "This is just like Ireland— it's amazing. Amazing!!" "Yes, dear," he mumbled, with forced patience.

The train clattered along; Aisling kept oohing and aahing for the rest of the journey. "I never thought England was like this," she bubbled, "but this is not anything like London." Rolling countryside and farmlands were everywhere. Cows in fields— even sheep. Aisling spotted kids playing near the tracks. "Oh. This is all very wonderful; I'm so happy, Bob. Aren't you happy, love?"

Maxwell laid his newspaper aside, looked at her and smiled, "Yes, I am happy." Putting his hand on her arm, a smile breaking through his usual forceful composure, he added, "Wait till you look at the sea," he murmured, "I booked us a room with a view, you know."

"Thanks, love," she cooed.

Aisling smiled; all the world was right. Pure and untroubled happiness settled over her like a warm comforter. She prayed it would last. The countryside rolled by in gentle waves of green and gold, and for a moment, the city, the job, and the drinking from the previous night seemed a lifetime away.

The taxi pulled up at the entrance of The Grand Brighton, the building rising before them like one of the grand landlord houses she remembered from back home, though this was larger, grander, and somehow more imposing. Its wide, sea weathered façade still clung to the ghost of its Victorian glory— balconies with wrought iron curls, rows of tall windows catching the late afternoon light. The doorman, in a stiff uniform and peaked cap, opened the cab door with a trained flourish. Aisling stepped out and felt her breath catch. The sharp scent and taste of sea salt in the air transported her, for a moment, to another place. She let her breath out slowly in awe. Back in the village where she'd grown up, the most prominent building was the church hall, and nothing in London, for all its bustle, had struck her quite like this place did.

The red carpet stretched toward the doors, and beyond them she could see the soft glow of chandeliers and hear the faint, distant notes of a piano. It was grand. Maybe too grand, really, for people like us, she thought. The sort of place she might have once said was overdone—a touch showy, a little pretentious. But the truth was, it thrilled her. The sense of occasion, of stepping into a world she'd only seen in photographs or grand hotels she passed but never entered in Dublin or London.

Maxwell was already paying the fare. Aisling straightened her shoulders, brushing invisible creases from her dress. She would not gape, like a girl fresh off the boat. Not in front of strangers. Still, as they walked through the doors into that grand, lamp-lit lobby, she allowed herself one quiet word under her breath.
"Jesus." And then she smiled.
The assistant manager appeared as they approached the desk, a man with thinning hair, a discreet paunch beneath his jacket, and a functional smile honed by years of dealing with guests he neither liked nor disliked. He neatly intercepted the young clerk and offered his own slippery greeting. "Good afternoon."

Maxwell had already measured him: a sycophant. He spotted the careful polish, the polite authority, the faint whiff of desperation that clung to men who spent their days pretending they were important in places that used them as though they didn't exist. "Good evening, Mr. and Mrs. Maxwell. A pleasure to have you with us."

Maxwell smiled, a shade too pointed to be entirely polite. "Detective Sergeant Maxwell, and Mrs. Maxwell."

Aisling kept her expression neutral, but she noted it—the small, aimed correction, the claim to rank. It was a habit she'd seen settle on him since the promotion, a faint tightening of the shoulders, a new weight in his voice when he spoke to men in uniforms or now, hotel employees. She said nothing. There was no point.

The assistant manager recovered quickly, offering a deferential nod. "Of course, Detective Sergeant. Your room is prepared—sea view, as requested."

Maxwell inclined his head—satisfied. And it hadn't escaped his notice that the assistant manager had sized them up, too. The sharp glance at Aisling's simple dress, the quick calculation of Maxwell's suit, the gleam of his wedding band, the quiet conclusion: newlyweds, some money, not old money. Possibly a provincial climber with ideas.

Maxwell moved to pick up their bags, when a flicker of movement at the edge of his peripheral vision caught him. The porter. Standing there—waiting. Maxwell's hand paused in midair; the gesture too fast to be called casual. He knew the assistant manager saw it too. Without missing a beat, he straightened, smoothing his jacket sleeve as if that had been his intention all along. "You can take those, young man?" he said to the porter, his tone friendly but carrying the weight of authority.

The porter nodded, politely.

Turning to Aisling, Maxwell said, "Shall we, dear?"

As they followed the porter to the elevators, Aisling, who had followed the entire exchange with amusement, nudged Maxwell with her elbow and whispered, "Detective Sergeant Maxwell." Even Maxwell found it funny.

The sea-view room was grander than anything Aisling had ever imagined. High ceilings crowned with ornate plasterwork, thick brocade curtains framing a wide bay window that looked out over the gray-blue sweep of the English Channel. A pair of wingback chairs sat by the window, their fabric a little worn, the pattern slightly faded by years of salt air and afternoon sun. The bed was vast, with crisp white linen and a heavy floral eiderdown folded at the foot. The soft scent of furniture polish and distant sea salt hung in the air. In the corner, an old walnut writing desk stood beside a vase of carnations. Maxwell noted the carnations with approval. *Nice touch*, he thought.

Aisling rubbed her hand gently across the eiderdown while Maxwell walked to the window. "Come, look at the view," he said enthusiastically. Aisling joined him and gasped. From the window, the promenade stretched in both directions, dotted with iron benches, lamp posts, and the distant glitter of Brighton Pier. The blue body of water shimmered in the sunlight, a glistening carpet of smooth, gleaming, almost honey-gold and silvery-gray pebbles. The sunlight danced across their rounded surfaces, each stone catching the light like tiny, scattered jewels. "This is heaven, Bob," she whispered as she snuggled into him.

They watched for a while until Maxwell became restless and said, "OK, let's go check this place out."

"Good," gushed Aisling. "Let's go for the afternoon tea."

"Only if you remember to crook your pinkie when you're drinking your tea," he joked.

Aisling curtsied. "Of course," she answered primly.

The afternoon sun slanted in through the tall windows of the lounge, catching the gleam of silver teapots and the sparkle of the chandeliers. Aisling sat upright, hands in her lap, taking in the room with wide, eager eyes. The velvet chairs, the soft clatter of fine china, the quiet hum of conversation. It looked like a world she'd only seen in films. *Agatha Christie*, she thought. She quietly enjoyed the scones and discreetly studied the other guests.

Maxwell, meanwhile, leaned back in his chair, watching the room through the eyes of a copper. He wasn't expecting trouble, but old habits kicked in. He noted the well-heeled older couple by the window, the flock of women in pearls, and a young man trying too hard to look like old money.

"You're studying them," Aisling said with a small smile.

"Force of habit," Maxwell replied. "Everyone's got a story. You can read it if you know how."

She liked that about him—the way he noticed things others didn't. Even if it made her a little uneasy sometimes. "Oh. I like to look too; I just think they look happy," she said softly.

Maxwell continued to look through slanted eyes. "Maybe," he said. "Or maybe they're just good at looking it."

Aisling laughed, a soft resigned sound, and shook her head. "You'll never leave the job behind, will you?"

He smiled then, bluntly. "Would you want me to?" She reached for his hand. "Not a chance."

As they entered the lavish traditional dining room, an impeccably groomed maître d' greeted them with disarming warmth, his eyes brimming with a knowing confidence. Every gesture was precise, every word measured, carrying just enough charm to mask the unmistakable trace of superiority. Aisling was flattered by the attention, but Maxwell eyed the arrogance. "Professional beggar," he muttered.

Maxwell's remark went right over Aisling's head; she was too engrossed in the surroundings—the stiff white tablecloths and waiters with napkins over their arms. Maxwell flicked a fork with his thumb, the silver ringing too loud in the quiet room. "Looks like you need a handbook for this lot," he grunted, Aisling sensed the caustic tone and smiled. "Just copy me, Detective Sergeant; you'll be grand," she teased.

Meanwhile, Maxwell was struggling with the menu: *Ballotine of Pigeon, Beef Wellington, Duck à l'orange.* Where's the Steak and Kidney Pudding or the pig's liver? Onions and mashed potatoes? He settled on the beef, and Aisling chose the duck.

A fawning waiter glides to their table with the practiced ease of a man half his age. "Ah, bonsoir, madame et monsieur, my name is Nico, I have de pleasure of being your waiter tonight." His hair was dyed an unnaturally glossy black and slicked back. The pencil mustache was visibly darker than his eyebrows. His rolled r's and mangled French were obvious, even to Aisling. "May I recommend zee chef's special pâté maison? Eet is… how you say… magnifique." He kissed his fingertips, then swept his hand gently toward the imaginary dish. They both declined the pâté and ordered the main dish, the beef for Maxwell and the duck for Aisling. After assuring them both that they had made excellent choices, Nico slithered away.

"Where the hell whorehouse did they get him?" said Maxwell, rolling his eyes.

"Oh, stop, Bob, you're awful!" laughed Aisling.

Within a few minutes, Nico returned with two glasses of champagne. With a flourish, he placed the glasses in front of them and said, "We understood… congratulations are in order. Your honeymoon, innit?"

Got you, thought Maxwell. "What part of Croydon are you from?"

Nico was gone. Aisling burst out laughing.

Aisling decided to try the dessert, but she wasn't able to pronounce any of them and didn't want to ask. The Chocolate Mousse caught her eye; that would do. The dark chocolate and whipped cream were just perfect. No coffee. Nico fluttered about their table like an eager hummingbird, wringing his hands over every course until Maxwell, amused, decided to let the poor man off the hook. The beef portion was laughably small, though what little there was melted richly on the tongue. The duck, by contrast, was mostly bone—a cruel promise of meat that never delivered.

Maxwell mulled over the last steak morsel and wondered. Maybe a good fish supper would do the trick. Aisling lingered over the dessert menu, frowning at the unpronounceable names.

She refused to ask for help, settling instead on the familiar. Chocolate Mousse. That one I know. It arrived silky and dark, crowned with a swirl of whipped cream. One spoonful and her face softened; it was exactly what she wanted.

They both waved away the offer of coffee.

When the attentive Nico discreetly placed the bill on the table, Maxwell didn't even glance at it. "Charge it to my room," he snapped—no "please," no eye contact.

"Very good, sir," answered Nico, still simmering beneath his composed exterior. As he walked from the table, he looked back and added, with questionable sincerity, "Have a good evening."

"Let's get out of here," whispered Maxwell as they stepped into the lobby. "Let's find a fish and chips stand; I'm starving." Aisling giggled as they headed off toward the pier. The aroma of cotton candy, along with the clang of slot machines, engulfed the air. Finally, the familiar smell of fish and chips filled his nostrils. He followed his nose like a bloodhound. They rounded a kiosk painted in gaudy stripes, where a steady stream of steam hissed as fat melted with batter. Maxwell stopped; his nostrils widened at the recognizable sound and smell of chips being salted and doused in vinegar. The vendor rolled the newspaper into a perfect cone. Maxwell watched impatiently as the vendor filled the cone with golden chips, followed by a battered cod fillet.

Walking hand in hand, they found a vacant bench overlooking the sea. Big chips, golden and steaming, crunched and flaked with each bite. But it was the hot, greasy perfection that truly tasted like home. Maxwell offered the chips to Aisling. "Just one," she said.

But one was followed by another until most of the chips were gone.

"Fancy duck," joked Maxwell as he headed back to the vendor.

It had turned into a beautiful evening, thought Aisling, as they headed back to the hotel. "Let's forget these high overblown dinners at the hotel."

"Yes," agreed Aisling. "What about bangers and mash?"

"Perfect," chirped Maxwell as he kissed her.

The remaining evenings were spent sightseeing and walking on the pier or beach. Aisling was happy; she thought it was a practical choice as she had plans for the house. Fish and chips on the beach was Aisling's favorite time. "You know, I think I could be like this.
Sun on my face, chips in my hand, no one demanding bedpans."

"Give it a week—you'd be bored," he smiled.

Aisling's eyes lingered on the horizon—an inner warmth settling within. "With you, love? No. Never," she whispered softly.

Mid-week, they took a bus trip to Devil's Dyke Walk. They walked the hills and spent quiet moments enjoying one another's company. Aisling was happy. Maxwell's mood brightened up; she noticed that some of the tension she had noticed lately was fading. As they sat on the grass looking over the South Downs, Maxwell was in a pensive mood. "My dad would've called this a waster's holiday," said Maxwell, almost to himself.

Aisling, sensing an inner sadness, linked her arm through his.
"You're building memories, Bob. That's something, isn't it?"

He didn't answer straight away. "Maybe," he murmured softly.

Aisling didn't rush him. They sat quietly; she finally eased to her feet, brushing grass from her jeans. "Shall we?" she asked gently, nodding toward the bus. He followed her gaze. Beyond the valley, the sun was dipping; evening came quietly, like a closing curtain. "Yeah," he murmured.

They sat quietly gazing at the rolling downs, each lost in their own thoughts. Maxwell broke the silence, "OK, let's go; I need a drink." They rose together and walked back along the ridge toward the bus stop. Within minutes, the bus appeared. It would carry them back to Brighton—the bus meandered slowly down the meandering road. Aisling could see the Brighton Palace Pier, its numerous, bright twinkling lights like distant stars set against the gray-streaked sky. Aisling watched the reflections flicker on the water beside them. Together, they watched the city light up around them—quiet, intimate, and beautifully suspended between day and night.

The King's Head Pub was half-empty, just a handful of locals gathered around the dartboard. The jukebox crooned a country ballad, and the air smelled faintly of old smoke and fried chips. Maxwell ordered a pint of Fuller's ESB ale. Aisling ordered her lemonade with ice. She chose the ice because she liked the taste— and because it was something she had never tried in Ireland.

Maxwell, she recognized, was in a talking mood. When the ale arrived, Maxwell lifted the pint, took an unhurried sip, and set it back down. For a moment, he stared into the glass, the amber liquid reflecting the light. An illusory picture mirrored an old brownish-yellow photograph. He couldn't look away from the faces and streets long forgotten for a few short moments.

He blinked and, with a half-smile, he murmured, "Funny thing. You take a sip and you're seventeen again, thinking you'll live forever."

He took another slow, pensive sip. "You know, back home I used to think I'd never amount to much. A boy from the wrong side of Derry—Londonderry," he corrected, "with no prospects— maybe a part-time job walking a greyhound or laboring somewhere."

Aisling looked at him fondly— a sigh of pity mingled with pride—and whispered, "Not much chance of that now."

There was something in her voice that touched a nerve. He felt the old reflex to hold her hand, to wait for a safer moment. But maybe the moment was now—perhaps it wasn't. He grinned and cleared his throat. "Just look at me now— Detective Sergeant Maxwell. And let me tell you, this is only the beginning. I intend to make Inspector before long." He paused. "Why not? I hear there are men in London looking out for lads like me: sharp, hungry, not afraid to get their hands dirty."

He caught sight of his reflection in the mirror behind the bar and straightened his tie. He was on a roll as he continued, "Give it a year or two, and we'll be having supper with superintendents. Maybe even some of the boys from Whitehall."

Aisling watched him with nervous admiration. "We don't need all that, Bob; we can be happy without chasing."

Maxwell's face darkened. "Not chasing—earning," he interrupted.

She leaned across the table, touched his knee, and lowered her voice. "OK, OK, but just don't forget who you are while you're at it."

There was a flicker of something—a quick curl of his upper lip crossed his face, but it was gone in a heartbeat.
Maxwell regained his composure. "I'll not forget you, anyhow."

Aisling smiled, clinking her lemonade glass against his ale. "I'll be happy with our lovely home and two or three babies."

He took a deep gulp of his ale. "Yeah, yeah, OK, time enough for that." Aisling sensed it was time to change the subject.
They walked back to the hotel in silence.

Maxwell awoke early. He reached for his watch; it was 5:15 a.m. As dawn gently broke, Maxwell sat by the window, the salty breeze floating softly through a slightly open window. The sun's first rays appeared low on the eastern horizon, a pale golden thread pushing through delicate clouds and the gentle haze of the early morning. The sky was a wash of pinks and oranges—hues that splashed against the horizon. The water was dotted here and there with a few small fishing boats, their fishermen beginning their day in the soft light. Maxwell could see a few early-rising joggers wrapped in warm sweaters, scattered along the pebbled beach below, and couples strolling with dogs.

Aisling stirred to the scent of salt and the distant cry of gulls. For a moment, she lay, listening to the hush of the waves breaking against the shore. She stretched. "Good morning, love."

"Morning. Come and look," he said, his eyes still watching the dog walkers.

She pulled on a robe and ran to join him. Maxwell sat there, silhouetted against the lightening sky, his gaze now fixed on the horizon as though searching for something. The sea glittered in the morning light. Aisling moved closer. "Couldn't sleep?" she asked softly. "Or are you still people watching?"

Maxwell turned, his face easing into a warm smile. "Didn't want to miss this," he replied, gesturing to the sunrise.

Seagulls screeched and impatiently circled, dipping to catch the occasional fish or simply gliding on the hunt. The sound of waves lapping steadily against the shore and the creak of the pier's wooden supports created a peaceful symphony that matched the calm of the moment.

"At home people believe they are harbingers of good news," said Aisling.

"Naw, they're just hungry bastards," retorted Maxwell. He sniffed and stood. "Talk about hungry, I'm starving. Let's go eat."

"Since we are planning dinner here tonight, let's keep our spending down," suggested Aisling.

"Right," agreed Maxwell. "I saw a few places on Preston Street that looked like they would have the right grub without costing an arm and a leg."

"The five-minute walk will do us good," enthused Aisling.

The Tudor House caught Aisling's eye. "It sounds posh, but likely not," laughed Maxwell. "We can impress our friends; they won't know."

Aisling giggled. The Tudor House Café sounded grander in fact than it looked. Inside, the air hung thick with the mingled scents of frying bacon, strong tea, and cheap detergent. Laminated menus lay on Formica-topped tables, their corners curled and sticky from years of greasy fingers. The plain round-backed chairs wobbled with age. Cheap prints of English countryside scenes clung to the nicotine-stained walls, their colors faded and smeared by time. It was a haven for holidaymakers on a tight budget, elderly couples heading out on coach trips, and builders chasing a fry-up before heading to a job. The clatter of plates and hiss of the grill provided a steady, working-class din.

The waitress, Val, late 40s, good figure, trying hard to hang on to fading good looks, looked bored. A cigarette drooped from her lips, angled downward, the discolored skin and fine puckering wrinkles around her mouth betraying years of habit and hard living. She spotted them right away— honeymooners—as they slid into a corner booth. She watched as they discussed the menu like two famished people—Aisling with her waistline in mind, Maxwell like a man who meant to get his money's worth.

When Maxwell set his menu aside, it was her signal to move. But Val held back. This was her game, and she played it her way. She'd wait. Finally, she sauntered over, order pad in one hand, a pencil stuck behind her ear into her blonde bleached hair.

"See anything you fancy?" she smirked, raising a flirtatious eye in Maxwell's direction.

Maxwell met her gaze, his expression giving nothing back. "What do you think, sweetheart?" he asked Aisling.

Aisling, unaware of the side-play, gave the menu one last glance. "Tea, toast, and a soft-boiled egg, please. Oh, and some strawberry jam, please."

Val replied, "Good choice, luv, we girls need to keep our figures." She jotted it down, then shot a quick look at Maxwell. "And you, big boy… what would you like?"

"The works," he said, without making eye contact. "Might as well do it properly."

Val flicked her cigarette with a smirk. "Hmm, thought so." Then she sauntered away—hips swaying just enough to make it clear she knew exactly who she was dealing with.

"I think she likes you," teased Aisling.

Val swaggered into the kitchen, barked the order at the fry cook without breaking stride. She leaned against the counter, took a long drag from her cigarette, and stubbed it out in a cracked saucer. Through the serving hatch, she watched Maxwell in the booth. Dot, another waitress—a few years older than Val but cut from the same cloth, with gray roots showing through the bleach-blonde hair—sidled up beside her.

"New face?" Dot asked, nodding toward Maxwell.   Val smirked. "Cop, I think. You can smell 'em."   Dot snorted. "Aye, I knew a few in my time."

Val winked. "Bet he's got a pair o' handcuffs in his pocket and a head full o' bad ideas."

Dot snorted. "Just my type."

Val grinned. "Mine too—it's been a while."

They chuckled before Val flicked her cigarette and moved back out onto the floor. She made her rounds of her tables until she arrived at the booth. The café clatter carried on—cutlery on china, the sizzle from the grill, the faint drone of a worn-out radio in the corner. She leaned a hand on the table's edge, the cheap, imitation bangles on her wrist jingling softly. Her eyes lingered on Maxwell's plate—near clean—and the untouched crusts on Aisling's.

"Food alright for ya, luv?" she asked Aisling, who smiled politely and nodded. "Lovely, thank you." Then, to Maxwell, she tipped her head, narrowing her eyes a touch, a half-smirk playing on her lips. "And you, darlin'? Hit the spot?"

"Just what I needed," Maxwell said, dabbing his mouth with a paper napkin.

Val drew a little closer, pressing herself against the table's edge, the reek of stale perfume and cigarettes floating with her. "Funny thing," she said, casual-like, "I'm good with faces. And types. Have I seen you before? You've got a bit of a copper's look about you. Am I warm?"

Aisling's eyes darted to Maxwell's, a flicker of tension in them. A slow, calm grin slid across his face. He'd fielded this one before. "I get that now and then."

Val chuckled, tapping her temple with a long nail. "Told ya. Never wrong." She straightened, patting the table once, then sniggered, tapping a nail against the tabletop. "You can frisk me anytime, darlin'."

Aisling gave a startled laugh—Maxwell stayed deadpan. Val straightened, satisfied, and with a wink to Aisling added, "Don't worry, love—I'm harmless these days."

She moved away, hips swaying with the kind of practiced ease that didn't need an audience. As she swaggered back to the counter, Val felt the eyes of the dockers on her. *Still got it*, she thought.

She hovered by the counter, idly wiping a spotless patch while keeping one eye on the booth in the corner and the line of newcomers. She'd served the honeymooners twice already— fresh tea, extra toast—enough to twig what was going on. The bloke had sharp eyes, the kind that didn't miss much. Definitely a cop. The girl was sweet—freckles, soft laugh, clearly enjoying herself. Val watched the way their heads leaned in close, the casual brush of her hand against his. *Hope she's not hurt*, she thought.

She waited for her moment, watching discreetly. Aisling pushed back from the table, dabbing her mouth with a paper napkin. Maxwell leaned back, arms stretched along the back of the booth seat. Like an actor hitting his cue, Val glided across the floor, lipstick fresh, the bill tucked in her apron pocket. "We gets a mixed crowd this time of year. Locals, Londoners, wedding couples… the odd gent from the Grand sneakin' in for a proper breakfast," she smirked, like it was a well-known Brighton secret. Staring directly at Maxwell, she added, "I've spent some good nights at the Grand with old gentlemen friends. Almost sure I've seen you."

Maxwell shifted in his seat. "Actually, I've been there on business."

"Yeah. Business. Same as me," she smirked. Then, with a glance at the queue, she softened it. "Hate to be a pest, loves, but we're a bit tight for tables just now. No rush. Just lettin' you know." She slid the bill onto the table, voice friendly but edged. "Whenever you're ready, loves. Got a few waitin' to park their fat backsides."

And off she went, already sizing up the next table. Aisling watched her go. "I like her. She's funny."

"Yeah. A real comedian," grunted Maxwell.

Aisling wasn't done. "You didn't tell me you'd been down here before."

Maxwell sighed, shifting his feet. "A while back. Strictly professional. Not much fun chasing bookies and bent councilors."

Aisling rolled her eyes but grinned, not sure what to make of it. Maxwell, dodging her look, pretended to study the bill. "Give her a good tip. She was nice," Aisling insisted.

He knew he had to save face. The bill came to 40p. He wanted to please Aisling and impress Val or avoid looking like a skinflint.

He laid a 50p piece on the bill. "Keep the change," he muttered.

Val raised a brow, impressed despite herself, though she hid it well. "Thanks, Detective," she purred.

Maxwell bristled. "Detective Sergeant, actually."
She didn't miss a beat. "Oh, my mistake. So sorry," she overstated, then turned and walked away.

As they left the café, Val watched them go. *You prick. I know your sort, mate. Got your number.*

Outside, Aisling took a deep breath. "Oh, isn't the salt air so refreshing?"

Maxwell had his own reasons for wanting to be outside. He grabbed the opportunity. "Let's do something different today. It's the last of our trip; this is your day. You choose." A twinge of guilt nagged at him. *Damn that bitch*, he thought.

Aisling paused, caught off guard by his thoughtfulness, then smiled. "Well… how about a walk through some antique shops and dinner at the hotel? I'd love that."

"You got it," Maxwell agreed, relieved that the café incident seemed to have passed.

They left the café behind and made their way down to the promenade. Aisling laughed as the seagulls swiped in and skyrocketed off with bits of breakfast scraps. She tucked her arm through Maxwell's; this was fun. "I'd love to poke around those little antique shops you mentioned, those tiny places down the old lanes you said were worth a look."

Maxwell moaned inwardly, but he had committed. The promenade slid into one of the boring lanes that zigzagged through the heart of old Brighton. The cobble streets lay uneven underfoot; the slightly tilting buildings with small grimy windows created a picture of earlier years.

Aisling's face lit up. "Oh, Max… this is gorgeous," she purred.
"It's like stepping back in time."

Shop after shop was a treasure trove. She turned slowly, her eyes darting from crooked doorways to peeling signs: *Antique Maps, Books Bought & Sold, Seafarer's Relics*. She let out a small, delighted laugh at a window filled with porcelain figurines and faded postcards. Maxwell kept his hands deep in his pockets, his jaw tight.

"It's just old junk," he muttered.

Aisling glanced at him, surprised by the sharpness in his tone. "No, no, it's all so charming. It's like a scene from a Dickens novel."

But Maxwell saw no beauty in it; he saw the dingy streets of Derry alleys that reeked of gas, things best forgotten. Aisling didn't notice the shift in his face. She was already moving toward a shop window displaying brass compasses and a battered naval telescope. "I love it," she said over her shoulder. "I could spend hours in a place like this."

"The bloody place should be bulldozed," he hissed.

"But, Bob, it's so unique to me; remember, I'm a country girl. Green fields and cows."

He groaned and let it go. Aisling had moved on.

"This one!" Aisling beamed, pointing at a bookshop with a crooked sign and a window full of yellowed hardbacks. "Let's have a look." She rushed inside while Maxwell hung back, watching people wander around the lane—some eager antique hunters expecting to find a hidden treasure, others sightseeing. Maxwell searched the faces, so many opportunities: pickpockets, shoplifters, con artists.

"Bob, Bob, look." It was Aisling. Her voice shrilled. "Look what I found!" She held a tattered hardback in the air like a winning trophy. The name of the book was *Esther Waters*, the author George A. Moore. "Look, this was my parents' favorite book. George Moore was from Mayo, you know. My father loved his books, used to quote one of his sayings all the time, I still remember it… A man travels the world over in search of what he needs and returns home to find it."

Maxwell hated the quote, hated the man, hated the place. "OK. Can we go now?"

Aisling noted the tone in his voice; she had sensed it before. "OK, dear, let's go."

They walked hand in hand along the weathered planks of Brighton Pier. Herring gulls shrieked overhead, their silvery-gray backs against puffy white clouds as they dived, brazenly nibbling at chips clutched in small sticky hands. The clatter and laughter of youngsters mingled with the distant hum of slot machines from the arcade at the pier's edge.

Maxwell's eyes caught the flicker of neon lights inside the arcade. His mood changed, the crumbling side street forgotten, as he steered Aisling toward the arcade. "Come on, love," he said joyfully. "Let's see if luck's on my side."

Inside, the air was thick with the scent of popcorn and a stale whiff of sweat and cigarettes. Rows of machines blinked and buzzed, promising fortunes to the desperate and the lucky. Sweaty punters hunched over one-armed bandits, faces damp and bleary, feeding in coins with frantic hope.

Maxwell zeroed in on a brightly colored game—one that promised quick wins and instant satisfaction. He dropped a coin in with confident anticipation. The reels spun, clicking rhythmically, then slowly came to a stop, but the jackpot eluded him. He tried again, and again he lost. His jaw tightened as he tried one more time. Aisling watched quietly, noting the sudden mood change that shadowed his face. She shivered slightly; it was a side she hadn't seen before.

She touched his arm. "Let's go, Bob; it's getting late, and I have to shower before dinner."

"Maybe one more try?" Maxwell muttered, with a trace of impatience. His hand fed the one-armed bandit one more time—reels spun, and again, failure. His heavy hand slammed down on the machine's edge, startling Aisling.

"I don't like losing," he snarled through gritted teeth.

Aisling touched him, her hand gentle on his closed fist. "We're on our honeymoon, Bob. It's just a game." He nodded slowly, the storm in his eyes slowly abating. "Yeah, just a game," he repeated.

They walked back to the hotel in silence. As they neared the hotel, Maxwell felt a twinge of guilt for his outburst at the slot machines. "Fancy Chinese tonight?" he asked, avoiding her eyes.

Aisling brightened immediately. "Oh yes, I've never had proper Chinese food before."

He forced a tight smile, trying for a joke. "Good. I don't think I could face another night of Nico."

Aisling laughed. "There's a place—Lotus House. Meant to be the best," he suggested.

As they stepped into the lift, an elderly couple joined them. Aisling nudged Maxwell and whispered, "I'll take a quick shower and get changed. Won't be long."

Maxwell washed up, changed his shirt, and headed for the bar. It was quiet at this hour—just a few lone drinkers nursing gin and tonics, a couple in deep conversation by the window. He ordered a Scotch, leaned against the polished counter, and stared out through the tall windows. The tide was coming in; the sea beyond was calm. Old habits had him scanning the room, logging faces, noting who came and went. No serious intent, just a reflex. A busman's holiday. He took a sip, letting the whisky settle in his throat as he tried to unwind.

Aisling would be a while. She always took her time getting ready. His gaze drifted back to the water, the tide inching closer to the promenade, the lights along the pier shimmering in the dusk. For a moment, he let it be just that—a drink, a quiet room, and the last evening of their trip. All quiet on the western front.

The bar door swung open, and there she was. Freshly showered, hair brushed out, a simple dress that somehow made her look even younger. She smiled as she spotted him. "Ready?" she asked.

Maxwell stubbed out his cigarette, downed the final sip of his Scotch. "Let's go."

They stepped out onto the promenade. The evening air had cooled, carrying the aroma of the sea and the distant hum of fairground music from the pier. Aisling slipped her arm through his; she was happy. He glanced down at her and managed a smile. "Lotus House is just up past the clock tower. Shouldn't take long. Hungry?"

She grinned. "I'm starving."

As they walked, the glow of shopfronts and passing headlights danced across the wet pavement. Maxwell kept his eyes moving, watching faces in the crowd. Old habit. He told himself to let it go—for tonight.

The walk to Lotus House took just a few minutes. Inside was warm and muggy; the low hum of conversation sounded welcoming. The decor of red paper lanterns, gold dragons, and lacquered screens completed the atmosphere. It was a new world to Aisling.

"Smells gorgeous," said Aisling as they followed the waiter to a small corner table. Maxwell took the chair facing the room without thinking about it. They were hungry—no lunch—and they ordered quickly: Sweet and Sour Chicken for him, something with prawns for her, egg fried rice to share, and a pot of Chinese style green tea. The food came fast, hot and inviting.

Aisling chatted, full of the day's little moments: the antique shops, her parents' favorite book. "Could you imagine?" She avoided any mention of the slot machines. Maxwell listened, saying little but keeping a half-smile on his face. In her excitement, Aisling had not noticed the small package in Maxwell's hand. He placed it on the table and pushed it toward her.

"A small gift," he whispered.

She ripped the paper off and muffled a squeal. "The book!! How did you?"

While she had been absorbed in scrutinizing old silverware in another shop, he had slipped back and bought the book. *The perfect night, the perfect…*, thought Aisling.

When they finished, he paid the bill and stood. "Back to the hotel?" he asked.

"Yeah, early start tomorrow," she said with a mock sad face.

They stepped out into the quiet street, the town settling into night. The air felt cooler now, the mist rolling in off the water. He linked her arm through his. "I'm sad in a way but looking forward to our own little love nest."

Neither spoke much on the rest of the walk back. Aisling was content, the last evening of their honeymoon winding down. Maxwell was lost in his own thoughts.

At the hotel, they crossed the lobby without a word and took the lift to their floor. Aisling stifled a yawn. "Nice night, nice week," she whispered softly as they reached the room.

"Yeah," Maxwell agreed, unlocking the door. "Not bad." And that was it—the last night in Brighton.

CHAPTER 14

After the Honeymoon

The kitchen was strangely silent when Maxwell left for work that first morning. He didn't take time for breakfast—a quick coffee, a hurried kiss, and he was gone. She watched through the window; he didn't look back. Aisling let out a soft breath of disappointment, turned away, and surveyed the boxes and wedding presents. The faint scent of putty and fresh paint was oddly reassuring. No time to waste. The place was a jumble— boxes from the old flat, a bag of laundry they'd forgotten to send out before the honeymoon.

She tied up her hair, rolled up her sleeves, and got to work.

The kitchen first. Aisling cleared a space on the counter and unwrapped the shelf paper she'd bought in Brighton—a pretty pale yellow with a tiny pattern of forget-me-nots. Maxwell would think it daft. She pulled open the cupboard doors, mentally mapping what would go where. Scissors niftily fashioned each piece; she then laid the paper carefully along each shelf, smoothing it flat with the side of her hand, taking quiet satisfaction in the small, orderly task. Cups and glasses over here, plates and bowls there. She folded the tea towels and stacked them neatly at the end of the counter. The first project complete, Aisling exhaled, satisfied as she stood back admiring her own handiwork.

By ten o'clock, she had the kitchen unpacked. Time for a break. She put the kettle on for a quick cuppa and opened her notebook. The tea was hot and sweet, just like home—and a twinge of homesickness caught her. She made a mental note to send thanks to everybody. Pen in hand, she pressed her lips together; her eyes lingered a moment longer before she scribbled a few items: curtains, curtain hooks, a small rug for the hallway, a lampshade for the spare room… herbs for the garden… plant some vegetables. She allowed herself a quiet moment, then was up again. The sitting room next.

She slowly unwrapped the wedding presents, her mind an evaluator—a silver frame, a too-fancy crystal bowl, a stack of linen napkins she'd never use. She made a pile of tissue paper and ribbons on the floor, stacking the useful things neatly, the impractical ones tucked to one side—maybe a regift?

The radio sat on the floor by the fireplace. She plugged it in and turned it on—just for the company of voices. As though on cue, Big Ben struck noon. The twelve o'clock news. She made another cup of tea and decided to listen. Kenneth Kendall's voice came on—measured, authoritative. She'd always liked him.

The news was grim: another incident in Londonderry. She switched it off. Hoped it wasn't a friend of Bob's. Then realized she didn't know any of Bob's Derry friends. Well, there was Father O'Kane. We should have him over for dinner, when I get the place straightened out.

She'd unpacked three boxes and started lining the wardrobe drawers. She found the news disturbing; the work steadied her. She decided not to mention it to Bob. There was no point. She tried to shake it off, forcing her thoughts into the house instead. She loved her new home; in the back of her mind, she was already seeing it: the way the place would look by Christmas… where they'd put a small tree in the front window… what color she might

paint the bedrooms. Three bedrooms: maybe three children. Two boys and a girl? No— two girls and a boy…
Bobby! She smiled to herself and reached for the next box.

The days after Brighton blurred into a quiet routine. Maxwell was back at work before the suitcases had been properly unpacked. He left early, came home late, and when he was there, his mind wasn't.

He talked about the job less than he used to, and when he did talk about work it was about new faces in the station. He was constantly suspicious that he might be being overlooked for promotion. Aisling filled her off-days with household chores. Evenings were quiet, where she laid out two cups—only one used.

Maxwell came home tired, poured himself a drink, made some wisecrack about his boss, and fell asleep in front of the wireless. Aisling never complained. She had her job, but at the end of a long, draining day she longed for company.

But in the evenings, she found herself missing something. A presence she could count on. Someone to talk with. It was one of those evenings—she was home from work alone, Maxwell was, as usual, "on a job"—when she thought of Fr. O'Kane. She had planned to have him for dinner once they got settled. She decided to ask Maxwell about it.

She waited for the right time. It was one of the rare evenings their shifts didn't clash. The house smelled of roast beef and onions, and the soft thump of the oven door opening and closing marked the final test of her efforts. She'd had a few disasters, but this time she hoped she had got it right.

Aisling stood by the stove, biting her lip as she peeked in at the Yorkshire puddings. They'd risen this time—golden, puffed rims catching just enough to promise a crisp bite. Better than last Sunday. Better than the sad, flat things from the week before that Maxwell had prodded with a fork and called "cowshit."

She set the plates out: thick slices of beef, roast potatoes—crisp and floury—peas, carrots, and those precious puddings nestled in a pool of gravy. Maxwell came in, loosening his tie and sniffed.

"Smells like a bleedin' pub carvery in here. What have you got?"

Aisling smiled, wiping her hands on a cloth. "Sit yourself down. And keep your comments to yourself until you've tasted it." He grinned. "Is it another attempt at them puddings?"

"You'll see," she said as she dished his plate and set it in front of him.

By the way he wolfed into the meal she knew she had won the day. Maxwell finished his plate, licked his lips and grinned.

"You did it, didn't you."

She waited until he poured himself a Scotch and sat back down. She sat opposite him.

"I was thinking," she began, stirring her tea, "we haven't really had anyone round since we moved in."

"So?"

"Well… I was thinking, maybe Fr. O'Kane. Just for Sunday dinner. Nothing grand. He married us, after all. And you two were friends back in school."

There was a flicker of a reaction. He looked up, one corner of his mouth pulling into a twisted grin.

"O'Kane, eh? I had forgotten about the unforgettable holy man."

Aisling pressed her case. "He did speak well of you at the wedding."

"Did he, now?"

"I wasn't listening."

He slackened off. "OK, it might be a bit of fun."

Aisling smiled gleefully. "So, you wouldn't mind, then? Just a bite to eat, a bit of company."

Maxwell finished his drink, stubbed out his cigarette, and picked up the *News of the World*.

"Mind? No. Could do with a bit of a laugh. Mind you, if he starts blessing the peas, I'm out."

"I'll send him a note tomorrow."

"Don't bother. I'll drop by the rectory and tell him."

CHAPTER 15

First Visit

The doorbell rang. Aisling, already in the hallway, smoothed her skirt, checked the top button of her blouse, and glanced at the mirror on the hall stand. Why so nervous? It's only Father O'Kane.

Still… she wanted everything just so. She opened the door.

Fr. O'Kane stood self-consciously on the step, a bunch of roses clutched awkwardly in one hand, a faint sheen on his brow. He was more handsome than Aisling remembered, or maybe she hadn't looked. His silhouette caught in the soft glow of the fading afternoon light. She saw him differently. She hadn't meant to notice, but the thought slipped in before she could push it away.

Aisling swallowed. "Father O'Kane—you're right on time! Come in, come in," she beamed.

"Thank you… thank you, Aisling," said O'Kane softly. He stepped inside, glanced around, taking in the warmth of the house—the aroma of roast beef, the scent of polished wood, a vase of fresh flowers on the sideboard. *I should have brought wine.* Maxwell's voice boomed from the sitting room: "Is that my old buddy?"

O'Kane tightened. Aisling, cheerful but her voice a notch higher than she intended, answered, "It is indeed!" She leaned in and under her breath, she whispered to the priest as she took the roses. "He's in a rare mood this afternoon. He spent the morning at the club." The faint scent of her perfume caught him off guard.

O'Kane gave her a small, polite smile before handing her the roses.

Maxwell appeared in the doorway, a tumbler in hand, grinning too broadly. "Well now, if it isn't the Reverend O'Kane."

O'Kane forced a tense smile. "Good to see you, Bob."

Maxwell sauntered over, clapping a clammy hand on the priest's shoulder, a touch harder than necessary. "Well now, Father, see we're still married, aren't we? Looks like your old mumbo jumbo works after all."

O'Kane smiled mildly. "It's the people saying the vows, and the hope that they keep them."

Maxwell snorted. "Aye, well… as long as she keeps making roast beef dinners, I'll hang in."

From the kitchen, Aisling's voice cut through, quick and perky. "And you'll be wearing it if you don't watch your lip."

Maxwell laughed, raising his glass toward the kitchen doorway. "See. Is that what you might call Divine justice?"

O'Kane gave a dry chuckle. A glitch in his gut warned him that things might become nasty. "Some things have a way of sorting themselves."

Aisling had come from the kitchen; she shot Maxwell a look. "Bob," she cautioned lightly.

O'Kane grabbed the chance to change course. "Thank you for the invitation. It's good to see you both."

Maxwell gave a sideways victory grin and raised his glass. "To old times, eh?" He took a long drink. "Aisling's been flapping about this all day. You'd swear the bloody Archbishop was coming."

Aisling rolled her eyes, stepping in to smooth the air. "Come through to the sitting room, Father. Can I take your coat?" He handed it over, murmuring his thanks, and followed Maxwell into the room.

The sitting room was cozy, a small fire crackling in the hearth. The good china set out, a decanter of sherry gleaming in the firelight. On the side table, a stack of Maxwell's newspapers—crime reports, political scandals, and the racing page.

Maxwell flopped into his chair with a grunt, gesturing toward the other seat. "Park yourself. You're among friends now."

O'Kane took the offered chair, close to the fire. Aisling set the roses in a jug of water, adjusting them for a moment longer than needed. "Nice flowers, Father," Maxwell teased. "Roses are red, violets are blue, honey is sweet, and so are you! Say thank you, dear."

Aisling ignored him, offering O'Kane a gentle smile. "Would you like a sherry, Father? Or something stronger?"

"Sherry's fine, thank you."

"No wimpy drinks for me," snorted Maxwell, hands up in protest. She poured and handed the sherry to the priest, their fingers brushing. He glanced up—just a flash, and it passed. "So, what's the sermon this week, then?" Maxwell asked, settling deeper into his chair. "Fire and brimstone? Or just the usual 'be kind to your neighbor' lark?"

O'Kane swallowed but smiled mildly. "A touch of kindness can go a long way."

Maxwell wasn't done. "Kindness won't stop a knife in the ribs. Or keep a wife from wandering, eh?" He shot a crooked grin at Aisling. Aisling's face flushed a little, the hand holding her glass tightened.

A nervous hush settled, a little too long. O'Kane cleared his throat, struggling for the right words. "It smells like an appetizing meal you're making, Aisling. I could smell it from the street."

She brightened. "Roast beef, Yorkshire pudding; it's Bob's favorite."

O'Kane managed a grin. "I'll consider myself spoiled. It's mine too."

Maxwell leaned forward, eyes glinting. "Aye, you'll have to say grace."

Aisling laughed, a soft nervous sound, grateful for the release. "I promise," O'Kane said, raising his glass. "But I'll keep it strictly secular."

Aisling stood. "Right, you two behave, while I see to the gravy."

As she left the room, the two men sat in the fire's glow. Maxwell took another long drink, then fixed O'Kane with a steady look and curled his tongue across his upper lip. "You haven't changed a bit, have you? Still the pious altar boy from school. It seems to have stuck."

O'Kane met his gaze, unflinching. "And you," he said softly, "still with a need to hurt."

A stare flashed between them—history, old hurts, unspoken things. Then Aisling's voice pierced the friction.

"Dinner's ready!"

Both men stood, eyes dropped, masks back in place and grinned. "Come on, let's eat."

There was a slur in his speech. And so they went, old rivals in new clothes, walking into the small, waiting dining room. Maxwell drained the last of his drink and pushed himself up, a little too fast. The glass clinked against the side table as he set it down. O'Kane noticed the slight sway.

Aisling was already at the table, setting down the gravy boat, her smile carefully in place. "Plenty for everyone," she said lightly, though her eyes shot to Maxwell, reading the signs as well as O'Kane had. They took their seats. Maxwell at the head of the table, O'Kane to his right, Aisling opposite. The table was neatly set, white tablecloth, polished cutlery, a small bowl of cut flowers at the center. O'Kane murmured, "It looks wonderful, Aisling."

She brightened a little. "Thank you, Father. It's nice to have someone appreciate it."

Maxwell snorted, reaching for the carving knife. "Are you flirtin' with the holy father now, Mrs. Maxwell? He's already taken."

Aisling's smile thinned, but she let it pass. O'Kane, eyes downcast, said nothing. Maxwell sawed into the roast with the enthusiasm of a man whose appetite came more from drink than hunger. "Right then. Who's hungry?"

O'Kane held his glass, watching Maxwell's hands: steady enough, but his face had reddened, his voice a shade too loud for the room. Aisling passed the vegetables. O'Kane asked polite questions about her work at the hospital and her mother.

When Aisling asked if he'd like a second helping, O'Kane noticed how her eyes lingered on him a fraction, searching for something in his expression. Complicity? Pity? Hope? He wasn't sure. He saw a trace of, maybe, desperation in her eyes. Maxwell had opened another bottle, poured another drink, muttering something about an easy life with no money worries.

O'Kane, sensing that the taunt was pointed at him, tugged at his knee and coughed, intending to change the direction of the conversation. "The home is beautiful; you've both done a great job."

Maxwell dropped his fork, mumbled something under his breath. His head jerked upward. "Oh aye, she's a great wee woman." Turning to Aisling, he slurred, "Why don't you take him upstairs and show him the bedrooms? I'm sure he'd like to see your sweet little bum as you go up the stairs."

Aisling teared up; she busied herself gathering the empty plates, avoiding eye contact, her movements brisk. She swallowed. "Dessert?" she asked too cheerfully.

"Not for me," O'Kane said gently.

Maxwell waved his glass. "I've got all the dessert I need right here." O'Kane remained silent, but his glance caught Aisling's again. This time, she looked away.

O'Kane set down his knife and fork, dabbing at his mouth with the napkin. The room felt smaller now, the fire's warmth oppressive rather than comforting. He could feel the sharp malice of Maxwell's smirking jabs, aimed at both of them now. Aisling's brittle brightness, the weight of things unsaid. He glanced at his watch, though he knew the time without looking.

"I should be heading back," he said, his voice quiet but firm. "Early start tomorrow."

Aisling looked up, her face showing slight disappointment. "So soon, Father? There's tea in the pot."

He gave her a small, apologetic smile. "Next time, perhaps."

Maxwell sneered, "Where's your rush? You don't have a date—do you?"

O'Kane refused the bait, rose to his feet, smoothing nonexistent crumbs from his jacket. "Good night, Bob."

Maxwell's head had slumped to the table. O'Kane turned to Aisling. "Thank you for a lovely meal, Aisling. Truly."

For a moment, something raced across her expression—gratitude, apology, maybe even relief. "I'll see you to the door," she said, setting down the teapot.

In the hallway, she retrieved his coat and helped him into it. The light was softer here, the light of the dining room fading behind them. "Thank you for coming," she murmured. "It meant a lot… to me."

O'Kane hesitated, then nodded. "Any time you need a quiet chat, a friendly face, Aisling."

Their eyes met, the quiet weight of the evening hanging between them. Then the sharp clatter of glass and Maxwell's slurred voice from the other room broke the moment. "Tell the Bishop I fixed that speeding ticket for him!" Maxwell roared.

O'Kane shook his head and managed to make a cheerless smile. "I'll be sure to mention it." Aisling opened the door. The night air was cool and clean. "Good night, Aisling."

"Good night, Father."

"Liam," muttered O'Kane. He hesitated, as though on the edge of saying something—and was gone.

Aisling pressed her forehead against the closed door. It was cool and soothing. She returned to the sitting room; Maxwell was sprawled in the armchair, asleep. She went to bed; the dishes could wait till the morning.

CHAPTER 16

Aftermath

The kitchen smelled of strong coffee, last night's dishes piled high in the sink. Aisling stood by the counter, her back to the door, one hand loosely cradling a cup, the other casually stirring Maxwell's mug. The window over the sink showed a gray, unpromising sky. She didn't look up when Maxwell shuffled in, freshly shaved but ashen, the strain of drink and poor sleep evident in his bloodshot eyes. The bravado of the night before was long gone.

He lingered a moment, watching her.

"Morning," he muttered, clearing his throat.

Aisling didn't turn. "Coffee's there." Her voice was flat, neutral.

He crossed the room, took the mug she'd set out for him, and held it between unsteady hands, as if steadying himself more than the drink. The silence lingered.

"I was out of order last night." The words were halting, more a reluctant admission than a statement of fact.

"You think?" said Aisling coldly.

He took a sip of coffee.

"I'll call him," Maxwell said quietly.

This time, she did look at him.

"Don't bother," she snapped. "He's a good man. He won't hold it against you."

Maxwell gave a short, unsmiling snort. "Probably thinks I'm a bloody eejit."

Aisling rolled her eyes and said nothing.

"I'll square it with him next time… if there is a next time." She turned sharply and placed her hands on the counter edge. "There will be a next time, Bob. I'll be inviting him again, whether you're here or not."

The silence thickened. Maxwell gave a short, awkward laugh.

"Course you will, love. O'Kane's a good fella. Sure, you know we're old mates, me and him." He forced a grin. "Listen, if I'm not here, bring that nice-looking friend of yours, Nurse Brennan. It'll give O'Kane a bit of a thrill."

Aisling didn't respond. She picked up her coat from the back of a chair and slung it on. The clock on the wall chimed six o'clock. She set her cup down with a decisive clink.

"I've work in half an hour," she said. "You see yourself out."

As she opened the door, he called after her. "We're alright though, aren't we, Ash?"

She paused, one hand on the handle. She didn't look at him. "You'll know when we are."

She left the room. The hallway door clicked shut. Maxwell stayed where he was, staring at the cup in his hands. The kitchen felt colder without her in it. For a moment he seemed on the verge of something—an apology, a thought, a reckoning—but it passed, swallowed by his old, familiar stubbornness.

He sat down heavily, rubbing his temple. "Bloody mess," he muttered.

Aisling, halfway down the street, felt none of it. She pulled her scarf tighter, her breath clouding the cold morning air. The ache in her chest hadn't eased since the night before. She walked faster.

Work would be easier than home today.

The soft patter of rain began against the windowpane.

The weeks slipped by in a blur of night shifts and gray afternoons. The days grew shorter, the air sharper. Aisling found herself moving aimlessly through lonely days by habit— tending to patients, making small talk at the nurses' station, and returning to an empty dwelling where Maxwell came and went on late shifts and mystery meetings.

Something between them had shifted. Not broken. Not yet. But shifted.

By December, the city had taken on that damp chill that clung to weary bones, shop windows strung with weary tinsel and tired paper decorations. She barely noticed.

CHAPTER 17

Christmas Morning

Another Christmas morning dawned gray and wet. The house was quiet, save for the distant sound of children's laughter drifting up the street. Aisling closed her ears against it—another reminder of the childless years slipping by, one after another. Maxwell had always said "not now"—too ambitious, too focused on climbing the ladder. She'd told herself she understood.

She threw a log on the fire and glanced at the cards on the side table, leafing through them slowly. She'd done it twice that morning, though she didn't know what she hoped to find; she knew each message. She picked up the last card in the stack; her fingers lingered on the one from home, tracing her mother's perfect penmanship, which she was so proud of. No one else she knew wrote like that anymore. She read the enclosed letter again.

The Dexter had a calf… it all went well.—Father's pains are back; it must be the cold and damp. Declan got a job at the creamery—how's Bob? The O'Rourke's youngest one is going to America to the oldest lad— hope you can get home this year for a week or so… Father says God bless.
Your Mother.

Her eyes stung. She folded the letter carefully and set it back among the cards, as though neatness might hold back what she felt.

Normally, Marie Brennan would have been there today— bright, fiery, full of laughter and mischief. But Marie had gone north to Liverpool, spending Christmas with her brother's family. Aisling hadn't told her she'd be alone today. Marie would've insisted she come along, or worse, stayed behind out of pity. Aisling didn't want either. She hadn't put her name down for duty. Pride, mostly. Now the idea of spending Christmas on the ward would have been better, at least with other people around— it seemed appealing.

She thought about Marie Brennan and smiled instantly, remembering the recklessness she had brought to her visits, especially when Fr. O'Kane was about. "Father," Marie would tease, eyes gleaming, "ever get a squeeze off them nuns—the ones with the dark eyes and guilty thoughts? No harm, as long as you don't get into the habit." Followed by a raucous guffaw. O'Kane's face would flush a deep, helpless red, though his laugh was always easy. "Ah, Marie, you'll have me in trouble with the Bishop yet." Without missing a beat Brennan quipped back, "Ah, not to worry, maybe your man has an eye on one of them young ones himself." Fr. O'Kane roared with laughter. The shocked Aisling screeched, "Wash your mouth, Marie Brennan—that's terrible talk." She secretly thought it was funny.

Her smile lingered a moment, then faded. She missed them both more than she'd dared admit. O'Kane had said he might stop by. "I'll try, Aisling, if I can." But the morning was slipping away. The sound of the children's laughter rose again. She set the cards aside and stared out at the gray, empty street.

The light outside had dulled to a wintry gray. Aisling had long since given up hope. She'd tidied the sitting room for no reason at all, lit a small fire, and poured herself a drop of sherry she didn't particularly want. The old clock ticked on, marking a day that was slipping away.

Then, a knock at the door. It was soft—almost apologetic. Her heart gave a small, foolish leap. She knew instinctively who it was. Or maybe she only hoped she did.

She paused by the hall stand, caught herself in the little mirror. A quick, self-conscious check of her hair. The faint trace of lipstick she'd put on earlier for no reason at all—or so she'd told herself.

And yet her hand lingered at her hair a moment longer.

She opened the door. And there he was.

But not quite as she expected. No clerical collar today. A dark gray jumper, open at the neck, a black polo shirt beneath. Dark trousers, neat but ordinary. He seemed to become more handsome each time she saw him, though she'd never let herself think of it.

He lifted a biscuit tin with a half-smile, the wind catching the hem of his coat. "Didn't forget about you," he said, his voice a little breathless, maybe from rushing… or maybe from something else.

She held his gaze a moment longer than she intended. "I was starting to think you had," she said quietly, stepping aside to let him in. He glanced down, a faint flush rising in his cheeks. "Never meant to be so late, I got delayed… a few stops along the way." The biscuit tin passed between them like a peace offering. She closed the door behind him.

"Not the collar today," she remarked, as she ushered him into the sitting room, her mood lighter now. O'Kane shrugged, as she placed the tin on the table.

"Man's allowed a day off now and then, isn't he?" She gave a small laugh. There was a short wave of unexpected happiness she hadn't felt all day. "Well, you're here now, and thanks for the biscuits." He smiled, properly this time, and for a brief moment, the room felt a little less empty.

They sat by the fire, the tin of biscuits between them, the flames catching little glints of gold on the brass fender. The room was warm, the world outside cold and gray. The talk was easy, if a little strained at first. They had never been alone before.

"What's going on with Marie Brennan? I thought she might be here for Christmas," O'Kane asked, pouring the sherry, careful not to spill any.

"No. She's in Liverpool this year. Visiting her brother. Left last week, dodging the worst of the weather."

"Lucky thing she took the week off." Aisling smiled. Although she meant it, she missed Marie's company. O'Kane smiled, stretched his legs toward the fire. "She could get a laugh out of a gravestone, that one." Aisling laughed softly at that, surprised at how easy it was to talk to him like this.

He gestured toward a small photo on the mantel. "Bob keeping well?" Aisling hesitated, the question catching her a little off guard. "He's… he's busy. The job, you know. Long nights. Sometimes… sometimes he's not home till late, or not at all." She caught the priest's glance. She said it lightly, like it didn't matter. It always sounded easier in the saying. O'Kane nodded, didn't press. Just sipped his drink. She wanted to change the conversation. "How is your mother?" she asked. "My mother moved to Donegal," he said, his voice softer—pondering. "The Derry home got sold after Daddy passed. Mammy wanted to be near her sister. Donegal is quieter—peaceful." She smiled, thinking how innocent and appealing it was to hear a grown man refer to his parents as he did as a child. "You get over much?" "When I can. Too long since, really. Always someone needing something." A shrug. No bitterness in it, just the way life went.

"How are all your folk doing?" he asked. "Have you been over recently?" "Oh, they're all grand, just got a letter from my mother. Like yourself, we haven't been over. Always something." She hoped he didn't notice the disappointment in her voice. The fire crackled between them. The easy, uncertain warmth of two people not quite sure why this moment mattered, but both a little grateful for it.

At last, he checked his watch. "I should go. Bridie Mulholland's expecting me, and she'll have words if I don't show." He stood, sighing, a little reluctant if either of them were honest. Aisling felt an unexplainable twinge of jealousy. "Of course," she murmured. "Thanks for the fire. And the drink."
"Thanks for calling."

There was another awkward moment at the door again, neither quite sure how to end it. Aisling's hand half-lifted like she might touch his arm, then it dropped. "Merry Christmas." "And you, Liam." There, she said it. And he was gone. She stood there for a moment longer than she meant to, listening to the soft crunch of his steps fade down the path. The house settling back into itself.

She poured one last sherry, glanced at the fire, and told herself it was just a visit. A kind gesture on a lonely day. Of course it was. But—

Somewhere down the street, a child laughed and a radio crackled into a carol. She stood very still.

CHAPTER 18

First Recruitment

Winter turned, and with it, Maxwell's restlessness grew. He wasn't due on until midnight, and there was no sense going back to a cold house and silence. He didn't even know if Aisling was working tonight. The Bell on Forest Road would do. The pub was busy for a Thursday—smoky, the air thick with Woodbine and Players. Voices rose and fell over the clink of pint glasses and the scrape of coins on the worn wooden bar.

In the snug at the back, in a cubbyhole for four and no one else, Detective Sergeant Maxwell nursed a half of mild, waiting for his shift to start.

The door opened and a man stepped in—gray suit, trilby, a folded *Evening Standard* tucked under one arm. Maxwell caught the movement in the mirror behind the bar before he saw him properly. The man looked slightly out of place—a lonely bank clerk, perhaps, a secret drinker, maybe a civil servant drifting in for a quick one. He ordered a gin, neat. No tonic. No ice. Then, as if by coincidence, he turned toward the snug.

"Mind if I…?"

Maxwell shrugged. The man sat, set his drink down, and opened the paper, but didn't read it. With his head still in the newspaper, the man whispered, "You're Maxwell. Greenleaf Road."

Maxwell tensed but kept his face neutral.
"That's right. And you are?"
"Let's just say I'm with the Yard. Special Duties section.

I've seen your file."

Maxwell raised an eyebrow, glancing toward the door.

"Didn't know I had one."

The man sniggered. "Everyone's got one, son."

Souser, Maxwell sniggered, catching the man's effort to iron out the Liverpool twang. "You keep your head down, don't cause no fuss. But you're sharp. Handled that business at the docks last month. A bit messy, but you read it right." Maxwell said nothing.

"There's a unit looking for a certain type," the man murmured. "Nothing official. Off-the-books stuff. Might be nothing. Might be a start. You interested in hearing more?"

Maxwell took a long swig of his mild, wiped his mouth with the back of his hand. "Always want to learn." A thin smile.

"Good lad. Tomorrow night, same time. I'll be here. You too."

He finished his gin, tipped a shilling on the table, and left. Maxwell stayed a moment longer, heart steady now, but the world subtly shifted around him. What just happened? A door had opened, but what lay on the other side?

Maxwell arrived early. He wasn't keen on the idea of being late for whatever this was. The pub was quieter than the night before— unusual for a Friday, but not empty. Two workmen in dusty overalls argued over the football pools; a pair of office girls giggled too loudly near the bar; the barmaid polished glasses, waiting for a rush that was slow in coming. Maxwell took the same seat in the snug—tucked away, half-private—and kept his eyes on the door.

At exactly seven-thirty, the man in the gray suit appeared. No newspaper this time, no hat. Same neutral expression. He carried two glasses, one gin, one mild, and placed the mild in front of Maxwell before sitting.

"Name's Carter," he said quietly. "You won't find it in any station log."

"I work for a branch of the service that doesn't exist— officially. Not CID, not Special Branch. Call it internal security. There are threats we don't put in the evening papers. Some wear a balaclava; some wear an Armani suit. Doesn't matter to us."

He checked the room—still quiet—then adjusted his glass and spoke quietly.

"There's chatter of something stirring. Irish groups; not the usual rent-a-crowd protest lot. New faces."

Maxwell's arm tightened. He kept his silence.

"We need people who can blend in, ask the right questions without sounding like they're asking. People who don't panic easy." Another pause as he scanned the bar.

"You interested?"

Maxwell took a sip. His heart quivered, but he masked it.

"What's the upside? Promotion? Money?"

A flicker of amusement crossed Carter's eyes. "It's always about the bread, isn't it? Well—better than a dick's wage. But it's not about that. It's about where you'll be when things calm down." He slid a slip of paper across the table. "Address in Fitzrovia. Monday night. Nine p.m. Say you're there for the library. Back entrance. I'll vouch for you."

Maxwell folded the paper and tucked it into his breast pocket.

"One more thing," Carter said. "You tell no one. Not your wife, your piece-on-the-side, your guv' at Forest Road, not your priest.

Nobody."

He stood and walked away.

Maxwell finished his drink in silence. The pub felt smaller now, the air heavier. He touched the folded paper in his pocket. Uneasy—exposed. Carter knew too much. Be careful what you wish for.

He stepped out into the night. A light drizzle had begun. He turned up the collar of his Burberry trench coat and took the side street behind the Bell—the shortcut that brought him out near the station.

Carter's words swirled in his head. *Not your priest.*

Had he been fishing? How did they know about O'Kane? An Irish priest in London was a name in a file, enough for suspicion, enough for gossip, enough for trouble.

He realized too late he'd walked the whole way in a semitrance. The streets he normally checked—alley mouths, parked motors, half-seen faces in doorways—tonight were a blur. Stupid. No good walking into the station like this. The Guv could spot nerves a mile off

The station was in semi-darkness. Most of the shift were out or holed up in the canteen. The air hung heavy with stale sweat, damp coats, and tobacco.

The Super's office door stood ajar. Through the sliver of light, Maxwell saw the broad shoulders bent over a filing cabinet, cigarette smoke curling like a halo above his head.

Tom Callan—old school, wily, sharp-eyed, meaner with age. Maxwell stepped inside.

"Hi, Bob. On for the late, are you?"

"Aye, Guv."

"Anything good tonight?"

"Not much. Couple of domestics, break-in on Leyton High. Sweeney's dealing. Should be a quiet one."

Then—casually, but dangerous: "Word is someone from the Yard's been sniffing round Forest Road. A few names getting bandied about."

The folded paper in Maxwell's pocket felt suddenly heavier.

"You heard anything?"

He thought about lying. Some quick throwaway line. But his throat was parched.

"Nah, Guv. Nothing worth passing on."

A slow nod from Callan. "Good lad. Keep it clean." Maxwell left, pulse unsteady.

Later in the early morning, home was no refuge. The place was quiet, the hall light spilling into the kitchen where Aisling sat at the table, a cup of cold tea beside her. She didn't look up when he entered.

He poured himself a strong coffee and sat opposite her. For a moment, neither spoke.

"How was your night?" she asked at last.

"The usual, same old shit."

"You seem in a mood. Anything wrong?"

"Job, job, job," he snapped. "It's always the job."

There was no accusation in her voice—something worse: sadness, weariness.

"You've been smoking too much lately."

"Station's tense," he muttered. It sounded like a plea.

"Anything wrong?"

He met her eyes. He wanted to tell her—the pressure of it, the strangeness of it—but Carter's warning was louder.

"Nah. Nothing worth talking about."

She looked away, then rose, grabbed her coat, and with a quick "Goodbye," she was gone.

Maxwell lit another cigarette, the flame unsteady on the first strike. He nibbled on a piece of toast without appetite. His head throbbed with unanswerable questions. He poured a drink, swallowed it in one go, dragged himself upstairs, and collapsed onto the bed.

Back at work, the station felt different. Same faces, same chatter, same old war stories—but something had shifted. Or was it paranoia?

Maxwell found himself watching the room more than usual. Not openly. Quick glances. Who stopped talking when he passed. Who lingered on the phone. When a question came twice in a minute, his nerves tightened.

The days crawled.

And suddenly, it was here.

Monday night came like a flash; his mind gripped by the prospect of what was ahead.

CHAPTER 19

Fitzrovia

Monday Night, 9 p.m.

Maxwell arrived early in Fitzrovia, just as the last commuters were spilling out of the tube and into the misty London streets. Fitzrovia was quieter than usual tonight, the usual buzz of conversation and cars muted under the damp, cold air.

He found the address easily: a row of Georgian buildings on a colorless street, their facades dimly lit by streetlights. The door was plain, unmarked, except for a tiny brass number on the doorframe. The brass 25 jumped against the black lacquered paint.

Maxwell glanced around, instincts kicking in, then knocked once, firm and deliberate. After a pause, the door opened just a crack. A pair of eyes peeked out.

"You're late," the voice said.

The door swung wider. "I'm not late," Maxwell muttered under his breath, stepping inside.

The air smelled of dust, old leather, and something faintly metallic. Carter—the man from The Bell—stood near the back, a dim lamp casting shadows across his pallid features.

"You made it," Carter said, as if it were nothing. "Good."

The door clicked shut behind Maxwell with the clunk of a prison cell door. The room was small, filled with mismatched furniture: a couple of chairs, a wooden table scattered with papers, and a half-open filing cabinet. A few men sat around the table— sharp faces, understated but expensive clothes.

Carter motioned to the empty chair. "This is where it begins."

Maxwell hesitated, then took the seat. He could feel their eyes on him—evaluating, measuring. He realized he had reached the point of no return. He steadied himself and glanced around the table, trying to establish the hierarchy—who was in charge, who followed.

One of the men across from him, older, with a hawkish nose and thin lips, was skimming through papers. Maxwell pegged him immediately as Number One. The man's piercing green eyes rose, fixing on Maxwell with surgical precision.

"Good evening, Mr. Maxwell. Do you mind if we call you Max?"

Trying to lighten the atmosphere, Maxwell replied, "You can call me what you like, as long as you don't call me too early in the morning."

Silence. Total. *Oh Christ. Stupid.* He shot a glance at Carter, who stared back like a slab of stone. Maxwell felt clammy—his shirt sticking to his back.

Without lifting his head, the hawk-nosed man said, voice like a scalpel, "We're not recruiting for the Bruce Forsyth Show, Mr. Maxwell." He paused, letting the words hang. Finally, "Shall we begin?"

Maxwell cleared his throat. "Sorry." His hands were sticky.

"You left Londonderry in '69. Why?" Sharp. Direct.

Maxwell blinked. "No work. Too raucous." "Raucous?" Number One echoed.

"Buddies in too much trouble. Wasn't my thing."

"You still in touch with any of them?"

Be careful, Maxwell warned himself. A slight hesitation. "Not since I left. Glad to be out of there…"

From the corner of his eye, he saw a third man at the table make a note.

Number One continued, rapid-fire: "You know the streets. Know who is or might be involved. Who hears things. Who might give up info. Who breaks under pressure. Who'd carry a message."

Maxwell bit his bottom lip—unsure how to answer—and ran his palms along his knees.

"Cat got your tongue, Mr. Maxwell?" It was Hawk-nose—eyes penetrating.

Maxwell crossed his arms, playing for time. "Yeah, I know the streets. Know the types. Money's tight—I'm sure it'd loosen a few tongues."

"What were your father's politics?"

Maxwell's stomach tightened. *Jesus—Carter asked me that. What did I say?* "He didn't have any," he muttered.

A quick flip of papers. "You told Carter 'Labor,'" Number One snapped.

Maxwell's mouth dried. "The truth is, the auld fella was more interested in dog racing. I told Carter that because he seemed to need an answer." He forced a sheepish grin toward Carter. Carter's face didn't move.

"I'd heard you think fast on your feet. Very well. Are you ready for this?"

Maxwell inhaled. "I'm ready and able for whatever the job takes."

"This isn't a job," Number One said. "It's a game of patience, persistence, and toughness. Your buddies back in Derry—or wherever—will not take kindly to your actions. Are you ready for that?"

"I'm ready."

"You talk a good game. What we need now is not just talk but action. When you see something, hear something, or meet someone you think might be trouble, you tell us—no matter how small." Maxwell swallowed, palms damp. "Understood."

"Good. We'll be in touch. Don't do anything stupid. And Maxwell"—Number One's eyes locked onto him like gun barrels— "this stays quiet. Between us."

Maxwell straightened, chest tightening, a twitch rising at the corner of his mouth. "Quiet as the grave."

The men exchanged a glance; a folder closed. The tension in the room loosened just enough for him to exhale. He was alone now—or as alone as a man could be in a room full of shadows. The weight of what he'd agreed to settled on him like wet wool. *Why did I say grave?* He had stepped over a line—a line he still couldn't quite see.

The MI5 man was testing Maxwell's usefulness, reliability, and instincts—gauging whether he was a street-smart lad worth cultivating—not quite ready to bring him in on any operations yet.

Maxwell stood in the quiet street. It was cold but he felt clammy—his shirt sticking to his back. His shoulders shuddered; coat pulled tight, he walked quickly. Hands in pockets, his fingers touched an unfamiliar paper. *How did that get there?* He read the note—48 Theobalds Road, Holborn.

Friday—same time.

CHAPTER 20

Holborn

The second summons led him to Holborn—a insignificant stretch of Theobalds Road lined with government leases and insurance offices. Drab—concrete block buildings.

The building was neither old nor new, just tired. A caretaker nodded him through without asking his name. Inside, a single clock ticked above a row of brown doors, all unmarked.

A bare office with no view, blinds drawn halfway, the hum of a fluorescent tube. He couldn't tell if it was morning or afternoon. The clock on the wall had stopped.

A cracked leather chair—no armrest—waited for him on the other side of a scuffed desk. The only decoration was a slightly crooked portrait of the Queen—the frame nicked and dusty.

Three men sat, grim-faced. One was the man from Fitzrovia—hook nose, the one that Maxwell had marked as Number One. The other two were new faces. Maxwell quickly recalculated and surmised that his earlier assessment was incorrect. The man in the middle did not look anything like a cop. He was in his early fifties with the forgettable face of a university don—gray suit.

He sat turning pages in a slim file. No nameplate. No rank. No badge.

When he spoke, his voice carried the dry authority of someone used to being obeyed. "Let's begin. Full name, please." Maxwell's answer was followed—fast, alert.

"You're from Londonderry, aren't you, Maxwell?"

"Aye," he said. "Born and bred."

They went through it again. Family. National Service. Posting to Walthamstow. Friends in Derry. Political leanings. Wife's details. Pub habits.

Maxwell felt the repetition. Tiny shifts in phrasing.

"You mentioned your father had Labor sympathies, correct?"

"Yes."

"Odd. Carter had him down as Independent."

A pause. The man didn't blink. Maxwell kept his voice steady.

"My father voted Labor, sir. I can't speak for how Carter wrote it down."

A brief curl at the corner of the middle man's mouth—not quite a smile.

He glanced up briefly. "You've been keeping yourself busy in Walthamstow. Certain people speak highly of you. Say you've a head for reading a room. You don't ask too many questions when it matters."

Maxwell stayed quiet.

The man studied him a brief moment longer, then closed the file—softly.

"You've been through one of these before," he said. "We like to be thorough. There's a situation developing—certain interests in London, certain faces from your home patch. We prefer to keep an eye."

He opened a drawer, drew out a plain envelope, and laid it on the desk between them.

"Inside's a name, a pub, and a time. You'll go there, have a drink, listen. Nothing more. You do well, we'll see about moving you along faster than the usual channels."

Maxwell weighed the envelope in his hand. "What department is this?"

The man's mouth moved—something close to a smile, but colder.

"You don't need to worry about departments. Just be where you're told, when you're told." He leaned forward slightly. "You're not in Walthamstow anymore, sergeant. There's a bigger game being played here."

Maxwell nodded slowly. "Understood."

"Good man."

As he turned to leave, the man said, "Maxwell—one more thing."

Maxwell paused in the doorway.

The man tapped the file with a finger. "You mentioned a name before. Gallagher."

Maxwell paused. *Shit, Gallagher? Did I mention him?* The name ricocheted around Maxwell's brain like a stray bullet. "Aye," Maxwell said carefully. "Brendan Gallagher. From our street. Tough bastard. Always had his nose into the politics. Left Derry not long before me. Word was he'd joined the Provos."

The man's expression didn't change. "We've heard the name. A bit of interest there ourselves. Disappeared a while back—South America. Or dead." He studied Maxwell's reaction, unblinking.

Maxwell met his stare. "You'd know him if you saw him?"

Maxwell gave a short snort. "Aye. Wouldn't forget Gallagher."

"If his name crosses your path—or anyone sniffing about for him—you let us know. Quietly. We're not asking you to chase ghosts. Just to know who's moving where." Maxwell nodded once. "Understood."

"Good lad," the man said, finally looking pleased. "It's handy when a man knows the streets he came from."

He reached for the next file, already finished with him. "We'll be in touch."

Maxwell turned to go—but the center man raised a hand slightly.

"One more round, Mr. Maxwell."

Maxwell paused, half-turned back toward the desk.

The man folded his hands. "Your wife—how would she describe you?"

"Hard-working. Cautious." *Why did he ask that?* "Who's the person you trust most in your life?"

Maxwell paused. "Myself."

The center man lowered his gaze; his eyebrows lifted a fraction. A silence stretched. The hawk-nosed officer made a small note.

"Tell me, Mr. Maxwell… is it ever right to break the law for the greater good?"

Maxwell swallowed—carefully, weighing the question— then shrugged lightly. "Depends who's writing the law."

The hawk-nosed man suppressed a smirk. The center man smoothed his palms together as though settling dust. The questions grew stranger.

"If a friend of yours were suspected of subversion?"

Maxwell was ready. "I'd want proof."

"And if proof came?"

"Then I'd do what was expected."

Each answer felt like stepping deeper into marshland.

Then came a deliberate trap: "Carter noted you left Brook Street in '69, yet here it says '70."

"Must be the paperwork, sir. '69's correct." There was defiance in his voice.

The colonel scribbled another slow note. Then came quiet. Long. Heavy. The clock ticked. Maxwell swallowed hard. He realized they were testing him—not for truth, but for stillness. For what he could hold back. He let the silence breathe.

At last, the center man closed the folder. "Well," he said softly, "you appear to know when to speak and when not to." He glanced at the others. "We can work with that."

The hawk-nosed officer leaned forward. "You'll be contacted, Maxwell. When and how shouldn't be your concern. You'll listen, report, and wait."

Maxwell nodded. "Understood."

"Good. One last thing," the older man added. "You've come this far—you might as well remember the golden rule." A long pause.

"Never assume you're the only one in the room who knows the true answer."

The words landed like a verdict. No handshake. No goodbye. The interview was simply over.

Maxwell left the office; the envelope tucked inside his coat.

Outside, the drizzle had turned to steady hail. Maxwell stepped into it, letting the cold pinpricks settle into his scalp and collar. He paused under a streetlamp, drawing in a slow breath before lighting a cigarette, shielding the flame with his hand.

The envelope felt heavier—as if the decision had already been made for him. He had gone in as a policeman. He came out feeling… claimed.

And somewhere behind him, in that bare little office, a file with his name on it had begun to thicken.

Whitehall bustled with its usual indifference. Maxwell stepped out into the street, the air damp and close, rain drifting sideways in a thin mist. He stopped beneath a streetlamp, lit a cigarette, and watched the glow flare at the tip. The city moved around him in its usual indifference, but something in the rhythm felt off—slightly delayed, slightly wrong.

A bus hissed past. A man in a dark coat hurried by without looking up. Ordinary things, but tonight they tugged at him.

He tightened the knot of his tie. The envelope inside his jacket rested against his ribs like a quiet accusation. He'd gone in as a policeman. He'd come out feeling claimed.

As he walked, he caught his reflection in a shop window— just a blur, but for a moment he thought he saw someone behind him. He turned. Nothing there. Only the wet pavement, the sodium glow, the echo of his own footsteps. He forged ahead relentlessly, with quiet resolve, a steady rhythm to his steps.

There was no going back now.

CHAPTER 21

Guv's Office

The station was quiet, rain tickling the windows. Maxwell had just finished his shift report when the word came down—"Guv wants a word." He knocked and stepped inside with controlled eagerness, posture straight, voice steady, careful not to let the thrill of his new post spill into swagger.

The Guv sat behind his desk, jacket off, sleeves rolled, a mug in hand. Across from him, a man from the Fitzrovia interviews— same gray suit, same dead eyes. Guv gestured to the chair. "Sit."   Maxwell did.

"Right," Guv went straight to it, glancing at the Fitzrovia man, whom Maxwell recognized as the note taker. "You've been seconded. Special Branch liaison, starting soon.
Temporary assignment. You'll get details later."

The Fitzrovia man gave Maxwell a thin smile. "You'll be briefed in due course. Discretion expected." He stood, closed the door softly behind him, and walked out—nothing. No handshake, no farewell.

Silence hung for a moment.

The Guv stared at the closed door, leaned back in his chair, rubbed a hand over his flushed face, and exhaled through his teeth.
"Every time one of them bastards leave a room the stink remains."   He
looked at Maxwell.

"Listen to me now. I don't like this. I don't like them. I've seen what happens to good men who get mixed up with these people. You're on your own the second you put your name to whatever they stick under your nose. They don't do loyalty. They don't do mates. You slip once, you're out, you're on your lonesome, and if you're lucky they'll just hang you out to dry." He picked up his mug, drank, and exhaled slow.

"You're a good copper, and from what I can see, a good man. So, mind yourself, keep your eyes open, be careful of their rules, and whatever you do—don't trust a bloody thing they say and, above all, don't become one of them."

Maxwell nodded. He listened carefully, though his eyes gave away the thrill.

"Understood, sir. I appreciate the caution. I won't let you down."

The Guv gave a tight nod. "Good. Now piss off before I get sentimental."

Maxwell stepped back into the corridor and smirked. *Let them watch. I'll turn their rules to my benefit.*

Later that afternoon—A Meeting of Detectives

Detectives' office, Walthamstow Police Station, late afternoon. A haze of cigarette smoke hung in the air. A couple of plain-clothes coppers nursed cups of tea, files spread out on wellworn desks.

The Guv stepped in—no ceremony.

"Right, listen up. Just so we're all clear—anyone wondering what was going on with his absences and interviews: there were no grounds for concern. Maxwell's been cleared. No case to answer. He's been seconded on special duties. I don't want to hear another bloody whisper about it. Where to is not your concern, nor mine.

You'll see him in the interim; there will be no questions. Just behave as normal. Is that clear?"

A few muttered "Right, Guv" and exchanged glances.

The Guv fixed them with a glare. "And if I catch wind of anyone spreading whispers or sticking their oar in, you'll find yourself walking a beat in bloody Stepney before you can say ransfer papers.' That clear?"

Detective Sergeant Quinn pursed his lower lip, halfsmirking.
Crystal, Guv."

The Guv glared. "Good. Now get back to work. This station

doesn't run itself."

CHAPTER 22

The Human Asset

Maxwell's initial transition to MI5 was not the glamor move he had imagined. The first few weeks were, as he saw it, bloody messager boy work—as he saw it—being asked to drop packages, collect envelopes, deliver sealed notes without knowing their contents. No explanations. No acknowledgement. *So much for trust.*

He was also assigned routine surveillance sweeps: shadowing minor persons of interest, trailing them through crowded pavements, watching who they drank with, who they argued with, who they avoided. Nothing dramatic. No confrontations. Just hours of quiet footsteps and cigarette smoke, slipping into pubs after them, taking mental notes while pretending not to notice when one of the senior watchers was clearly following him. "Don't contact us, we'll contact you," they told him. The brushoff.

The debrief sessions irritated him most. He would sit in the corner while junior analysts—boys who had never worked a beat— pored over maps, times, faces, and Maxwell's reports with the certainty of exam markers. He held his tongue, but in his head he corrected them. He could have run half the briefings better. He knew the streets; they were guessing at them. But he nodded, stayed quiet, played the good soldier.

Meanwhile, Maxwell was anxious for an important assignment, something with action—a tail with teeth, an interrogation, a door to kick in. The King's Head had become his office. He had to be out of the house, not wanting Aisling to know he was not reporting to the station. Over long, drawn-out pints he planned—who he knew and how he could get information about back home, which pubs he should frequent.

O'Kane came to mind. A priest sees things, hears things. People spill their guts to them. Especially Irish lads far from home, with loose tongues and guilty hearts. *Who knows what might drop into O'Kane's lap—and by extension, into mine.*

Maxwell's thoughts turned on how O'Kane's softness might make him pliable—easy to lean on, if conscience or circumstance applied the right pressure. He tucked the notion away.

Aisling noticed the change at once. His moods had grown darker, more morose, as if a weight she couldn't name had settled on him. There was more pressure at the station, she told herself— more late hours, sudden disappearances, unexplained trips. He no longer drank at home, though the cigarette smoke hung thicker. The talk of work and promotion had dried up, and when she tried to broach it, he changed the subject and looked away.

She began to wonder if he had lost his job… or if there was someone else. The late-night calls unsettled her most—the rings that ended in silence, only dead air and a click. They gnawed at her in the quiet hours, feeding doubts she couldn't push aside.

Several weeks passed, and Aisling noticed a palpable change in Maxwell's mood. She was at a loss but glad for it and assumed that the pressure at work had eased. The late-night absences continued, but she appreciated the new tone. She had long since stopped asking him about his movements.

One evening, as Aisling stood folding laundry, she was pleasantly surprised when Maxwell came through the door in a rare, buoyant mood. He loosened his tie, flicked on the TV, and poured a generous whiskey before kicking off his black shoes. Then he sprawled into his favorite armchair with the ease of a man without a care in the world.

"I hope you've cooked something good tonight, Ash honey." His voice was cheery.

She smiled, happy to see him so bubbly, but she wasn't ready for complete absolution.

"Well, we might have if I knew what hour or day you might appear." She tried to keep her tone light, but the edge was there. Aisling had started to prepare a meal—bacon and eggs. She saw this was her opportunity.

"I saw Fr. O'Kane this morning," she said, trying to be casual. Maxwell's antenna went up, but he feigned disinterest.

"Really," he grunted.

Aisling continued, "He asked after you. Said it's been a while since he called by."

Maxwell held his breath, forcing self-control. He took a short sip. "You know, he's right. Maybe you should ask him over."

She stopped—surprised. "Really? Since when? You two never had much to say to each other, and when you do, it usually doesn't end well."

"Oh, leave it be. Different times, different times. It never hurts to be civil."

Aisling looked askance, her eyes squinting, curious at the sudden change. "Why now?"

He gave her a look—half-suspecting, half-culpable. Aisling sighed and let it drop, but her wariness lingered.

A few evenings later Aisling arrived home from work, tired and lonely. The house always seemed chilly and empty when she was alone. Bob's mood had improved but his work schedule seemed to have become more grueling. He claimed it was a special assignment—more money—but she wondered if it was worth it.

Marie Brennan had gotten a new boyfriend that seemed to take up all her off-duty time. Fr. O'Kane hadn't been around for months. As a result, life had become very lonesome.

The evening crept in. Aisling sat at the kitchen table, her fingers circling a single teacup before her, staring blankly ahead. She felt sorry for herself but determined to get out of the funk. *Maybe I should ask Fr. O'Kane… maybe Marie and the boyfriend if she can't make it without him.*

She thought about Bob. *Why was he so anxious to have Father over?*

Maybe it was nothing. *Yes. I will invite them. Bob might not even be here.*

CHAPTER 23

The Dinner

It took several weeks before Aisling could coordinate a suitable time with Marie. She hoped that Fr. O'Kane would be more flexible. Marie was glad that her boyfriend had been invited, as she wanted to show him off. She had repeated several times that she met him in Tralee last year when they were both home for a week in July. They were both pleased when they learned that they lived within a mile of one another in Kilburn. According to Marie, he had left Ireland after serving his apprenticeship as a bricky and had built a good little business in London. Aisling was happy for Marie and glad she would be a neighbor in the years ahead.

When they arrived, Aisling could see by the sparkle in Marie's eyes why she was attracted to the big Kerry man. He was square shouldered and well-built, his broad face carrying a warmth that made him instantly likable. Marie bounced in with her usual glee. "Where's Fr. O'Kane?" she cried excitedly.

Aisling, overcome by her exuberance, smiled. "Well, hello—aren't you going to introduce us?"

"Oh, I'm sorry!" Marie's hand flew to her mouth with a giggle. "This is Tim. Tim Flynn, the best-looking man in Kerry—just ask him." Turning to Tim she added, "Tim, this is Aisling, my now-and-forever best friend."

Aisling turned back to Marie, still smiling. "Now I can answer your question. Father O'Kane is running a wee bit late, but he's coming." With a polite nod to Tim she added, "You're very welcome, Tim. Come on in and meet Bob; he's in the sitting room."

Bob Maxwell had heard the commotion in the hallway and was standing. He and Marie exchanged chilly greetings, although he extended a hand to Tim. "Always good to meet another Irishman." Tim joined him in a hefty glass of whiskey as the two women withdrew to the kitchen.

Before Aisling reached the oven, the front doorbell rang apologetically—just one short ding. Aisling's heart jumped. "That's him now," she blurted, too excitedly.

Marie gave a swift, puzzled glance. "Go get it."

Aisling pulled her apron off, touched her hair, and rushed to the door. She opened it, and there he stood—a shy smile, eyes blue with a glazed wetness. She gulped. For an extended heartbeat, neither spoke. Aisling felt the awkward weight of the moment. A hug? A handshake? She half-raised a hand, then changed her mind, her smile doing its best to cover the flutter in her chest.

"You made it," she said, a little breathless.

"Wouldn't miss it," O'Kane murmured.

Before either could bridge the strange little gap between them, Marie's voice rang out from the kitchen, sharp and playful. "Well, are you keeping the poor man out there all night or what?"

Aisling laughed, grateful for the intrusion. O'Kane gave a bashful grin and handed a brown bag to her. Marie caught sight of the pair as they entered the kitchen. For a split second, something about the way Aisling looked at him—or how neither seemed quite sure of themselves—made her hesitate. She started to open her mouth, some cheeky quip about priests and married women on the tip of her tongue, then stopped herself. *Not now. Not the time.*

Instead, she grinned and hugged O'Kane. "Well, look who the wind blew in. About time." She stopped with mock shock— hands raised. "Do I have to go to confession for hugging you, Father?"

O'Kane laughed, relieved at the ordinary welcome, and Marie let the Aisling greeting pass—though she made a mental note. Something was up. She didn't know what. Maybe Aisling would talk about it.

Aisling slipped the whiskey from the bag with an inner glow and set it aside before gently guiding O'Kane toward the sitting room. "Come on, Father, at least have a glass of wine," she said, forcing a brightness she hoped would soften the edges she feared might come.

Tim Flynn rose as the priest entered, his chair scraping the floor—his nod stiff but respectful, the gesture of a man honoring the cloth without yet knowing the man who wore it. Bob, however, didn't stir. He kept his gaze on the amber swirl in his glass, topping it up with a steady hand. Not a glance, not a word— just the silence of a man struggling between hostility and need.

Aisling sensed the air tighten between them, but she forced a smile all the same, smoothing the moment as best she could. "Glad to meet you, Father, I've heard a lot about you," boomed Flynn with a warm smile.

"Nothing good, if it came from Marie," chuckled O'Kane.

"Oh, I could tell you the dark secrets about my old schoolmate," interjected Maxwell with a forced laugh. "How are you, old friend?" he finally threw to O'Kane.

O'Kane gave a demure smile. "Good to see you, Bob. Thanks for having me."

"Not at all—good to have you. Have a drink. What'll it be? Whiskey?"

"No thanks, Bob, I'll have a glass of wine if I may."

Maxwell glanced at Tim and shrugged as he handed O'Kane the wine.

The table had been set with care—a simple roast chicken, potatoes, green beans, and a trifle waiting in the fridge for later. Aisling insisted everyone sit where they pleased. Marie made a show of steering Tim beside her at one end. O'Kane settled at the lower end, leaving Aisling alone across from Marie and Tim. Maxwell took the head of the table.

"Right," announced Aisling, pouring wine and raising her glass. "To old friends and new."

Glasses clinked, and conversation tripped slowly into life. Bob Maxwell led the way. "So, Tim," he began, leaning back, glass in hand. "I hear you're in the building trade?"

"Bricky by trade," Tim grinned with a tint of pride. "These days I mostly chase the big contractors and lads leaning on their tools. The big fellas don't want to pay their bills—and sure, no wonder, they're buying villas in Spain."

Marie laughed. "Well, they need a love nest for the girlfriends. Right, Father?"

"Aye—and the drugs," muttered Maxwell, his jaw tightening.

O'Kane shook his head, half in amusement at Marie's antics. He took a sip of wine—listening, content to stay out of the opening tête-à-tête.

"Father O'Kane," Tim turned toward the priest with an easy smile. "And yourself—how long have you been in London?"

"Longer than I expected—but I go where they send me," O'Kane replied with a soft grin.

Aisling smiled, glad for the momentary ease. "I know the parishioners are glad you're here." Marie caught the glance.

Maxwell steered the conversation. "You know, me and the good Father go back long before London. Grew up in Lon—" his gaze flicked around the table, "—Derry, didn't we, Liam?" O'Kane's fork paused mid-air; he nodded. "That we did, Bob."

Maxwell ignored the shrewd implication in his voice. "You wouldn't believe the scrapes this lad could get into."

O'Kane gave a tight smile. "Lessons well earned, I suppose."

Marie grasped something in the exchange—a trace of an old, unfinished conflict—and quickly changed direction. "Do you go back often?"

Before the priest could answer, Maxwell's fist tightened— the childhood animosity stirred. He glared at O'Kane through glazed eyes. "Aye, I'm sure he keeps in touch."

Marie was talking again. "And Aisling should be voted 'Best Hostess of the Year.'"

"Your turn next time, Marie," Aisling countered, glad for the distraction. She wasn't sure what had just transpired, but she sensed it was ominous.

Tim, oblivious, grinned. "Ah, and a good plate of spuds, cabbage, and a shoulder of the best bacon at Marie's table."

Laughter broke the tension for a moment. Plates were passed, second helpings offered. For a while, the conversation turned to safer ground—rising petrol prices, strikes, politics. Maxwell watched the big-mouthed Kerry man work his way through both the meal and the whiskey; the man had an opinion about every subject. The more whiskey he consumed, the more opinionated he became. Maxwell branded him—a talker.

When Maxwell mentioned the scandalous state of the Irish football team, Tim was adamant. "Sure, how could a small island like ours field two teams? Them bloody loyalists in the north won't agree to having one team."

Maxwell saw his opening. "I'm sure there's plenty feel the same way, Tim. How do you feel about it?" he said, addressing O'Kane.

O'Kane sensed the trap. "I'm not into sports very much— maybe a wee bit of fishing now and then."

"You still see many of the old crowd?" Bob asked casually, refilling his glass.

"Not really," O'Kane said. "People scatter."

Maxwell saw the door slightly open. "Some names stay in touch though, surely. What about Gallagher—he was a good friend of yours."

O'Kane felt a twinge of guilt. "No, not for years. I went off to Saint Patrick's in Armagh—we lost contact."

Aisling, catching the strain in his expression, rose from the table. "Trifle, anyone? Come help me, Marie."

It was an excuse for Maxwell to top up Tim Flynn's glass. "I'm glad Wilson got in. What's your thoughts on it?" Maxwell asked them both.

Tim had a ready answer. "Ah, I used to be a Labor man, but since I made a few bob I'm more leaning Conservative." Maxwell's interrogation juices were flowing. "I thought Labor would be better for Ireland?"

"Not at all—sure they cracked down just as hard on the lads."

Maxwell pushed. "I see there was some bombing in Birmingham last week."

"Aye—Belfast lads, I hear… all got away back," boasted Flynn.

"You're well in the know, Tim. Where do you get your information?" quizzed Maxwell, eyes targeting.

Flynn was beginning to slur. "Ah, you know… there's talk at the pubs or on the sites."

"Tell me this now—where does a fella like you find a decent pint these nights, or do you drink much?" joked Flynn.

Maxwell shrugged and sneered. "Now and again. Depends who's buyin'."

Tim elbowed O'Kane as he roared with laughter. "That's the way of it, isn't it? As they say in Kerry—a poor man's whiskey tastes sweeter when it's someone else's coin."

Fr. O'Kane had sat quietly listening. Maxwell held his gaze—assessing. Then, turning to Tim: "I'll have to get the lay of the land, so I will. Haven't had much chance since I came back this side of town."

Tim leaned over, lowering his voice. "There's a place— The Killarney Bar, on Kilburn High Road. Thursday nights— proper crowd. Bit of a session if you catch the right night. Sure, you might know half the faces yourself. A lot of northern lads."

Maxwell chuckled. "You know, I might take you up on that."

O'Kane sipped his wine and watched the exchange in silence. Aisling and Marie cleared the dishes away, deep in their own conversation, oblivious to the undercurrent.

Maxwell pushed back in his chair and turned his attention to O'Kane. "You're very quiet, Father. What have you to say about all this?"

Fr. O'Kane steepled his fingers, looked from one to the other before speaking. "My politics are confined to my parishioners— and that's political enough for me."

Maxwell noted how deftly the priest had fended off the question. He stared, fish-eyed, at O'Kane. *This is going to be a harder nut to crack than I'd thought.* Maxwell took a drink and turned his attention to Flynn. He spoke casually. "Tim, you must know a few of the Irish lot knocking around the Kilburn pubs—The Shamrock, O'Leary's, that new one on the High Road?"

Flynn's speech was getting looser as he warmed to the subject. "I haven't been to O'Leary's or the Shamrock, but all the in-the-know crowd hang out in The Killarney. Come down some night and I'll introduce you to some of the northern lads."

O'Kane gnawed on his inner cheek, taking a quick glance at both men, relieved when Aisling and Marie arrived with the trifle. Aisling, cheerful and masking the earlier tension, announced, "Right—who's for trifle? Plenty to go 'round."

Bleary-eyed Tim grinned, raising his empty glass. "Ah, Jaysus, Ash, you'll have to roll me home at this rate!"

Marie's eyes flashed wide. "Watch your manners, Tim Flynn. It's Aisling or Mrs. Maxwell to you."

Tim blinked, confused. "Well, sure, that's what Bob calls her."

"Well, you're not Bob."

Aisling smiled. Marie glanced at O'Kane. "Father, go easy on the trifle. All that sugar can't be good for your testosterone—mind that oul' sex drive."

Everyone laughed except Aisling. O'Kane crossed himself in jest. Marie teased, "Tell me, Father—ever tempted to chuck it all and go wild? Bet there's a rogue in you."

"There's a rogue in every man, Marie. The trick is knowing when to leash it," O'Kane replied.

Tim lifted his glass again—slurred but cheerful. "To old friends… new friends… and the lads that never got caught!" O'Kane raised his glass. "To friends."

Marie touched Tim's shoulder. "Right, time to go before I insult Father O'Kane again and get excommunicated." "One more for the road!" Tim pleaded.

"You'll have it at home," she laughed.

At the door she tossed one final jab: "Mind yourself, Father—Aisling might have that trifle laced."

"Too late for that," O'Kane blushed. Aisling felt a twinge.

The door closed. Silence fell.

"Would you like a coffee before you go, Father?"

"A coffee might be in order. I've a bit of a buzz."

Maxwell cut in quickly. "Yes, and I'd like your thoughts on a thing or two."

"I can't stay long," O'Kane said.

Aisling went to the kitchen. Maxwell topped up his whiskey. "You always steer clear of the whiskey."

"Never felt the need."

"Just like the women, eh?" Maxwell chuckled. O'Kane ignored the remark.

"Heard a fella from Stanley's Walk got into bother last week. Jamie Coyle—you know the name?"

"No."

O'Kane continued lightly. "You know the last time I was home I was talking with a woman from Fahan Street—Mrs. Quigley—and I asked her what I thought was an innocent question about the rumors I had heard—and she said, 'You know, Father, that there'—" he tapped his nose, "—gets you that there—" he tapped his knee.

Maxwell smirked, understanding the message. He tried again. "Some old names pop up now and then. A name like Gallagher."

"I've no word of him; I told you that."

Maxwell lit a cigarette. "Likely for the best. Not all friends travel the same road."

"It's a small world. Names get around," O'Kane replied.

Maxwell probed. "Funny hearing Tim rattling on. Some things never change."

"And some do."

Maxwell shifted in his chair, unsure who was winning the word game. "Always wondered where you'd land."

"Never thought you cared," O'Kane retorted quickly.

O'Kane shifted, anticipating another trap. "You know, Bob—you should take up fishing. You might be good at it."

Maxwell's eyes hardened—just a fraction. "The world's a funny place," he murmured.

"Coffee's ready!" Aisling called.

"You go ahead," Maxwell said. "I'll finish my drink."   In the kitchen, Aisling poured coffee and sat opposite the priest.

"Thank you, Aisling," O'Kane said. He caught himself— careful.

"So, what did you make of Tim?"

"Talks enough for three. Harmless."

"Marie thinks he's a keeper."

"That's a pair. She'll keep him in line."

"You've a way of rattling him."

"Who? Tim? I rattle a lot of people."
"Not Tim. Bob."

Aisling leaned in, voice low. "He's not the man I married. He's quieter. Watching. Like he's somewhere else."

"Maybe it's the job. He's strained."

"He watches you," she whispered. "Even when he smiles."

O'Kane touched her shoulder gently. "Pressures of work can change men."

Her eyes filled. "Listen to me—I'll be crying into your coffee."

"I understand loneliness," O'Kane said softly. "Even in parish chaos. I'll pray for you."

She touched his hand. "Thank you, Liam."

Sensing the danger, he finished his coffee. "This has been a beautiful evening, Aisling. Thank you. Wonderful to see you all."

At the door, she kissed him lightly on the cheek. "Take care of yourself, Ash," he said, turning quickly.

Aisling stood in the hallway, staring into the mirror—a face caught between worlds she dared not imagine. She walked toward the sitting room, then changed her mind and climbed the stairs—drained.

CHAPTER 24

First Night at The Killarney

The Killarney Bar was heavy with cigarette smoke, the hum of conversation rising above the clink of pint glasses and the occasional burst of laughter. A popular Wolfe Tones tune played from a jukebox in the corner. Maxwell stepped inside, taking a swift sweep of the room under the pretense of looking for someone in particular. No recognizable face, except Tim Flynn, already at the bar, waving him over with a broad grin. Maxwell acknowledged him but wished the Kerry man wasn't so boisterous.

"Max! Over here! I thought because of the wife you'd chickened out!" Flynn boomed, guffawing. Several heads turned; a few faces gave a quick glance toward Maxwell before returning to their pints. As he approached the group clustered around Flynn, Maxwell grinned, but inwardly he thought, *I wish the bastard would keep his voice down—but I'll play along.* Clapping him on the shoulder, Flynn announced, "Lads, this is Max I've been telling you about. I've known this man since we were young fellas, so I have. Lost track of one another and only reunited again recently. Kicked the shite out of each other many a time. He played for Derry when I togged out for Kerry—and I needn't tell you who won!" He threw back his head laughing.

Maxwell made an attempt to answer, but Flynn cut him short.

"What'll you have, Max—a pint, is it?" Maxwell nodded, and a pint of Guinness was on the counter as though already waiting.

He looked at the men and raised his glass.

Maxwell sensed that one of the group seemed less exuberant about his arrival. The man eased his way beside him.

"What part of Derry are you from?"

Maxwell tensed but covered it. "Bogside—do you know it?"

"I've heard of it."

"Hasn't the world," chuckled Maxwell.

The man pushed on. "You still a beat cop?"

"Naw, stuck at a desk for now. Not many openings for a fella with my accent, if you get my drift," Maxwell answered, letting that hang for a moment. He shrugged. "But you never know—opportunities sometimes come along. No harm in knowing which way the wind's blowing."

Flynn noticed the two conversing in low tones. "Are you two planning a risin'?" he laughed. "Micky, Max is a sound man. One of our own, so he is. Max, you met Mickey Devine… come meet a few of the other lads."

He introduced names—some first names only. As Flynn made the rounds, Maxwell shook hands, mentally filing each face away.

He reminded himself of his plan: get in, set the stage, and get out.

Maxwell struggled to remain neutral. His nerves crawled; every new arrival seemed menacing. He couldn't watch everyone, but he knew he was a target—Dougherty's eyes. He sipped his pint slowly, casual, waiting for the moment. He ordered a round.

He looked at his watch. "Jeez, Tim, I have to get going. I promised Aisling I'd take her to the pictures."

"A bloody Derry man henpecked! Would you believe it?" Flynn laughed.

Maxwell smirked. "Your day will come."

The others chuckled. He turned to the group. "Good to meet ye, lads. Hope to see you again soon. I only dropped by to say hello." When he stepped into the street, Maxwell took a deep breath. Ice broken. He looked left, then right, and began walking, head down, collar up. He took several steps, giving his mind room to clear. A strange adrenaline dump hit him. He hadn't realized— not until now—that he'd been nervous in there.

What had he actually learned? Nothing really. Names, or bits of them.

Flynn was too loud, too eager, over-embellished everything. Probably meant well—but a liability all the same. If these were real players, and they might be, would they have copped it? The others… Devine. Was that a name worth keeping? Sharp, keen eyes. Quick to test him, slow to trust. Be careful. Dougherty… hard to read… quiet, clocked everything. Those types weren't bystanders—readers. Maxwell sensed he was storing it away, but for whom? Himself? Someone higher?

The rest—first names only—didn't give much away. Paddy, Seamus, the Tyrone lad needing work. Was it cover? Code talk? Or genuinely brickies and laborers with nothing more than opinions, listening to old rebel songs and playing soldiers? Hard to tell—but one thing was certain: they knew people. Then again, they could be a bunch of harmless wannabes collecting money in pubs for "the Cause."

A few remarks kept rattling around his head: "Things heating up again." "A lad sent back to Belfast." Nothing concrete. Nothing you could pin to paper. But in certain places, words weren't thrown about for the sake of it. It was something—but nothing.

The question was: should he report it? But what was there to report? A few pints, a couple of names, a bit of drink bravado talk?

If he reported this now, it'd land on some manager's desk, gather dust, and when something did go down they'd wonder why he'd wasted their time with pub gossip. And then someone else would be sent in—someone with no instinct for the talk that wasn't being said. Someone who couldn't read the Irish way of speaking. And if this did turn into something, it'd be snatched away before he had the chance to see it through.

Fuck them, he thought. Let it simmer—steer it his own way.

He scoured the street as he walked—no tails, no watchers. Just the steady mist settling over the pavements and the amber glow of the lamps.

As he reached his street, a flash of doubt. Was this a risky play? Maybe—but better than handing it to some upper-office penpusher who'd kill it stone dead. And besides, this was the first thing that smelled like a proper job since Fitzrovia.

Maxwell gave a tight smile to no one in particular, pulled his coat in against the cold, and kept walking. Aisling was surprised to see him home so early.

When Maxwell was gone, Flynn lowered his voice. "Lads, ye need to have no doubts about Max. He's grand—a sound skin. He knows what's what." He paused, then winked. "He could turn out to be handy for the lads."

Devine glanced at Dougherty. The conversation shifted.

The talk continued about a lad being sent back to Belfast last week, a few muttered mentions of things heating up again. One of the group asked Flynn about work for the Tyrone man needing a job for a month or two.

"Sure, sure," promised Flynn. "We'll fit him in somewhere."

The conversation turned to football and a building job in Cricklewood.

CHAPTER 25

The Check-In

The next morning, Maxwell checked his mail. Not at the post office, but at the bookmaker's shop off Camden High Street, his drop-off point. The message was terse: "2:30 tomorrow." Maxwell raised an eyebrow. The Service liked to keep its checkins on a regular schedule, even when nothing much was happening. But this one felt different. Not a courtesy—a tether.

The afternoon was gray and clammy as he made his way to the meet. Same place, a rented room above the bookmaker's shop. No signs, no names. Just a dingy door with a stiff hinge. The room had a musty reek of old damp brick. The Section Head was already there. Maxwell had met him at the initial briefing but hadn't got a proper measure of the man. The face was bland, soft-featured— but not forgettable. The eyes marked him: sharp, piercing, analytical; the kind that evaluated a man in an instant.

His coat was carelessly hung over a broken chair. On the table lay a folded newspaper, a few loose pages tucked snugly inside. No briefcase.

"Maxwell." He nodded, voice flat, detached.

Maxwell sat without removing his coat. No reason to settle in. This wouldn't take long.

The Head leafed through the newspaper, drew out a single page, glanced at it with steel-gray eyes. "Anything worth noting this past week?"

Maxwell kept his tone neutral. He was ready for this. "Nothing yet. Same faces. Some pub talk."

The Head didn't look up. "Where'd you go?"

It came rapid. Maxwell swallowed hard. "The Killarney Pub."

There was a pause.

"It's time you made yourself known in a few more of the Irish pubs. There's chatter; something's afoot."

A small jolt hit Maxwell's gut. Was that speculation? Or a veiled nudge? What did they know about the Killarney?

He shrugged slightly. "As I say—maybe pub talk."

"Maybe not." The Section Head kept his eyes down. The reply was sharp.

A brief, uneasy silence. The Section Head tightened his jaw, scratched his chin, and fixed Maxwell for an instant. "Even so… there's movement. Low-level, maybe, but we take notice."

He scribbled a notation, folded the paper over, and slid it into the newspaper. "If something's coming, we want to hear about it first. Before it's a plan, if possible."

Maxwell gave a short nod. "If there's an in, I'll find it."

"Do… And Maxwell… don't get drawn in too deep. You know what happens to lads who forget which team they're on."

Maxwell held his gaze, gave a faint smile. "I know where I stand."

The meeting ended without ceremony. The rustle of paper. A sharp nod. Dismissed.

Maxwell made his way down the unsteady, creaking stairs.

174

As he stepped onto the street, he replayed the exchange in his mind. No mention of the Killarney. No mention of Flynn. Not even a sideways glance to suggest they knew where he'd been. Either they were genuinely fishing… or they were testing what he'd volunteer.

He wasn't giving them a damn thing.

He walked briskly, but not too fast, pausing at the corner before turning into a side laneway. The Head's phrasing stuck with him—*Irish pubs… chatter… movement.* All intentionally vague. Nothing actionable. Nothing verifiable. But enough to signal that they'd caught a scent of something and wanted him to chase it.

Fine. He'd chase it—but on his own terms.

The absence of specifics told him more than any briefing could have. If they had solid intelligence, they would have pushed him harder. If they knew about Flynn, they would have asked directly. They hadn't.

Which suited him perfectly. It meant the ground was still his to claim.

He needed an excuse to get back in with the Irish group.
But casual—not too eager. A luncheon at his place might do it. Aisling could arrange it easily enough; she and Marie were thick as thieves. Flynn wouldn't think twice about an invite. Maxwell would feign being busy at work but promise to drop by the Killarney soon.

Let Aisling suggest it. Yes. That would work.

CHAPTER 26

The Seed Planted

Aisling had noticed a pleasant change in Bob's schedule. He seemed to be home earlier, and the long night duties appeared to have eased. He had muttered something about a cold case finally being wrapped up, though for political reasons it was being kept quiet. That, he said, explained why it hadn't hit the papers.

Friday evening came, and Aisling dragged herself home after a long day at the hospital. Eight surgeries. Easy for the surgeons; they could take a few days off. When she opened the door, she was hit by the smell of frying onions hanging in the air. She paused in the hall. The wireless hummed softly, a traditional fiddle tune drifting from Radio Éireann. She smiled. When she entered the kitchen…

Bob stood at the stove with a wooden spatula in hand.

"Surprise," he beamed.

Aisling shot him a gleeful smile. "Where did you come from?"

"Finished early," Maxwell said, still smiling. "Thought I'd surprise you."

Exhausted but thrilled, Aisling kissed him. "Let me take a shower."

When she returned, he had set the table and made a pot of tea. They sat down to a palate-pleasing meal of bacon, bangers, and eggs smothered with fried onions.

"What's the occasion?" Aisling asked.

"Nothing. Just thought you needed a break," he said lightly.

The conversation moved easily. Maxwell flicked ash from his cigarette, shrugged as if remembering something only now.

"I forgot to mention—I ran into Flynn yesterday. Said we'd catch a pint one of these days. I was surprised he was sober."

Aisling laughed. "You know, it wouldn't be the worst idea. Marie's been on about catching up. And you never make time for people…"

Maxwell gave a sheepish grin. "I'll try. I promise. Wouldn't stop you if you invited them."

She smirked. "Next week maybe. Sandwiches and tea. I'll ring Marie."

Maxwell shrugged, feigning indifference. "Up to you." But in his head, the move was already made.

CHAPTER 27

Entrapment

aturday came with a planned purpose. Maxwell had cleared his calendar, hough not without calculation; he meant to arrive after Marie and Flynn, to t them settle before making his entrance.

Aisling, meanwhile, had been in motion since dawn. The kitchen filled ith the warm scent of baking—scones turning golden, eclairs cooling on the ack, an apple tart with a remarkably flaky crust gleaming with sugared glaze. y midday her apron was spotted with flour and her face moist—hair pinned astily back, yet her hands never stopped moving. She lined plates with neat iangles of sandwiches, rushing against the clock, determined that everything e ready before the first knock at the door.

On the two o'clock chime, the doorbell rang.

Aisling pulled off her apron and ran to the door. Giggles erupted nmediately. She tried, unsuccessfully, to avoid Flynn's bear hug—she could mell that he had been drinking already. She and Marie exchanged girlish ecks, even though they had seen one another at work the previous day. isling ushered them into the dining room, toward the blazing fire. She ondered where Maxwell had gone—he'd promised.

As they sat at the table, there was a rattle at the door; Maxwell entered ooking flustered.

"Sorry I'm late."

Flynn rose to shake hands. "Busy man… a bank robbery?" he laughed.

"Always something—busier all the time." Maxwell glanced at isling. Turning to Marie, he nodded aloofly, "Marie."

Marie answered coolly, "Bob," exchanging a quick glance with Aisling.

They sat. Aisling poured the tea. Flynn positioned himself at the end of the table, sleeves rolled up, the second sandwich already disappearing into his mouth. He jabbed a thick finger across the table—mouth full.

"Now, there's a man gone either shy or snobbish on us. Thought you were too good for the Killarney these days, Bob."

The table laughed. Maxwell raised a brow, feigning mock offense. "Too good for the Killarney? Me?"

Flynn grinned wider, elbowing Marie. "Aye! Gone all respectable, he has. And a good Derry man, too. Be grand to see you back down there with the rest of the paddies, instead of giving out parking tickets."

Marie chuckled—another telling glance at Aisling, as if testing the temperature. "Careful, Tim," she said. "You'll have him thinking you miss him."

"Course I miss him," Flynn declared, grabbing another sandwich. "He owes me a pint, doesn't he?"

Maxwell grinned—satisfied his plan was unfolding naturally. "Work's been a bastard lately. Next week maybe. I'll stick my head in, buy the first round."

Flynn slapped the table. "That's a promise now!"
Maxwell poured whiskeys for both and tipped his glass in mock solemnity. "You've my word on it."

And just like that, it was all set. No pressure, no push. A public promise made in good company—the perfect next step.

They ate on. Talk drifted to football, hospital gossip. Flynn boasted that he had pulled in a big contract. Maxwell mentioned that a fellow from the docks had been nicked for stealing tools. He kept the talk easy, the drinks coming, and his eyes on Flynn— noting who he mentioned, and who he didn't.

Aisling gathered the cups, smiling faintly. The room still hummed with laughter, but a faint chill had crept into the air.

CHAPTER 28

The Crack in the Door

Maxwell let two weeks pass before going to the Killarney. It was approaching closing time. *Let them get oiled.* The place was packed and loud. A young singer was trying his best to sing "Kevin Barry" to an indifferent crowd. Maxwell spotted them straight away and made his way over—removing his coat on the way. Flynn, towering over his group, saw him.

"Look who's decided to grace us," he roared, raising his glass.

Maxwell grinned. "Sorry I'm late. Hope I'm not interrupting." He skimmed quickly for a reaction.

Flynn grinned wide—he was well into the sauce. "I thought you'd fallen into a hole. Hi lads—ye remember Max, the Derry man. What will it be, Max?"

"My turn," insisted Maxwell, turning to the bar. His eyes flicked. Same faces, a few new ones. Two men deep in conversation by the snug—heads close together. Noted.

He ordered two pints of Guinness and chasers. Flynn grabbed the Guinness and raised it.

"Thanks, mate. Sláinte."

"I thought for sure you'd never come," mumbled Flynn, his words slurred and thick.

Maxwell chuckled. "Work—you know how it is."

"Aye, feckin' slave drivers," one of the men muttered, glancing at Flynn.

Maxwell lifted his glass. "To the working man."

"To the working man!" they echoed, slamming their pints together. "Sláinte."

Maxwell studied the group—Devine was absent.

"Where's my friend Devine tonight?" he whispered to Flynn.

Flynn sidled in closer, lowering his voice just a shade. "He's away back on a bit of business, not sure—Dublin or Belfast." He moved closer still. "A word to the wise. Your timing is good, lad. Might be a bit of something on the go soon. Word is."

Maxwell's heart skipped, but he gave a casual nod. "Sure, if I can be of any assistance."

"Good man," Flynn whispered, smiling over his pint. "I'll keep you in mind."

He winked. Maxwell let the moment hang, then tipped his glass back and grinned. "Appreciate it."

And that was it. The first crack in the door.

The rest of the group got involved with a darts game. Maxwell turned his attention to the singer, but his focus was on the pair near the snug. The older man left first and was followed shortly after by the younger one. There was a tension in the air— Maxwell could taste it.

Flynn was listing sideways now, chin slipping toward his chest as sleep overtook him.

Maxwell decided to leave. His work here was done. He knew the hook had landed—the game was starting to play his way.

Maxwell came in shortly before midnight. Aisling was still on the sofa, the book she'd been pretending to read lying open on her lap.

Relief washed over her at the turn of the key, followed by the rasp of his smoker's cough. *If only he'd give them up.*

"You're late," she said, managing a smile.

"I couldn't just run in and out," he explained, crossing to the sideboard. He poured a drink, loosened his tie, and dropped into his armchair as if sinking into himself—the tired ritual of a man who had done this too many nights before.

Aisling watched him, quiet for a moment. "I worry about you down there, y'know."

Her voice was low, almost to herself. He looked over.

"At the Killarney?"

"At places like the Killarney. Lads like Flynn." She exhaled sharply. "It's not the same anymore, Bob. There's talk—police watching certain homes, certain fellas. And the Service sniffing at every Irish accent they hear."

Maxwell kept his face still, only the glass moving to his lips. "It's a drink and a few songs, love. Nothing more."

"I'm not daft, Bob." She closed the book, tapping it against her knee. "And Marie… I worry about her too. She's crazy about Flynn. That galoot will drag her into trouble, if she's not careful."

"Ah, he's a blowhard, Ash. Full of piss and vinegar. He wouldn't last five minutes if it came to anything."

"That's what worries me. It's the loud ones who get noticed. And the ones hanging around them." She stood, crossing to the window, pulling aside the curtain just a crack. "You don't have to be doing anything to get yourself on someone's list these days. Being in the wrong pub, talking to the wrong *amadán*—you get painted with the same brush. You're a copper, Bob. You know it better than most."

He came up behind her, rested his hands on her shoulders. "You've nothing to fret over. I'm careful."

She turned to face him—her brow creased. "You'd better be."

"I'll have a word with Marie tomorrow," Aisling whispered softer now. "See what's in her head about that big gobshite."

Maxwell smiled faintly, brushing a strand of hair from her cheek. "You're wasted on us mortals, you know that?"

"I know." She kissed him and gave a small grin, but the worry didn't leave her eyes. She lifted the book and went to bed.

Later, when the kitchen had gone quiet and Aisling's breathing settled into sleep, Maxwell sat alone in the front room, a cigarette burning down to the filter in the ashtray. The glow of the streetlamp through the curtain stripes made the room feel closed in—caged. The whiskey sat, untouched.

He replayed the night at the Killarney in his mind: the flick of Flynn's eyes when Devine's name came up, the hesitation before he leaned in. *Might be something on the go soon. Word is… Belfast or Dublin…* It was never the words that mattered. It was the thought behind them.

Maxwell knew men like Flynn—useful idiots, braggarts, always chasing approval. On the fringe, the peripheral dwellers, always pretending they were deeper in than they were. Dangerous, not for what they might do, but because they could be deliberately fed false information, and they'd pass it on eagerly, believing themselves insiders.

And then there were the other two. The older fella and the young buck by the snug. That was business, not piss-up talk. Something passed between them—not in words but in the way the younger one's jaw tightened when the older man left. Maxwell read it. The sort of tension you only see when something's about to shift. But what?

The Killarney was heating up. Too much talk, too many pints, and the wrong ears in the wrong corners.

Maxwell leaned back, rubbed his face. Aisling wasn't wrong. The political wind had changed in London. MI5 was watching everything that smelled of Ulster. Special Branch too—but those lads didn't have his nose for it.

Flynn would break sooner or later. They always did. The trick was to be standing close when it happened.

He stubbed out the cigarette, reached for the whiskey— and stopped. *Careful.* He lit another cigarette instead. There were nights you drank, and nights you didn't. This wasn't one for drinking.

Maxwell took a long drag, the smoke curling in the dim room. The Section Head's steady gaze at their last meeting kept returning to him—the way the man's eyes fixated just a fraction when Maxwell stalled around certain topics.

Did he suspect I was holding something back?

Intelligence officers knew silence. Too much bred suspicion.

Maybe it's time to feed him a morsel, Maxwell thought. Not the whole truth. Just enough to show I'm playing ball, that I'm tracking the right people. But timing was everything. Reveal too much, and Flynn and the others might catch wind. Too little, and the brass might start watching him instead of the targets.

He exhaled—ash falling on the new carpet.

He'd give them the pair from the snug—innocuous enough, and far from anything that could lead back to him.

CHAPTER 29

The Blunder

More than a week had passed since the last Section meeting. Maxwell began to be concerned. *Is there a problem?* he wondered as he lit his fourth cigarette. The scrambled eggs and toast that Aisling had prepared for him before going to work sat halfeaten.

He was startled by the shrill ring of the phone. He let it ring three times before lifting it. The voice, flat and nondescript, spoke. "Is this 2453500?" Maxwell's pulse barely moved. The number meant nothing to anyone else. He glanced at the clock on the mantel. 10:05. The message was clear. 2:45, location three. Friday. "No," Maxwell said. "You've got the wrong number." "Ah. Sorry about that." Click. Maxwell cradled the receiver, his face giving nothing away. He lit a cigarette, exhaled through his nose. The meet was on—tomorrow. Was that good or bad?

Maxwell took the long way around—eyes habitually sweeping every corner. The Friday meet had been well chosen. Red Lion Street was always busier at the end of the week. Clerks knocking off early, tradesmen ducking in for a trim before the weekend; another casual face would be swallowed in the bustle. Standard Service practice: don't hide—disappear into the noise.

Maxwell arrived five minutes early, slipping through the street toward the barber shop on a quiet corner near Holborn. Inside, the place was in full swing with the usual mid-afternoon crowd. Heads buried in *The Racing News*, exchanging tips and small talk. The gentle, hypnotic rhythm of humming clippers and snipping scissors played a familiar soundtrack. The scent of talcum powder and aftershave mixed with the faint suggestion of cigarette smoke.

No one paid Maxwell any notice as he stepped inside. The barber—a stocky man with a tired comb-over, sleeves rolled up—glanced up and gave the briefest of nods toward the back.

Maxwell made his way down the narrow corridor and pushed open the door to the small plain room beyond. A single table. Two chairs. A darkened window cracked open to let out the stale air.

The Section Head was already there, seated neatly with a folded newspaper and a cup of tea. No sign of haste, no mark of irritation. The man gave no hint that he'd seen Maxwell enter.

"Maxwell," he said, with the faintest inclination of his head. "On time. Punctuality is good."

Maxwell took the chair opposite without a word.

A moment passed before the Section Head spoke again, setting his paper aside with careful precision. "Anything new to report?"

Maxwell offered a mild shrug. "Been back to the Killarney, same faces. Same voices. A few louder than others."

The Section Head's gaze rested on him—steady, patient, the kind of look that invited conversation without forcing it. "Nothing stays the same for long," the boss said mildly. "Times change. People shift. And sometimes, when they do, interesting things fall loose. So, you saw no change?"

Maxwell knew the tone. An invitation to speak. He chose his reply carefully.

"Well, there were a couple of new faces in the snug. Older fella and a young one. Didn't get names. But something passed between them."

"Older? What do you mean older?"

Maxwell swallowed, hoping it went unnoticed. "About fifty, I'd say."

The Section Head raised a brow, intrigued but not convinced. "And your impression?"

Maxwell lit a cigarette, took his time. "Business. Not drink talk. When the older one left, the young lad's jaw set tight. Seen it before. A job's coming."

"You keep saying older—too old to carry a bomb, too old to build a bomb?"

Maxwell could feel the sweat on his back. "I mean older than the other one."

A small, peeved smile slinked across the Section Head's lips— not warmth, but recognition. "Interesting." He let the word hang, then sipped his tea. "And Flynn?"

Maxwell froze. *Did I mention Flynn before?* He couldn't remember. "Making noise as usual. Dropping Devine's name. But I'm keeping an ear to it."

The Section Head pounced. "Who's Devine?"

Maxwell felt himself drowning. "Oh, just noise. Flynn's a blabbermouth—just noise. Devine's a bricky, he didn't turn up." The Section Head tapped one long finger against the cup. "Noise can be useful, in its own way. Sometimes a man's nonsense disguises someone else's intent."

Maxwell held his gaze. The seat became uncomfortable. "I'll keep close."

The Section Head nodded. "You do that. Very good." Then reached for his newspaper. "Same arrangement. Until we need a change."

Maxwell stood. No handshake, no farewell. As he walked to the door, he felt the eyes on his back.

"Oh, Maxwell—who did you say Devine is?"

Maxwell felt the jerk of the tether. "A bricky," he blurted.

The Section Head deliberated, then turned away. Maxwell caught the note being scribbled.

He let himself out into the hum of the shop. The Section Head remained seated.

Outside, the city hubbub hit him like a hurricane. Footsteps on wet paving stones, the hum of voices, the mournful clang of a tram bell drifting through the afternoon. It all added a sense of intense irritability and anger. He had no control over the noise nor his future.

Maxwell walked without direction, his mind a muddled tangle. The meeting hadn't gone well. He could feel it in his gut. The way the Section Head's questions came a smidgen too smooth, the way he'd circled back—laid those small traps—let the silences stretch. And Maxwell, fool that he was, had stepped into them. *Devine!! How the hell did I let that slip?* He hadn't meant to mention the name. It had slipped out in the middle of Flynn's nonsense, and the Head had seized on it like a cat on a mouse.

He could still hear the quiet question in his ear. "Who's Devine?" And his feeble, hurried answer, "A bricky, didn't turn up." How stupid. The Service didn't care about brickies who missed a round at the pub. The Section Head had filed it away—unfinished details—they would come back. They always did.

He crossed the street, found a doorway, lit another cigarette with unsteady fingers. He'd let the Head steer him, and worse, he'd realized it too late. He felt outfoxed. Outmaneuvered. Too quick. Too loose. What did it mean? Was he being tested? Or was the Section Head already halfway convinced Maxwell was holding something back. Either way, the rope was tightening.

He sucked deep on the cigarette, the smoke hitting sharp in his lungs. He'd have to be sharper next time. Watch every word, every pause, be prepared. Something was heating up, and the Service's patience wore thin when heat rose. But where was it happening? The Killarney Pub, the men at the snug, Devine? Maybe it's all a diversion. He took another long drag. *Can I still land this? Or am I already under the microscope?*

Time would tell. But one thing was certain, tonight wasn't a night for pints. It was a night for keeping to the shadows. He flicked the cigarette into the gutter and moved on. He decided to go home but first he'd take a walk in the park to clear his head.

He let himself into the house a little after seven. The place was empty; Aisling hadn't arrived from work. He turned the radio on— *The Archers* was playing. The cold remains of the breakfast sat on the plate. He poured a whiskey, then tipped it down the sink, lit a cigarette, and made tea instead.

The day had been a disaster. The meeting still weighed in his gut. Devine's name. The Head's eyes. The screw-up of it. Now the dwelling felt too small. He turned off the radio and sat in silence.

CHAPTER 30

The Proposition

Aisling came through the door at eight o'clock sharp. She looked exhausted, a strand of hair stuck to her temple. He could see it had been a bad shift—a face too pale, drawn, the slight slump of her shoulders. "You're home," she said, surprised.

Maxwell managed a grin. "Pulled a short straw, it seems. One of the lads took my shift." It was a prepared cover.

She gave him a sidelong look. "That's twice this month," she said.

Maxwell shrugged, heading to the cupboard. "Must have felt sorry for my sorry ass, after all them all-nighters." He poured her a cuppa without asking and set it on the counter beside her. "How was it?" he asked, though he already knew.

"Don't ask," she said, sipping the tea. "One fatal, two eejits who took a tumble off a scaffolding, and a lad with half a hand after a lathe accident. It was a madhouse all day. I don't know what it is about Friday, but it's always the worst."

Maxwell muttered a soft word of sympathy, hiding the rawness of his own nerves.

She studied him as she hung up her coat. "And you, not going out? No pints with the lads?"

"Not tonight." He forced a smirk. "I'm sure the Killarney would be packed with Paddys, rushing to spend their hard-earned money." Aisling raised an eyebrow. "Or are you hiding from Flynn

again? I'm sure he'll be looking for you and him full to the gills."
Maxwell chuckled. "You're not wrong."

She was watching him, eyes focusing just a touch. She always
could sense when things were unsettled in him.
"Everything alright, Bob?"

He hesitated a fraction. "Yeah. Just a long week. Same old
crap, same noise."

She reached out, brushed a hand over his cheek. "You worry
too much, take that job too serious."

He chuckled. "You should talk."

"Go put your feet up," he said softly. "I'll make another pot
of tea."

Aisling gave him a tired smile. "Maybe a bath," she whispered,
and headed upstairs.

Maxwell turned the radio back on. He flicked the knob,
anything to keep his mind off the Section Head.

Aisling came back down about half an hour later. She was in
her dressing gown; her hair still damp from the bath. Maxwell was
still in the kitchen; a cigarette burned to the nub in the ashtray—
the tea beside him gone cold. "You didn't drink yours," she said,
pouring it down the sink. She filled the kettle, watching his
reflection in the window. "Didn't fancy it," he muttered
absentmindedly. She gave him a look—one of those tired but
knowing glances wives reserve for men who think they're hiding
things. But she decided to let it pass.

"I spoke to Marie earlier," Aisling said as she leaned against
the counter, cradling a fresh cup of tea. "On the phone.
Before I left for my shift."

Maxwell flicked ash into the tray. "Oh aye?"

"She's more serious about Flynn than I thought. Can't see sense for it. I told her straight, keep clear of his nonsense. He's all mouth, but loose talk like his brings trouble down on all of us these days."

Maxwell's stomach tightened, but his face stayed still. "Was she listening?"

Aisling sighed. "Sorta half. Said I was fussing. You know how she gets. Laughs it off. 'Sure, it's only a bit of craic, Aish.' I told her, there's coppers listening to every Irish voice in London now. The wrong word in the wrong pub and it's your name in a notebook, or worse."

"But was she listening?" repeated Maxwell.

"It's hard to tell with Marie, you know how she is, everything's a joke, but she did say she was thinking of going back to Ireland," finished Aisling.

Maxwell took a long pull from his cigarette. "You did right. Did she have anything more to say about that?"

"I don't trust that Flynn, Bob. He's the sort that gets people hurt. Big mouths are dangerous in times like these."

Maxwell managed a dry smile. "You should've joined the force."

She smirked back. "Someone's got to do the thinking around here. Am I right?"

He forced a weary smile. "Of course you are, love." She reached for his cheek, rough from the day's stubble. "You look like you've gone ten rounds yourself."

"Long week," he muttered, stifling a yawn. She didn't press it. "Come on. Let's have an early night."

Maxwell stubbed out the cigarette, followed her upstairs, the words still gnawing at him. *Big mouths are dangerous in times like these.* He knew that better than anyone. And in the back of his mind, one name circled like a shark—Devine.

A few nights later Maxwell's nerves were still raw, but he knew he needed something to report. He wasn't planning to stay long. Just a pint, enough to take the edge off the last forty-eight hours, and the Killarney was close. The place was its usual haze of smoke and chatter, though tonight he sensed a restless energy drifting over the regulars. Was it real, or just his own mind playing tricks?

Flynn was alone—already well into his cups, perched at the bar, his voice carrying above the din. When he spotted Maxwell, his face lit up like a Christmas tree. "Max, ya aul bollocks! Get over here, will ya!"

Maxwell drew a steady breath and crossed to him, sliding onto the stool at his side. *Better to be seen with him than to look like I was avoiding him.* "What's the story, Tim?"

The big man dropped his voice, leaning in, the reek of drink strong on him. "Listen, bucko... you remember saying you'd help out if we needed you?" The hair at the back of Maxwell's neck stirred. "I need a hand with a wee thing.
Nothin' foolish now. Just a run out to the country, bit of a job. You'd be perfect—clean face, solid head. No one'd look twice at you. If you could wear the uniform it'd be bang on."

Maxwell kept his tone even. "What kind of run? Where and with who?"

Flynn grinned, looked around, voice a whisper. "Aw, just the two of us, tight like. You know… a bit of gear. Only holdin' it mind you. Two days, tops. There's a few… two or three crates need movin'. At the moment they're down past Croydon. No money in it mind you… all for the Cause, don't ya know. Our bit for aul Ireland… exciting right?"

Maxwell felt the blood pumping at his temples. "You've lost the run of yourself, Tim," he said, his voice lowered to a whisper. "This isn't pints and songs. This'll get you ten years, or worse."

But Flynn was too far gone, too flattered to be trusted. He wasn't bragging this time; he was delivering a message. Someone else had set the terms. He winked again, pleased with himself. "They'll be meetin' us Tuesday night—give us the final details—a safe-house near Wapping. You don't have to lift a finger. Just be there with me."

Maxwell felt the trap closing around him. This wasn't a loose boast—Flynn had set something in motion he couldn't simply step away from.

"Can't do it, Tim."

Flynn's face fell. "What?... Are you fucking serious?"

"I'm telling you Tim, leave it. Whoever you're workin' with; they'll hang you out to dry soon as look at you."

Flynn's grin hardened. "Easy, Max. Be careful. Do you know who you're talking about? These are Irish patriots… These are not the kind of men who hang their comrades out to dry."

Maxwell realized there was no refusing now, not without exposing himself—or worse. "It's too late now, pal. My word's given. You're in."

Maxwell's stomach sank. The Section Head's words echoed: *Even fools can be useful.*

He finished his pint and stood. "I'll see you, Tim."

Flynn grabbed his sleeve. "Tuesday night, Max. Don't be a prick now."

Maxwell shook free and walked out into the cold night air.

CHAPTER 31

The Intimidator

As he stood outside the pub, Maxwell was in a reflective mood. Was he too quick to rebuff Flynn's ask? Did he overstep the "hang you out to dry" comment? Should he go back and make amends? He replayed the scene at the bar: Flynn, well-oiled, voice too loud. *A wee run, Max. Three, maybe four crates. No big deal. Just holdin' them.* Maxwell had told him straight, "Count me out, Tim. I'm not touching it."

And he meant it. Or he thought he did—but was that the correct decision? Now, out here in the cool of the night with no definite plan, the certainty wavered.

What is the end-game here? Why did I scheme to win Flynn's confidence? *Stupid, stupid.* Three or four crates. Nothing. Could be a few old Enfields, maybe a Thompson or two. Nothing game-changing. He took a long pull on the cigarette, watching the tip glow in the darkness.

The smart move—the one drilled into him—was to report it. No freelancers. Get word to the Section Head first thing. Let them decide whether to shut it down, flip Flynn, or let it run its course. Maybe they'd take it over.

But there was a nagging itch under his skin.

What if this is bigger than it sounds? What if this is the gem you've been waiting to find?

He didn't trust Flynn's loose tongue, that was for sure. But if he was involved in a run—a useful idiot—someone clever was behind it. That meant a name, a face, a place. And Maxwell's pride wasn't about to let that pass through London without him knowing who was carrying it.

Maybe I tread in a little further. No harm in hearing the pitch. Keep my distance. Find out who else is at the table. Could be worth something—maybe it's a bloody disaster waiting to happen.

And if I don't report it, it's my neck.

He ground out the cigarette with his heel. Either way, I can't leave it sitting.

He kept walking, still undecided. He was running the numbers.

Report it now. Play the good boy. Let the Service scoop it up. Couldn't hurt after last month's sit-down with the Section Head. A lead like this, even from a fool like Flynn, could mend fences— or at least buy breathing room.

Then again… what if it's worth more to me than to them?

He took a long drag on another cigarette. How many was that today? Aisling is right. Maybe next Monday. Maybe after this thing ends. He tossed the cigarette away.

Three or four crates. Could be nothing. Could be something. I've turned worse scrapes into my advantage. Who says I can't again? Decision made. Not a final one—not yet— but enough to walk a little further down the road. See what shakes loose.

And if it goes bad… I'll decide then. It's not over till I say it is.

He took the note from his pocket—the one Flynn had given him: *11 Maiden's Court, off Watney Street, Stepney E1.*

Maxwell made a slow circuit of the backstreets before approaching the address The dark street off Watney Street was quiet at this hour. An old man and his dog walked leisurely, adjusting their gaits to each other as they passed the end of the street. Maxwell tabbed him as harmless.

The curtains in most homes were drawn, lights on in one or two windows. On the second pass, everything checked out. The home itself was modest but tidy—a two-story terrace, paint a little faded but clean. Lace curtains in the windows. A potted plant on the sill. The kind of commonplace residence you'd pass a hundred times without seeing.

As instructed, Maxwell knocked twice, then once. Almost immediately Flynn opened the door. No grin now—just a tight nod.

Maxwell stepped abruptly into the hallway. The interior smelled of polish and pipe tobacco. Framed photographs lined the wall—a young couple on their wedding day, a soldier in uniform. The place felt guardedly silent.

"In and through," Flynn muttered, leading him to the sitting room. It was frugally furnished but comfortable. Fire unlit. Aging carpet—clean. Armchairs with crochet covers on the headrests. The curtains were drawn, the clock on the mantel ticking steadily, demanding quiet.

A man sat at the dining table in the corner. Mid-thirties. Salt and-pepper crew cut. Steely green eyes. Lean face. "This him?" he asked, eyes never leaving Maxwell. The accent Northern, clipped and controlled. Not Belfast… not Derry… somewhere between.

Flynn gave a small, tense nod.

The man didn't rise. Maxwell scrutinized him—5'10", 180 pounds. Muscular frame under a well-cut, charcoal-gray, doublebreasted suit. He could have been a company executive. His voice was calm, unruffled, deliberate.

Maxwell reached for a cigarette, but before his hand found his pocket the man spoke—flat, quiet. "No smoking."

He placed a folded slip of paper in front of them. "No names. No talk after tonight. You'll follow what's on this. Read it. Memorize it. Burn it. No one carries paper."

A pause. "Any questions?"

Maxwell unfolded the slip. The handwriting was small, precise.

Thursday. Dock 17.

Ten crates. Marked farm machinery.

Collect 23:00 hrs.

Transport to shed off Sanderson Lane, Stepney.

Rear of Sheedy's Auto Repairs.

No talk. No delays. No mistakes.

He read it twice, his gut tightening. "Ten crates?" he burst out.

"Flynn said three, maybe four." He glared at Flynn.

Flynn was already watching—the easy swagger gone. Now only fear. The ghost of panic behind his eyes. He glanced at Maxwell. "I… I didn't know, Max. I swear. I thought it was just a run, a few bits. Christ."

The man ignored the exchange. He checked the clock. "Change of plan." His steely gaze locked on Maxwell. "If you're sloppy—if you draw attention—you'll answer for it. When we're done, you leave one at a time. Ten, fifteen-minute gaps.   No standing about. No talk in the street. Straight on your way. The old couple will be back by ten. I don't want a chair out of place."

He rose, buttoned his coat, and slipped out without a sound.

Flynn let out a long breath, wiping the sweat from his upper lip. "Fecking hell, Max… that bastard gives me the bloody creeps." He fumbled for a cigarette.

"No smoking," Maxwell snapped.

Flynn shoved it back in his pocket like a chastised schoolboy. "I've met hard men on sites and pubs… but that fella's for real. He doesn't need big talk. The way he looks at you—like he's already decided if you'll be standing in an hour or in a sack at the bottom of some river somewhere."

Maxwell was barely listening. He read the note again. Flynn saw the anger rise in him. "I swear to my mother's grave, I didn't know it was ten crates. I'd never have agreed if I thought it was this size. That's a serious move. Heavy stuff. Ten crates? That's not bits and pieces—that's a fucking war chest." Maxwell glanced at the clock, mind racing. "It's time to get out of here. You go first. We'll meet to make a plan."

"Great idea, Max… I need a drink. Let's meet at the Killarney."

"No. Not the Killarney," Maxwell snapped. "The Golden Heart in Spitalfields. No one will know us there. Just one pint— do you hear me?"

Flynn nodded and all but bolted from the house.

Maxwell sat thinking over what just happened. He felt trapped—between the Section Head and the Intimidator. The words echoing through his head: *"Don't forget which team you're on"*—*"If you're sloppy—if you draw attention—you'll answer for it."*

He took out his handkerchief, wiped the table, adjusted the chairs, and waited the full fifteen minutes before he left.

CHAPTER 32

The Golden Heart

The Golden Heart pub was an ideal choice—a classic, unpretentious, working-class West End hostelry. It heaved with noise and bodies on the Friday night, wall-to-wall with dockers, tally clerks, market lads, warehousemen, and the odd chancer in a shiny suit trying to look like he belonged. The L-shaped bar, brass footrail dulled by thousands of boots, was packed three deep; jars of pickled eggs and onions sat clouded under the yellowish light.

Dim brass wall lamps cast shadows that clung to the nicotine-stained ceiling. Cigarette smoke drifted in slow, stubborn layers, smearing the mirrors advertising Truman, Charrington, Watney's— old breweries fading into memory. A low rumble of Cockney voices rose and fell like machinery in motion.

When Flynn arrived, he paused inside the door, blinking into the hazy gloom, searching for a free table. A few heads turned, sizing him up, but once they saw the workman's clothes and scuffed boots, they dismissed him as one of their own. He edged toward the bar—instantly distracted by the ample cleavage of the voluptuous barmaids. For a moment, he forgot why he'd come. He ordered a pint of ale and scanned the room again. Most of the crowd hovered around the bar, leaving several tables near the back surprisingly free.

He chose a table with a clear view of the front door and waited. He didn't wait long.

The pub had grown more crowded when Maxwell shouldered his way inside. He shook off the cold with a brisk sweep of the eyes; the noise seemed to bend around him. At the bar a barmaid with auburn-dyed beehive hair and a form-clinging top leaned toward him.

"Cor, you're a big one. What can I get ya?" she purred.

Maxwell wasn't in the mood. "Courage Best Bitter," he muttered.

"Courage Best? Blimey—someone's feelin' brave tonight," she teased, but Maxwell's focus was already fixed on Flynn.

He crossed to the table and sat heavily, pinning Flynn with a stare that carried no warmth.

"We're in deep now. You realize that, don't you?"

Flynn swallowed. "Aye."

"We'll need a lorry," Maxwell said, his voice dry, like the words wrestled in his throat. Flynn nodded again, but his gaze drifted—the distance in his eyes betraying fear he was too afraid to name.

Maxwell's fingers drummed a sharp rhythm on the table, leaned in, lowering his voice. "Right. Listen up. Forty-five minutes after ten you'll be at Draper's Yard—off Cable Street. Go tomorrow. Walk it. Learn every inch. It's at the north end, behind the old tannery. You'll see a lamp-post—that's your mark for the lift. I'll spot you. The dock's just round the corner. When I pass; you follow. If I'm not there in ten minutes, you walk away. Understand?"

Flynn drained his pint, Adam's apple bobbing. "And the lorry?"

Maxwell's eyes hardened. "You don't worry about the lorry. Don't ask where it came from, who owns it—nothing.

You see it when it rolls in. You help shift those fucking crates. We drop them at Sheedy's. Then you never mention any of it to me again. Clear?"

Sweat trickled from Flynn's hairline. He nodded. "Clear."

Maxwell finished his pint in two long gulps. "Good. And one more thing—no drinking. Keep out of the Killarney. If you start blathering now, we're both dead men. Now let's get the hell out of here. You go first."

He watched Flynn weave out of the pub—shoulders rounded like a man walking into a storm. Maxwell rubbed both hands over his face. *How did I ever think this was a good idea?* For a moment he considered ordering another pint, anything to steady his thoughts, but the notion passed. There were too many details to pull into place.

He stepped into the cool night air and turned up Cable Street, his mind already leaping ahead—Fennick's Yard, the lorry, the plates, the route, the timing, the patrol gaps. Every piece needed to align or the whole thing would explode in his face. The plan seemed to settle around him like a rope tightening at his ribs.

It's still not too late to call this into Section.
He pushed the thought away. No risk, no reward.

He ran through the checklist again: Fennick's tomorrow. Find plates—something clean, not too new, not too old. Commercial. Believable. Check the yard—watchman? dogs? lights? Which trucks get dumped? Pick one. Tools: screwdriver, nail file, gloves, cap. No one sees you. No one remembers you.
But what if there's a guard? Then improvise.

The thought was menacing, though in some corner of his mind he found it exhilarating.

The house was empty when he arrived; Aisling had night duty. He moved quietly, collected a screwdriver from the shed, a nail file from the bathroom, and slipped into bed—the weight of the night pressing heavily on his chest.

CHAPTER 33

The Plates Change

The next day stretched long, his nerves strung thin. By the afternoon he couldn't sit still, so he took a walk through the side streets, hands buried in his pockets, keeping his head down. It eased nothing—every step only turned his thoughts back to Flynn and the job ahead. By the time he circled back, the lamps were coming on, and the air had grown cold, the skies overcast.

When Maxwell arrived home he was relieved that Aisling had gone to her work. He checked the fridge knowing she had left a meal for him. He stuck it in the oven to reheat. Something dogged him. It was Flynn. He couldn't get the man out of his head. He saw him as weak, inept and worst of all traitorous. His gut told him that he was completely undependable, but for better or worse he was stuck with him.

It was 7:00pm, he'd take a short nap and be prepared for what lay ahead.

It had started to rain when Maxwell left the house just before half-eleven. The street was dead quiet, save for the occasional hum of a distant car on the

Woodford New Road. He was relieved Aisling was on late shift — no one to explain himself to.

He locked up, pulled at his collar, and walked down Hale End Road. The street was dark — silent. A black cat shot across the road ahead of him and vanished under a car. His eyes followed, he felt a shudder down his spine. He pulled his collar tighter against the damp night air and took the long way round, avoiding the main road for as long as he could. Not because anyone was looking for him — old habits, that was all. He passed the corner shop, shutters down, a few empty crisp packets fluttering along the gutter. Somewhere a dog barked once, then went quiet again.

At the bus stop near the top of Hale End Road, an old enamel sign clung to the post, half the letters worn away. He waited, back against the wall, keeping to the shadows, scanning both ends of the road. No one about. A single motor hummed past, an electric bread van cruised past heading toward Chingford. The last bus rumbled up a few minutes later.

The half-empty bus was eerily quiet. The driver didn't say a word when Maxwell climbed on. "Bethnal Green," he murmured, voice low. He dropped his fare in the box and took a seat upstairs, right at the back. He settled back, fingers drumming against his thigh, already going over the job ahead. The bus sputtered by quiet streets, darkened shops, the odd late drunk stumbling home. He kept his head down and his eyes on the streetlights. Maxwell checked his watch. 12:20 a.m.
Good timing.

The bus droned on through Walthamstow and
Clapton, heading south. It wasn't quick, but it was quiet. No one else on the top deck. Just Maxwell and the stale smell of old tobacco clinging to the seats.

He got off near Bethnal Green, a good half-mile from where he needed to be. No sense getting too close. Not on wheels, anyway. The driver didn't look at him as he stepped off. Maxwell gave a nod, kept walking. He stuck to the back streets, cutting down a obscured alley behind a row of lockups, then across a bit of waste ground where an old mattress lay half-buried in muck. The night was still, the air thick with the heavy smell of soot and rotted garbage. Now and then a light would flicker in an upstairs window.

By the time he reached Cable Street, it was one o'clock. He crossed over, keeping his head down, and made his way towards the yard. The place sat desolate, quiet behind rusted iron gates, the old sign hanging crooked, letters flaked and rusted. In a dark corner between a pile of oil drums and a fence panel that was half off its brackets he saw several batteries. He waited a moment, listening. The alley was suddenly filled with the eerie wailing of two cats locked in a fierce battle. A dog barked somewhere in the distance.

A cab hissed past at the far end of the street. Then nothing. Maxwell took a breath, rolled his shoulders, and moved.

The yard was a mess of burnt-out shells of wrecked cars, lorries and vans, piled high like a crash pileup. Maxwell crouches low beside a rusted car shell. He moved quietly between them, eyes adjusting to the dark. The rain picked up.

It took him a few minutes to find what he needed; a stack of number plates piled on a wooden palate, old, scorched, half of them bent or rusted. He picked through, found a couple of them that were commercial — matching ones that might do. He cleaned the worst of the muck off and slipped them into his holdall. It was too easy, but now, find the other two.

He rifled through a greasy pile of old plates. Metal clatters. Plates scrape. Too noisy. A dog barks. He ducked for cover. He took a look around. No one. No dog, no watchman. Back to the rummaging, digs deeper, plates sliding and rattling, every scrape like an alarm bell in his ears. His hands are slippery in the pelting rain.

He finds one – a front plate — wrong code, tosses it aside. Another — bent.

Another — no.

His fingers slick with rain and oil. *Shit.* He cuts his finger on a twisted plate. Panic. He hears footsteps, getting closer. His heart pounding. A voice shouts something he can't make out. He waits – silence – and back to the hunting. Finally, under a threadbare tire — the second front plate — scratched, but a match. No time to admire it. He scoops up all four, shoved them into his hold-all, and moved fast, keeping low, slipping between wrecks toward the side fence.

He left the same way he came in; back over the broken side fence, dropping to the ground, remaining in the shadows.   He walked steady, not hurrying, not wanting to draw attention. A few streets over, he cut through an alley behind a pub — kept going until the yard was well behind him. It was past two thirty by now.

The odd cab started to appear, but nothing else. When he hit a main road near Cambridge Heath, he stuck his hand out as a black cab came dawdling along. It pulled over. "Where to, mate?". "Highams Park", Maxwell said. "But drop us off by the Green, not the house". The cabbie gave a knowing look.

"Been out where you shouldn't, have ya?". Maxwell smirked, shook his head. "Got to get home before the missus gets home

from her shift. If she finds the bed cold, I'll get a pan to the head."
The cabbie chuckled. "Ain't that the way of it all. Hop in". The cab
pulled away, and Maxwell settled in the back seat — sodium
streetlights penetrating the smog outside the window."

He let his eyes close, the first job down, a few more to go.
He took a deep breath — his mouth was dry. They reached
Highams Park not long before four o'clock. He paid cash, told the
driver to keep the change, got out by the Green, and walked the
last couple of streets alone. It started to rain again, an odd bus
rolled by the tires squealing in the persistent rain.

The house was dark and quiet. He slipped the key in the lock
and stepped inside. He removed his coat and stashed the hold-all
in the tool shed, stuck the kettle on and took a quick wash. When
the water boiled he made a cup of tea. As he sat smoking he drank
the tea while mulling over the night's significance. *Too late to pull
out.*

He washed his cup with cold water, rinsed the kettle under the
cold tap. By the time Aisling came through the door at eight-thirty,
he was in bed, half asleep, with the job a mile behind him.

Maxwell woke later than he intended. He snuck out of bed,
managing to avoid wakening Aisling. He shaved and washed up
and went downstairs. He moved quietly around the kitchen. He
wasn't hungry, but expecting it to be a long night, he decided on
bacon and eggs. He cursed under his breath as the pan clattered on
the gas cooker. Upstairs, he heard the faint sound of the bedroom
door creak and Aisling's voice, soft with sleep but edged with
concern. "Max? What time is it?" "Half nine," he called back,

lighting a cigarette and exhaling toward the cracked window. "Had a call—need to check something down the docks. Nothing serious."

There was a pause. He could picture her now, sitting on the edge of the bed in her dressing gown, hair a tangle from the night shift. She'd come off duty at the hospital hours after he'd rolled in from the scrapyard. He'd been asleep and she had been too tired to ask questions anyway, but now she was alert enough to feel something off in his voice. The smell of frying bacon reached her nostrils. She tied her hair back and came down stairs. "I'll do this," she said, "you sit down." He sat and watched. He felt deserted needed someone to talk to, someone he could trust. *Should I tell her? She's got a good head on her shoulders; I can trust her.* "Aisling," he started and held back.
He felt vulnerable. She turned. "Thanks for everything," he muttered. She gave a small, puzzled smile, then went back to the stove.

When the breakfast was ready he ate it without hesitation. Aisling returned upstairs which gave him the opportunity to go to the tool shed. He checked the duffle bag… two number plates. Snatching up his cigarette pack and the bundle of odds and ends he'd set aside the night before — gloves, screwdriver, a small nail file, and his badge.

Maxwell's lies had piled up so thick he hardly noticed them anymore. Today's was "check at the docks," nothing more than a cover to stretch the hours at home before he finally stepped out in the afternoon.

He stepped purposefully off the tube at Whitechapel and made his way down Bethnal Green Road, the late afternoon light already beginning to fade. He found the place easy enough—a grim cluttered costume shop tucked between a pawn broker and a boarded-up café. The cracked sign above the door read ***Albert's Theatrical Supplies***, though no one had bothered repainting it in years.

Inside, the air was thick with mothballs and old greasepaint. A muddle of false beards, tattered, pink feather boas, and a novelty policeman helmet hung from a hook. Behind the counter, sat a heavyset woman with **dyed post-box red hair, a cigarette hanging loosely from lips caked in lipstick. She barely looked up from the tattered book she was reading.**

Maxwell plucked a short, dark brown stick-on moustache from a wire rack, grabbed a tiny tin of spirit gum, and dropped them on the counter. He paid cash, no name, no change, and was out within minutes.

Back in a murky side street, he ducked into the doorway of a boarded-up chemist, peeled the backing off the moustache, daubed on the glue, and stuck it above his lip. He glanced at the reflection in the grubby window. It wasn't David Nevin, but it would do. He adjusted his jacket, made sure his badge was within easy reach, and headed for Wapping Freight Services.

The yard was as shabby as he remembered it. The rusted fencing, uneven concrete, and the stench of diesel hanging thick in the air. The gate sagged on rusted hinges; one half held in place by a length of chain; a padlock that looked older than the watchman guarding it. The old man glanced up from his spot on a three legged stool. He was in his late sixties, a heavy drinker by the look of his blotchy face and bloodshot eyes. Maxwell tagged him as an old ex-con.

Maxwell didn't bother with small talk. He flashed the badge just long enough to catch the light. "Detective Sergeant Wilson," he said crisply. "Following up on a hit-and-run report. Witness thought it might've been a Bedford TK box van. Just need a quick look around". The old man squinted, taking in the badge, and the tone of voice. He straightened. "Ain't no one's been in or out since lunch", the watchman muttered, waving a nicotine stained hand toward the yard. "'elp yourself, guv".

Maxwell stepped inside, the gate creaking behind him. He made a show of glancing over the line of vans, pausing by the Bedford TK he'd earmarked. Tires looked good. No visible damage. Papers on the dash, just as he hoped. "Mind if I ask about the schedule on these? Particularly the Bedford. How often is it used? Was it out recently? Any planned runs this weekend?" He rapped a knuckle against the side panel, pretending to check the bodywork. "Anyone report any panel damage or repairs lately?" he asked casually.

The old man gave a lazy shrug. "Panel damage?. Not that I've 'eard. Why?" Maxwell flashed him a sharp look. The old pickpocket realized he had overstepped the mark and cleared his throat. "Well, that one's mostly on the weekend market runs; if it's not needed Friday night, it usually sits till Monday. I think it's in fairly good nick, the brakes were last done two months ago, a few hiccups, but nothing too serious." Maxwell nodded slowly, filing the details away. *Good. Plenty of downtime to move it. The brakes being recently serviced means it won't raise any mechanical alarms.*

Maxwell eased off, "Thanks, mate, just routine". He turned to go and turned casually, "Like a good pal, if you hear of anything, give the local station a ring". The old man nodded, already reaching for his cigarettes again. Maxwell gave a thin smile, stepped back out the gate, and vanished down the street in silence. He smiled inwardly, thinking he had gotten exactly what he needed. The moustache came off three streets away and dropped into a drain.

He lit a cigarette and let the taste of it settle his nerves.

He exhaled a long slow breath —*Another job done.*

Maxwell slept late; he rose at 6:00 PM. He didn't bother to shave, grabbed a quick cup of tea, and headed out to the tool shed. Clearing off the workbench, he laid out his inventory one more time. A worn towel was spread across the bench, and the four number plates were carefully rolled into it to keep them from clattering. He placed them neatly in the hold-all. Next, the screwdriver, nail file, and small flashlight were bundled into a rag and set on the towel, followed by a bottle of water, a cap, a pair of gloves, and a packet of cigarettes.

When he returned to the kitchen, Aisling was busy at the stove.

"Another late night." Was it a question or a statement?

Maxwell reached for the soap. "Yeah, that cold case I told you about is heating up. Out tonight again."

She didn't answer; she had heard it all before. "There's stew in the pot. Heat it up before you go out." "Thanks, Ash," he smiled, kissing her cheek.

She pulled her head away, grabbed her coat, and headed to the hallway. Within a second she popped her head back in.

"What's in the hold-all?"

He stalled a moment but recovered. He grinned, raised an eyebrow. "You wouldn't want to know."

Aisling flashed an unsmiling look. "I should have known better."

The house settled into silence after the door slammed. He liked it better when she was on night shift—less to explain, fewer questions. Maxwell poured another cup of tea and stood by the window, watching the rain streak down the glass. The street was quiet, the slick pavement reflecting the glow of a single streetlamp. He checked his watch. It was too early. He hated waiting.

He turned on the gas, lifted the lid on the pot, inhaling the appetizing aroma. Aisling could cook when she wasn't too knackered. He ladled some of the heated stew into a bowl and ate it standing at the counter, the steady rattle of rain against the window a soothing rhythm to his stress. It was coming down harder now. *Good. Fewer people about.* Less chance of some nosy sod hanging around where he didn't belong.

When he was done, he rinsed the bowl, left it in the sink, and fetched the hold-all from the hallway. One last check of the contents—plates, tools, gloves, flashlight, water, smokes.

Everything in its place. He drew the curtains, killed the kitchen light, and slipped his cap on. It was 9:15 PM. Time to go. He grabbed his kit and left.

The dull gray Hillman Hunter MI5 unmarked pool car was parked at the side of his house. Maxwell checked his watch: 9:18 PM. He slipped out of the driveway and headed to Walthamstow, then on to Hackney, before ending up in Stepney. Using the backstreets, he found a quiet side street, grabbed the hold-all, and left the Hillman. He tugged his collar—more reflex than need. The rain was saturating the cap and running down his neck. The seven minute walk through back lanes toward the freight services yard was a grind. Slow, steady, keeping to the shadows. He checked his watch: 9:40 PM.

Maxwell climbed through the broken fence and headed for the van, hoping it had not been moved. Crouching behind a rusting oil barrel, he had a clear view of the yard guard's shed. The door was ajar, a nicotine-stained bulb hanging from the ceiling the only source of light. He shifted his position and saw the bent head. It was the old man he had encountered before.
The head was stooped—either asleep or drunk.
Maxwell moved on, his pace quickening. There it was at the end of a row of lorries and vans, the Bedford just as he'd spotted it the night before. He tried the handle; it opened. He threw the hold all on the seat and slid into the driver's position. The cab stank of old oil, moldy canvas, and the strong, putrid reek of decayed cabbage. His throat tightened and he gulped through his mouth. He found the nail file in the rag and slipped it into the ignition. He jiggled it back and forth.

He froze. *Stop. The plates.*

The nail file still in the ignition, he gripped the towel, screwdriver, and flashlight. Time to finish the job.

Out of the van in seconds, the towel, screwdriver, and flashlight in hand. He dropped the towel on the wet ground, fingers fumbling to unwrap the plates. The flashlight bounced between his teeth, casting a thin beam over the wet blacktop. A sudden noise made him freeze, heart pounding. He listened. Just a discarded metal sheet rattling in the sudden squall.

Maxwell worked fast despite the heavy rain pounding down around him. He already had two sets on hand, making sure one was a perfect match. A quick glance—the perfect match. Screws twisted free, rain slicking his palms. The old plates came off, swapped fast with the false set. He wrapped the originals tight. With the new plates fitted and screws tightened down, he was ready.

The nail file was already in the ignition. A quick twist— and the engine coughed, then caught. Maxwell gave the choke a nudge to steady the idle, pressed the accelerator to confirm the sputtering would stop and be replaced by a steady hum. He eased off the handbrake.

His boot squelched against something soft as he reached for the gear lever. He glanced down. A wilted cabbage leaf, graygreen and rank, was pinned beneath his boot. He brushed it aside with the edge of his boot, eyes already back on the road.
He clutched and shifted into gear.

The van pushed into the wet street; he glanced right and turned left. The van crept forward, tires whispering over the wet tarmac. At the gate, he paused for one more check. The street was clear. Then he tossed the unused set of plates aside. He exhaled, tension releasing. He allowed himself the faintest smile, slipped the van into gear—ready to disappear into the stormy night. Moving out discreetly, sticking to back streets.

The wipers struggled to clear the heavy rain.

His gaze remained fixed on the road, knuckles white as he navigated the slick cobblestones. The rain was easing up. The Bedford bounced along the cobbles of Cable Street, the fog thickening ahead. Maxwell flicked the headlights off and let the mist swallow the van. The hold-all on the passenger seat sagged to one side with each bump—a dark, silent weight. The only sounds were the engine's uneven cough and the wet slap of tires on cobblestones.

Maxwell kept an eye on the mist-blurred pavements, the boarded-up shopfronts, the glimmer of a pub's upstairs window, a small beacon in the gloom. The van took a sharp right pivot off Cable Street onto Draper's Yard. The expected lamppost stood solitary on the corner, the light casting a hazy halo glow, its rays diffused by the gentle drizzle.

"You. Bastard." His fist hammered the steering wheel.

No Flynn.

CHAPTER 34
Dock-17

Maxwell's brain froze. He made another drive-by; his foot pressed the accelerator. *Wait ten minutes.*

The van jerked forward and he found an unlit lane on his right which curved back to Cable Street. At the end of the lane, he braked hard, the van's tyres skimming the slick cobbles. The mist clung low, swallowing the street. Nothing moved. No figures. No sign of life. No Flynn.

A scuttling rat with glinting eyes darted from an old, deserted warehouse across the cobblestones, its shape flickering like a warning. Maxwell watched it vanish into the fog, unease prickling at his neck. He checked his watch. Three minutes to eleven. Too long.

Too bloody long.

He gritted his teeth and swung the van round, back toward Draper's Yard, easing it past the crooked row of shuttered tailor and barber shops. The lamppost was still there, solitary in the drizzle, its pool of yellow light mirrored in the fog. No Flynn.

Maxwell swallowed hard, his throat suddenly parched. He could feel it now—a crawling shiver slinking beneath his skin: the game had changed, and he was on the losing end. His hand darted instinctively to where a Smith & Wesson should have been beneath his coat—a reflex, nothing more. No gun. Using one wasn't part of the plan. Old habits die hard.

Was it a set-up? Had Flynn never intended to go through with it? Was Flynn already picked up? Or worse—had he talked to Special Branch or MI5?

A voice in his head hissed: Walk away now… burn the van… get back to Highams Park, wash your hands. Report what you know.

But it was too late. The van was stolen. The job half started. No telling who was watching, who was waiting.

A car horn sounded faintly somewhere beyond the warehouses, a single sharp note swallowed quickly by the fog. Maxwell stiffened. Sound played tricks in the mist, bouncing off metal and brick, turning every echo into a footstep, every drip into a whispered warning. He shifted in the seat, suddenly aware of how exposed he was. Too exposed.

Maxwell took a long breath, wiped his palm on his coat, and pulled the van into the dockyard.

It was empty. Just a litter of old crates, a stack of pallets, and a length of rusting chain drooping from a hook. The rain began again, hissing softly in the puddles. Where was 17?

For a moment he wondered whether the number meant anything at all, whether Flynn had thrown it out as bait. He tightened his grip on the wheel. If this was a trap, it was a bloody patient one.

"We're in deep now. You realize that don't you?" another dishonor dodged. Promotion, clearance, clout. He could finally step out of the shadows of men like Carter.

He exhaled into the gloom. Even the air felt heavier here, as though the docks themselves were holding their breath.

Then—movement.

At the end of the dock a light flashed. Two young, muscular men stepped out of the mist. Heavy coats and caps pulled low. No names. No glances. No need.

One peeled back the canvas. The rear double doors of the old van opened with a groan, the rusting hinges protesting the overused movement. Damp air rushed in. The other grabbed one end of a crate. Too heavy. The second moved in, sharing the lift. They worked fast, in silence.

Maxwell kept his gaze locked on the windscreen, staring into the darkness beyond the docks. Every muscle in his neck ached to turn, to check the shadows, but he forced himself still. He listened instead—the scrape of wood, the grunt of effort as the crate shifted. He caught the way the men's shoulders tightened with the lift. The first crate hit the floor of the van with a solid thud, the old Bedford's springs squeaking under the weight. A second followed, then a third. The metal chassis gave a weary creak with each load, sagging visibly by the fourth.

Heavier than I figured.

A gust of cold air slid into the van, carrying with it the faint, oily tang of the river. It reminded him of nights on surveillance— long, dead hours where nothing moved but your imagination. He felt that same pressure now, settling on his shoulders, urging him to get out, get clear, vanish before the fog lifted.

One of the men muttered something low. *What was the accent? Was it English? Eastern European?* Did it matter? Something about the rhythm of it clawed at him, a reminder that he was a bystander in his own job.

Maxwell sucked a sharp breath as another crate was manhandled aboard. Whatever was in the crates, it wasn't Christmas toys.

And if they knew who he was, what he was, they wouldn't be loading this van at all.

Maxwell's fingers hovered near the screwdriver under the towel. His other hand tightened on the wheel. Get it loaded. Get gone. Don't ask, don't count.

The last crate was the heaviest of all. The two men heaved it aboard with grunts, the old Bedford slumping deeper under the load. The springs gave a long, tortured groan. The doors slammed shut with a hollow clang. No words, no goodbyes. The two men vanished back into the mist like they'd never been there. The dock was wrapped in darkness.

The van rolled out of Dock-17—pregnant.

CHAPTER 35

The Crates Drop

Maxwell eased the van into gear, feeling every creak and groan in the frame like a shouted warning. The weight behind him pressed against the Bedford, against his nerves, against the thin thread of luck he was riding.

He nosed the van through the gates of Dock 17, rain hammering the windscreen, wipers smearing muddy streaks. The Bedford bucked under the load, tyres hissing through puddles, the wheel stiff in his grip. He took the first corner wide, the steering heavy—fighting him. A pothole sent the crates lurching in the back. He flinched, instinctively glancing at the mirror. Nothing but wet cobbles and mist. The area was near deserted, but the wrong face in the wrong place could finish him.

In the distance, the streetlights blotted the drenched stones. A fire engine wailed somewhere close by. The streets were shrouded in shadow. Maxwell kept the Bedford in second, letting the engine burble instead of roar. A lorry stood at the exit, brakes hissing, driver smoking with his elbows out.

Good—cover. Maxwell tucked up behind a tar-spattered tipper. His leg worked the brake, each movement setting the load swaying; every sway felt like a warning. The leaf springs strained. The tipper eased ahead—Maxwell rolled forward a foot. Then stopped. A Port constable strolled past, truncheon tucked in his belt. He tapped the Bedford's side panels out of habit—one, two.

The suspension sighed. *Don't bounce, don't bounce.* Maxwell drained a breath and fed a whisper of throttle to steady the chassis.

He hugged the tipper's tailboard, using its bulk to hide the Bedford's slump, indicators ticking. Out through the dock mouth, past the last stacks of pallets and the last smell of rope tar and fish meal, into the city's orange glow.

Left with the tipper. Right without it. Under a dripping rail bridge where water fell from girders. He let a bus lumber past; a police car slid into the other lane and away on some other mission. Maxwell exhaled—relieved—almost.

Clutch—second—third. The Bedford settled into the night traffic like a party crasher. Maxwell exhaled again, then finally breathed. The docks fell behind him like a bad dream.

His jaw clenched. The van rode low—too low. A slumping load, stuck out like a sore thumb. Bound to catch the eye of some fresh-nosed copper looking to fill his book. He checked the mirror—dimmed headlights behind. Two blocks later—still there. A tail? He took another look; the lights turned off into a side street. A long, shaky breath left him, half-sigh, half whimper. A nervous bubble of laughter climbed his throat; he swallowed it down.

The traffic light showed green. A figure ahead—blurred in the downpour Maxwell's gut tightened. Beat copper? No—just a drunk—coat flapping open to the rain.

The van crawled past, gears grinding. Sweat ran cold down his back as the crates shifted again. The engine labored; each gear change was a wrestle; each turn a risk.

At a junction, a patrol car idled at the curb, steam rising from the exhaust, blue lamp strobing the rain. Maxwell kept the Bedford steady, eyes front. The copper stared at nothing in particular.

Maxwell took a wide turn into a side street and checked the mirror. Still nothing. Another hundred yards.

Another pothole. The crates knocked with a dull, sickening clunk. He coaxed the van on—left into a narrow side street, tyres skimming pooled water.

At last, the yard. Figures waited in the rain. No sign of welcome. Maxwell edged the van through the gate. He cut the engine; the hiss of rain replaced the sound. He stayed behind the wheel, listening. No tail. Clean. Almost relaxed. *Finish it. Get out of here.*

As he killed the lights, a small dark saloon nosed in behind and idled. A young woman sat at the wheel, her pale face lit by the dash glow. She didn't move. Maxwell's shoulders tensed. *How did I miss her?* He hadn't heard an engine—hadn't heard tyres on the wet stones. But the men in the yard didn't so much as glance her way.

Four men stood ready. Heavy rain jackets, hoods low, hands gloved. They gave nothing away and seemed uninterested in him. A fifth stood apart—older, thick through the shoulders, a streaked beard showing beneath a sou'wester. He moved with a limp— slow, deliberate, each step dragging a fraction. A crowbar hung loose from his hand. One nod. The rear doors swung wide; rusted hinges protested. Rain hammered the crates as the men moved in, two to a box, careful but quick. Well-drilled. Silent.

The limping man levered the first lid. Nails shrieked. Maxwell glanced in the rearview mirror—hands tightening on the stirring wheel. The limp peeled back sodden packing; steel caught the thin light. A rifle. He checked the markings, gave a small nod, and the work resumed. Boots on wet stone, rain on canvas, wood on metal—the only sounds.

Maxwell stayed in the cab, sweat prickling between his shoulder blades. His part was done—almost. But he still worried. *How did I miss her? A woman as wheel-man—clever.* Four men… or six? He took another quick look in the mirror—Four men… or six? The limp again, touching a lid. Maxwell stiffened. The unloading paused. Nails shrieked; wood creaked. He strained to hear the chatter—only rain.

The inspection done, the lift resumed. The last crate hit the ground with a dull thud. No orders. No farewells. One by one the men melted into the dark, collars up, rain and night swallowing them. None looked back. The saloon was gone; he hadn't seen it leave.

Maxwell stayed in the van, his hands gripping—tension tight in his gut. *Go? Wait?* Nothing.

Maxwell waited in silence, let the stillness settle. *Screw this. I'm out of here.* Then turned the key. The engine coughed and caught. No headlights. The Bedford eased for the gate, tyres whispering over wet cobbles.

If trouble was coming, it wasn't here. Not yet.

CHAPTER 36

The Vanishing

The van whooshed along the wet streets, Maxwell's eyes flicking to the mirrors every few seconds. The rain had eased to a fine mist, a greasy sheen on the roadway, and the fog hung low, clinging to gutters and doorways. London after midnight—half dead but still dangerous.

A little further on, he spotted it: a dark alley between a boarded-up pawnbroker and a rundown warehouse. No lights. No foot traffic. The kind of place you might get knifed for no reason other than being there.

He cut the engine, the sudden hush pressing in around him. No sound but the soft hiss of water trickling down a broken drainpipe. The alley stretched left and right— slim, boxed in by high walls, a rusted fire escape clinging precariously to the side of the derelict warehouse. A broken crate lay against one wall, sodden cardboard spilling from its side.

Maxwell moved a few paces from the van, pausing at the corner where the alley met a side lane. He checked both ways. Nothing. A burned-out streetlamp flickered faintly at the far end, its glow barely cutting the fog. He crouched briefly, checking beneath the van and behind a skip. No sign of life. No prying eyes. Satisfied, he straightened—then, a sudden sound.

An exhale. Footsteps. Not heavy, not hurried—but wrong in the fog. Somewhere in the mist a shape moved, a figure where there shouldn't be one. Maxwell stop in his tracks, heart hammering. A cop? A watchman? Or worse—someone cleaning up unfinished business. The silhouette hesitated. A match flared, briefly painting a hollowed face in quivering orange light.

Not a threat—just some poor sod crouched against the wall, a strip of foil balanced across his knees, the dark smear of something ugly bubbling under the flame. A thin roll of paper at his lips. He dragged deep, the smoke curling as he exhaled with a long, contented sigh. Eyes met. No words. No nod. Just a dead, indifferent stare through the haze. Then the junkie looked away, sinking back into whatever world he was chasing.

Maxwell moved on, pulse still hammering, the sickly-sweet stink clinging to the damp air behind him. He let out a trapped breath—one he hadn't realized he'd been holding prisoner. Another sweep of the alley. Nothing. Satisfied it was clear; he slipped back to the van. The wet metal of the door pressed against his gloved palm as he swung it open and slid inside. Fumbling, he found the plates in the towel, their chipped paint dull under the dim dashboard light. He pulled them free—a quick precautionary wipe.

He worked fast. The flashlight askew between his teeth, the wet gloves slowing the unscrewing of the stolen plates. The mist beaded on his jacket; the worst of the rain had passed, though the air still hung heavy and damp. The original Freight Services numbers in hand—damp but clean. Plates switched, rag wipe, stuffed back into his pocket. Maxwell slid behind the wheel. The van's cab stank: a heavy tang of oil and wet canvas battling the sour reek of rotted cabbage. He checked his watch. 12:19. He was still inside the planed window—barely.

When the job was done, he leaned back, eyes darting to the alley's mouth. A heavy sigh exhaled for what felt like the first time in an hour and let the van roll forward, tyres murmuring. The night wasn't done with him yet—but for now, the rain had shown a little mercy. He took the long route back.

No point in being clever, just quiet.

At this hour, a bored copper might pull a van over just for the chat. The rain held off, a fine damp hanging in the air, soft as a whisper. *Too early? Too late? Too quiet?* The thought chewed at him as he drove. The yard sometimes stirred before dawn with market runs heading to Billingsgate or Covent Garden. Too many vans moving about—too many eyes. Or worse—too few.
Coming back early could look wrong.

Killing time might make sense. Just enough to let the clock roll closer to twelve-forty, twelve-forty-five—a safer, less suspicious window. A lone cab trundled past. One more slow circuit—not to waste time, but to check for patrols or trouble spots.
12:30. Time enough.

He turned down the tight lane that led to the Freight Services yard. The rusted gates stood part-open. Light filtered weakly from the doorway of the watchman's hut. A figure was there now—the old yardman, hunched and broad, a cigarette flare bright in the gloom. Maxwell tugged his cap lower, hands steady on the wheel— a casual wave as he passed. The yardman squinted, one bleary eye catching the van's outline.

Maxwell's jaw stiffened. He steered past, slid the Bedford into its customary spot, tyres hissing on damp stone. Engine off.

Quick check—no one watching. The door shut with a soft click. Without a glance back, he crossed the yard, moving toward the broken fence panel he'd slipped through hours before. The fence creaked faintly under his weight. The mist snaked around him which felt like a living thing.

London swallowed him whole.

12:34. Job done.

Time to make the call.

Chapter 37

Damaged Goods

He moved briskly now, boots striking wet pavement in tempo. Traffic was sparse, the mist dissolving to reveal the grim outlines of shuttered buildings. He kept to the shadows, eyes scanning for movement, ears tuned to every faint sound. The job was done—for better or worse—but the night hadn't released him yet. *Cover my tracks.*

Ahead, a dim red glow caught his eye—a phone box. Its paint was chipped, its glass smeared with graffiti. The door hung heavy as he pushed it open. A stale stink of urine and tobacco hit him; cigarette butts and Watney's cans littered the floor.

He closed the door behind him and dropped a coin into the slot, praying for a dial tone.

Two rings. Then the voice—calm, precise.

"Yes?"

Maxwell swallowed, keeping his tone even. "Got a tip about a weapons move tonight. Thought it worth following up quietly. Was able to embed myself." A pause, "Go on."

Before he could answer, another question cut through.

"When did this come in?"

"Turned out solid," Maxwell said quickly. "Arms shipment. Crates moved through a Freight Services yard down in Rotherhithe. I became attached. Van's back. Plates switched.

No issues." The words came rehearsed—too rehearsed.

Another pause. Sharper now.

"I repeat…. when did this come in?"

Maxwell hesitated. *I should have prepared better.*

"Yesterday evening. Pub talk. Something I'd been working. Timing was crucial—I had to act fast." Silence. Maxwell felt the heat.

Then: "Where are you now?"

"Phone box, Albion Street. By the old church." Another pause—longer this time.

"Stay there. Someone will collect you in five minutes."

Maxwell blinked, gripping the receiver tighter. "I thought I'd—"

"Stay there."

The line went dead.

He stared at the receiver, pulse hammering. The mist outside seemed heavier now, pressing in on every side. He replaced the handset, wiped his palm on his coat, and stepped into the clammy air. He reached for a cigarette—dropped it— cursed—lit another.

He waited in the fog, each minute stretching rigid with unease. His mind raced through the night's events: the crates, the faces, the saloon woman, the limp. Everything suddenly felt lopsided, wrong, like a move made on a board he hadn't realized he was playing.

Prepare—careful—not too slick. What a bloody cock-up.

A low purr approached. Headlights cut. A dark Wolseley rolled to a stop at the curb. The driver's window slid down.

"Get in."

Maxwell obeyed—and stiffened. Someone was already there.

A new face.

A Section man—silent, unreadable, face half-shadowed— his fellow passenger.

The figure sat motionless in the far corner, offering no greeting. Just the slow turn of a head and the brief glint of watchful eyes. No coat steaming, no sense of rush. As if he'd been waiting all night.

Maxwell's breath caught. Not fear—not yet—but something cold unfurled in his chest. He didn't know this man. The cut of the suit, the stillness—too calm, too controlled. A watcher. Or worse— an auditor.

The door thumped shut before he could speak. The car moved off.

No one said a word. Not the man beside him. Not the driver. Only the hum of the engine and the slap of tyres on wet road broke the silence. Maxwell felt himself shrinking inward, every nerve tuned to the slightest shift beside him.

He stared straight ahead, hands clasped tight in his lap, mouth dry. The familiar streets slid past in the dispersing fog. He didn't need to ask where they were going. Feeny's Yard.

Ten minutes. Maybe more. The car slowed. The wrought iron gates came into view—half-open. Floodlights slanting across gravel, cutting deep shadows. They rolled in.

Men were already there: dark coats, low voices, quick movements doing nothing obvious but everything necessary. Maxwell stepped out. The man from the car stayed behind, face still as stone.

A figure raised a hand—flat, horizontal. The message clear. Empty—Weapons gone.

Maxwell's stomach dropped—a taste of bile. The air felt suddenly thin. He scanned the yard, incredulous—shadows, cigarette smoke, boot prints in the mud. Crates had been here, but not for long. No splinters, no tarps, no wheel marks. A military level clean.

This was no follow-up. This was containment.

Trust. Weapons. Ambition. All gone.

He swallowed—stomach turning—lungs burned as the oxygen had been sucked out. "Nothing here? The crates were here—I saw them. Ten crates." His voice cracked. No one answered.

Then, from the darkness behind him, a voice:

"Report to the Section Head. 0800

Maxwell turned to explain—but the speaker was already walking away.

No questions. No explanations. Just the time.

0800 hours.

He stood alone in the damp yard—gutted. The silence pressed in, louder than ever. Engines faded into the muddle until only the drip of water and the hollow rasp of his breathing remained.

        The night devoured him like a phantom.

Damaged goods.

CHAPTER 38

Dangerous Meeting

The key turned softly in the lock. Maxwell stepped into the house, careful not to let the door snap shut behind him.

The place was still—immersed in the quiet of mid-morning.

Aisling's shift would've ended hours ago—she'd be asleep now.
He moved upstairs without a sound, avoiding the eighth step. A weak light glowed beneath the bedroom door. He paused. Aisling lay curled under the duvet, hair an undistinguishable tangle on the pillow. Even in sleep, her face carried the haggard look and weariness of a long night on the ward. She shifted slightly, eyes squinting open.

"You're back early."

Maxwell forced a smile. "Yeah. They gave me some leave. Cold case wrapped up. He gave us the runaround, but we got the bugger in the end."

"You need it. You've been running ragged lately," she mumbled, half-asleep.

He slipped out of the bedroom and down the stairs. The haunting words followed him.

Compromised judgement—intractable.

The words returned uninvited, caustic and deflating. He'd sat in that chair like a schoolboy, enduring the Section Head's clipped rebuke. A file had been snapped shut, the sound sharp as a slap. No defense. No denials.

"You've been a liability, Maxwell. We're reviewing your full record. Stand down until the hearing."

The butter tore through the toast. He dropped the knife in the sink—the clatter louder than he intended—and reached for his coffee instead.

Another echo—Flynn—*Why?*

The loudmouth who had pulled him into the weapons lift— swore it was clean, humdrum. Then the no-show. *No excuse. Nothing. Where the hell did he go—and why? Is he I.R.A., or MI5? Or something worse?*

He needed answers, but how? Aisling would ask questions if he pushed too hard, but Marie would know. She always knew where Flynn was drinking or hiding. Had he been picked up by MI5? Maybe he'd find out tomorrow, asking casually.

There had been no word, no show, just silence. He'd have to talk to Aisling, she wouldn't know, but Marie—Flynn's girlfriend— might know something for sure. The thought brought a flicker of hope, or perhaps despair—a tense foreboding tightened in his gut..

Maxwell killed time over the next few days in routine activities—polishing his already shined shoes—rearranging the tool shed, lining up tools with pointless precision. All disguising the rising unease that was eating him.

He wandered down to the Killarney Pub on unplanned evenings, nursing a pint and listening for a hint of a sign, but nothing came. The regulars chatted about football and work, but not a word about Flynn. Eyes sharp, ears sharper—still nothing.

Flynn's crew were nowhere to be seen. *Where is Devine?*

At home, he kept things light with Aisling—brewing her tea, asking after her shifts, mentioning Marie's name just often enough to sound casual. No pressure, just little nudges. If Marie had called, he wanted to know. If Flynn had been mentioned, even in passing, he was listening.

Days turned to weeks, still without mention of Marie. It was time for more purposeful action.

Maxwell had prepared breakfast. The unmistakable smell of frying bacon and fresh tea filled the air. Aisling, worn out from a night shift at the hospital, dragged in quietly.
Maxwell was ready with a small smile.

"Morning. Thought I'd get a jump on breakfast today.
Figured you'd appreciate it after an exhausting night."
Aisling, with a drained sigh, mumbled, "That's thoughtful.
Thanks. It's been a challenging one."
They ate in comfortable silence. Maxwell watched her,
then casually refilled her cup.
"Any news from Marie lately—she hasn't been around?"
he asked with casual interest.
Aisling added sugar. "Actually, I talked with her today.
She had a lot of news."
Maxwell kept eating—all ears.
"She mentioned Flynn's sold his little building business—
he has headed back home to Kerry. Seems they're planning
a wedding."
Maxwell swallowed hard—his attempt at casualness faltered.
"Kerry? When?" He held his jaw—covering the quiver.

Aisling, oblivious to the panic her news had created said, "He sold and moved a few weeks ago."

Maxwell drained his cup. The tea tasted bitter— his mind racing. Flynn back in Kerry? Distance… cover… or running from something?

He needed time to think. *Is this good or bad news?*

Maxwell clenched his fist under the table, and with a sudden, steely calm in his voice he said.

"It's time you got your rest; I'll clear up." He waited till the stair board creaked. He needed to think.

CHAPTER 39

The Code

The days mingled one into another. Hope and questioning tangled through the daylight hours; despair and futility ruled the nights. Maxwell woke each morning with the same heaviness in his chest, a tight band tightening each time he checked his phone for a message that never came.

The silence from the Service was louder than any reprimand.

He'd told Aisling he was on leave. Technically, it wasn't a lie. She'd accepted it easily enough—said he deserved the time. With her working nights and him rattling around the house alone, the walls seemed to shrink by the hour.

By early dawn that morning, he couldn't bear them any longer. While Aisling was still at the hospital, he dressed, buttoned his coat, and stepped into the chill air. The streets were damp, washed by a passing shower, and the sky was just beginning to brighten. London stirred—purposeful, indifferent— while he felt none of its get-up-and-go.

His steps carried him toward the park, half-conscious, habit more than choice. Mist hovered over the grass, last night's rain soaking the pea gravel. A woman in a red coat tossed a ball for her spaniel. An old man fed ducks beneath the bridge. A young boy struggled to fly a kite. Life persisted—oblivious to the storm inside Maxwell's head.

He walked slowly, hands rammed into his pockets. The hearing was weeks ago and still nothing—no clearance, no summons, no decision. Each day he waited for the phone to ring. Each evening the silence settled heavier. It felt like banishment.

Near the far gate, a scent cut through the damp. Coffee. Rich, bitter, unmistakable.

He followed it down a side street to a small café tucked beneath a brick arch. Inside, a handful of early risers lingered over pastries and papers. Maxwell ordered a black coffee and chose a seat by the window, the posture of a man waiting for something that might never come.

The hum of the espresso machine softened the quiet. Jazz murmured from a radio. His fingers tapped the saucer. Should've bought a paper. His breath clouded faintly above the cup as he stared out at people who had purpose, direction— something he had been denied.

The bell above the door jingled.

An elderly woman shuffled in, bundled in mismatched layers, the cuffs of her coat frayed. Two overstuffed shopping bags swung from her arms. She picked up her coffee, cast a sweeping glance over the café, then made a slow, deliberate path toward him.

"Mind if I sit, love?" Her voice was warm, cracked like old fine china.

Maxwell nodded, quietly startled.

Something about her—the upright posture, the measured tone—hinted at an old-school decorum. Not just manners. Discipline, maybe.

She sipped her coffee, then leaned forward as if adjusting her napkin. Her hand slid a small, folded square under the edge of his saucer, quick and practiced. She finished the cup in two firm gulps, adjusted her scarf, and rose.

"Be seeing you, love. You take care now," she said, already moving toward the door. The bell jingled again. She was gone.

Maxwell waited in astonishment. He looked around, then calmly lifted the saucer.

A folded note. Three numbers: **5, 11, 3**.

Something clicked back into place inside him—sharp as a gear engaging. No hesitation. The meaning was immediate. A directive. A summons. A silent confirmed acknowledgment that he hadn't been cast out entirely. Not yet.

But one troubling thought chilled him: *How did she know I was here?*

He watched for further movement, slid the note deep into his pocket, and stepped out into the morning. The park was waking properly now—joggers cutting determined paths, dog walkers calling softly after their pets. The world turned on, unaware of the coded spark flickering back to life inside him.

Still, the muddle inside him hadn't entirely lifted. The numbers circled his mind—simple, but sharp, slicing through weeks of uncertainty.

5-11-3

A return to the codebook. A meeting. An instruction. A test?

He followed aimlessly through no set path, letting the city lead him. Through the wrought-iron gates, down rain-dulled pavements. He drifted into a boutique arcade off the main road.

The air was thick with perfume and the sweet tang of confectionery. For a moment he lingered before a window, staring without seeing. A reflection moved behind him—a figure in a raincoat—and vanished as quickly as it appeared.

A tremor ran down his spine. He walked on, not hurried, but less slow—watching.

By late afternoon he had almost convinced himself it was nothing. A shadow, a trick of light, a ghost conjured by weeks of isolation. Then a flicker of optimism surfaced—small but real. They wouldn't have used the code unless it meant something. Not with him. Not now.

A clock chimed across the square—five slow, deliberate notes echoing against budding trees and wrought-iron railings. Spring light lingered, stretching shadows thin.

Maxwell paused at the edge of the square and rattled the coins in his pocket. He wasn't ready to go home. Not yet. The house, in Aisling's absence, would feel too empty. Too expectant. He needed the muffled comfort of strangers around him—the illusion of company.

A young couple crossed the far side, laughing effortlessly. A boy chased pigeons near the war memorial. The sight tugged at something deep, a faint ache of lost youth and choices long made. Regrets? Maybe. Discarded.

A wooden sign creaked in the breeze—*Wendell's News &* *Tobacco*. A holdover from another age. Inside, the shop smelled of printer's ink, licorice, and damp. A battered fan hummed behind the counter.

Maxwell scanned the shelves—humbugs, pipe tobacco, outdated magazines—then grabbed an *Evening News*. A Cabinet reshuffle screamed across the front page. Irrelevant, but grounding. Solid. Ordinary. He folded it crisply and handed a coin to the shopkeeper, who nodded as if Maxwell were a familiar face.

Back outside, the square had settled into a muted hush. A gull cried overhead, the sound cutting through the quiet.
Maxwell tightened his grip on the folded paper.

Maybe he'd grab a pint. Sit. Read. Pretend he wasn't waiting.

Waiting for what?

His fingers brushed the fold of the note in his coat pocket.

5-11-3.

A summons. Or a warning?

Either way, the silence had finally fractured.

CHAPTER 40

The Morning After

Aisling was worn out, shoulders drooped—looking like she'd been dragged through the wringer of a twelve-hour shift. Left with only the energy to flop into the nearest chair, her scrubs lying over the back. She had scarcely settled when Maxwell arrived. He poured himself a stiff drink and watched her with guilt for a long moment before speaking.

"I might pop into the office tomorrow," he said, keeping his tone light. "They rang earlier. Something about tying up a few loose ends."

Aisling looked up from her tea, weary-eyed—one brow slightly raised. "I thought you were on leave. I was hoping we could do something on my days off, you know."

He raised a defensive hand. "I am on leave," he blurted too quickly. "This is just... routine. Administrative stuff. They want someone who knows the files. I promise I'll make it up to you. Anyhow, it may not take too long."

She gave a small, long-suffering nod—too tired to argue. He could tell by the subtle tightening of her lips that she didn't quite believe him, but she let it pass.

He ran a hand through his hair and glanced out the window, the weight of waiting still pressing down. The evening dragged, the message drilling into his brain. **5. 11. 3.** He'd be there— prepared. Just in case. He tried—too hard—to convince himself it was routine.

For a moment, a flicker of something close to hope stirred. Maybe this was the thread to pull. Maybe this was the beginning of an end. But as the hours passed, the weight of doubt returned— slow and grinding.

The kitchen was quiet now. Aisling had gone to bed, her footsteps soft, the quiet creak of the stair board marking her ascent. Maxwell sat in the semi-darkness. The *Evening Standard* lay unread on the armrest, its front page shadowed by the streetlight. The city beyond was alive in slivers of sound— muffled sirens, the occasional dog bark, a car humming past. All unnerving.

He poured himself another whiskey. Not out of thirst— more habit. One sip was enough. The taste—a dull, sour layer that coated his tongue. The stress and nicotine dulled his senses; only the harsh tang remained, a constant reminder of the day's anxieties.

He climbed the stairs with long strides, avoiding the second to-last step, and undressed in silence, careful not to wake Aisling. She stirred slightly, turning toward the wall. The clock ticked past midnight. He lay on his back, eyes to the ceiling. **5. 11. 3.**—the numbers embedded in the plaster. The night stretched ahead, long and restless. He closed his eyes, but the numbers remained— menacing. He shifted and opened his eyes again.

Now, in the dark, he lay beside Aisling, eyes open to the ceiling. The room was warm, the window cracked for air, letting in the occasional hum of a car or the aggressive screech of cats down some distant alley. London—never quite asleep. Hours dragged.

He floated somewhere between memory and regret, past missions flashing like unedited film reels. Names without faces. Faces without names. The weight of what wasn't said— ad hoc actions. Flynn— crates—the man with the limp—*"If you draw   attention, you'll answer for it"*—*"You've been a liability."* The words flooded his mind. Sleep was impossible.

A soft gray light began to inch along the edges of the blinds. The alarm clock read five o'clock. Morning, or something like it. Maxwell swung his legs over the side of the bed and sat, elbows on knees, rubbing his temples. Aisling breathed evenly behind him.

He stared at the floor for a long while—dreams rewinding.
Still—he hadn't fallen apart. That had to count for something.

The meeting. The flick through the codebook for number 5.
He had no plan yet. No certainty. Just a meeting—play it by ear.

He slipped from the bed quietly, toes curling on the cold floorboards. The weight of the day settled on his shoulders before he even reached the bathroom. The tap struggled and sputtered chilly water. He cupped his hands, splashed his face, and stared at the man looking back—bloodshot eyes, jaw clenched like a fist. He stood before the mirror, razor in hand. The pale morning light seeped through thin cotton curtains.

He lathered up, fingers working the soap into his skin like muscle memory. The mirror fogged; a quick rub with his free hand didn't quite clear it. The first stroke of the razor was cautious— down the cheek, familiar ground. But as he moved closer, around the mouth, the blade caught. A sharp nick just on the corner of his lip.

"Damn it," he hissed, dabbing at the bead of blood with a dry finger. Always that same spot.

A few quick, practiced strokes, a double-check of the usual patches— then done. The cut was still bleeding, faintly, repaired with a bit of toilet paper. He rinsed the blade under the cold tap, his jaw alerted by the sting of aftershave. He cleaned up the cut as best he could. It had stopped bleeding, mostly. He ran a damp hand through his thick, disheveled hair and left the bathroom.

The scent of toast and fried eggs hit him before he reached the kitchen. Aisling was at the stove, barefoot, still in her robe. Her hair was pulled back, messy, and beautiful. Maxwell thought for a mini-second—regret. She didn't turn. "You're not going anywhere on an empty stomach."

"I said I'm only clearing up loose ends," he muttered.

"You'll need your strength to do even that," she said, flipping an egg with the flat of a knife. "You haven't eaten properly in days."

He sat down, checked the clock above the mantle, and reached for a cigarette. Just past eight. He still had some wiggle room.

"Don't light that cigarette." It was Aisling, as if she had eyes in the back of her head.

She brought over a plate—eggs, toast, bacon, a fried tomato. "Eat."

He nodded quietly, grateful. She sat opposite, nursing a mug of tea in cupped hands.

"You slept a bit better?" she asked, her voice gentler now. "Didn't hear you toss as much."

He gave a noncommittal grunt, cutting into the egg.

He finished the meal in silence. The eggs were the way he liked them—sunny-side up, the toast perfectly crisp—but it might as well have been cardboard. He didn't taste a thing. His mood was anything but sunny; his mind was already walking the streets ahead of him, trying to read signs that hadn't yet appeared.

By half past eight, he was dressed—dark jacket, collar turned slightly against the breeze, black leather shoes polished to a dull shine. Aisling handed him a sandwich wrapped in greaseproof paper.   "In case you get stuck."

He gave a weak smile and kissed her forehead. "Thanks." His hand lingered on her arm.

"Is everything alright, Bob?"

He felt unmasked. "I'm fine."

And with the door clicking shut behind him, the day finally began—the day everything might change.

Aisling watched his departure, furrowed brow—lips pursed.

God, he's leaving—and something is about to happen.

CHAPTER 41

The Bookshop

Outside, the city was stretching awake. The air had that faint snap of early spring—not quite warm, but softer than winter. A light breeze stirred the branches, and here and there, tight green buds hinted at the season's slow return. The wind coming off the reservoir had a bite to it, despite the sun trying to climb through the cloud.

Maxwell took the short walk to Highams Park station, collar up, eyes on the ground. No one paid him any attention— just another man heading into the city, suit too plain to question. Still, every footstep behind him felt a shade too close, a scrape on the pavement half a beat out of time. He told himself not to look back. He looked back anyway—nothing. He boarded the next train, the 8:52 AM, to Liverpool Street, and took a window seat. The carriage smelled of tobacco and old coffee. Around him, the usual shuffle of commuters— quiet, hunched into corduroy coats or bomber jackets, some getting a jump on the news, others planning the day ahead.

The train clattered through Walthamstow, then Hackney Downs. He watched the rooftops flash past—chimney pots, washing lines, graffiti crawled on walls. By the time they pulled into Liverpool Street just after 9:20, he was no closer to knowing what he'd say when he got to Holborn. No one would listen.

Their minds were made up—closed.

He changed to the Central Line. The platform was crowded, a wave of bodies moving in instructed rhythm— zombies. He stayed near the doors, and gripping the pole. The city had its own smell—metal, oil, sweat, perfume. From there, the stops were a countdown. Three... two... one.

At Chancery Lane, he surfaced. The traffic was already heavy. Crowded buses lumbered past. A courier on a bike clipped a wing mirror and swore loud enough to turn heads. He checked his watch. Nearly ten. He wasn't due until eleven. That gave him time.

He walked. An hour to kill. Not enough time to do anything useful. Too much time to do nothing. His life was all about waiting—filling time, watching, listening. Parked cars, pubs, and cafés were his usual lookouts, but not today. The idea of sitting still, sipping weak coffee, pretending to read a newspaper, only sharpened the edge in his gut. So, he walked. Not far—just enough to move, enough to clear the fog.

The city was changing gears—late-opening shopkeepers dragging out displays, a bin lorry rumbling past, an old man swearing at a cab that wouldn't stop. He cut through a side street, then another. No destination. He circled the same row of shops twice, not caring. Eventually, he found a bench across from a vegetable stand, sat, and watched an affluent woman squeezing tomatoes before purchasing. At ten-forty, he checked his watch. Still early. But waiting on the street felt worse than walking. He rose slowly. Walked past the bookshop, knowing it would be there—he'd double back.

At ten-fifty, he crossed the road toward the shop. There it was. The old bookshop sat wedged between a tailor's and a chemist's. It looked forgotten—the kind of place you passed a hundred times without noticing. The front window was dusty, its display uneven. A tired copy of *Decline and Fall* leaned against *A Room of One's Own*. The floor of the window was cluttered with yellowed paperbacks and an orphaned plant in a cracked pot—a single bud rising from dry soil. A brass book hung precariously above the door. The lettering on the glass had long since peeled away, leaving only a faint trace of a name.

A quick check of the street behind him. No tails. No watchers. Just traffic and silence. Still, the hair at the back of his neck bristled, as though someone had just stepped out of sight.

Maxwell paused outside, steadied himself, then pushed it open. The aging bell above the door gave a reluctant, wobbly *tuktuk* as he stepped inside.

Dust and cobwebs hung in the air like ghost stories. Behind the counter, a thin man with a neatly trimmed beard and spectacles halfway down his nose glanced up from a leatherbound volume. The uneven floor groaned with every step. The scent of old paper, glue, and something faintly medicinal filled the air. A thin beam of pale light slanted through the grimy window, catching drifting motes of dust that swirled like tiny planets.

Maxwell studied him. He hadn't seen the man before, but the quiet, measured way he carried himself marked him as a "Joe"—semi-retired, perhaps, but one of the Service's own.

Maxwell cleared his throat. "Morning. I'm looking for something a bit... off the beaten path."

The man, dressed in well-tailored tweeds that had seen better days, slowly closed his book, rose, and approached with a quizzical glint. The probe unnerved Maxwell—did he misread the code? The old man noticed—amused. He grinned. "You've come to the right place, then. Beaten paths are for people who know where they're going."

Maxwell felt queasy—there was something intimidating about this old man, not physical but an inner strength. "Right now, I'm not so sure I do," he said cautiously. "Any recommendations for a man at a crossroads?"

The bookseller steepled his fingers, touching them to his lips while tilting his head. "Crossroads, hmm?" He thought for a moment, then reached for a worn paperback. "This one. *The Broken Compass*. Not well-known, but... curious timing, you asking."

Maxwell, still off-balance, took the book and flipped it over. "What's it about?"

"A man who thinks he's out—but finds the road keeps circling back. He starts reading his enemies to find himself. Or maybe to lose himself better. Hard to say."

Maxwell avoided the old man's eyes. *He knows.* He pushed a half-smirk. "Sounds cheerful."

The old man leaned back. "Depends who's reading it." "How much?" Maxwell asked.

The old man straightened, taller than Maxwell first thought.

"That one? On the house. It's not really the kind of book you buy. More like… the kind that waits for the right hands."

Maxwell got the message and swallowed hard. He is a "Joe"— of course he is. He raised his eyebrow and flicked through the book. Searching for an exit line, he muttered,

"Right, well, cheers."

The old man was already back in his chair, opening his book—but watched Maxwell through the corner of his glasses. He raised a bony, arthritic finger and gestured. "The last owner scribbled some editorial notes on page 250."

The reluctant jangle of the doorbell was a dismissal.

Maxwell stepped out into the street, the book tucked safely in his pocket—his hand resting over it like a bodyguard shielding a client. He walked briskly, head low, weaving between pedestrians without really seeing them. A pushchair squeaked over uneven paving, and someone laughed loudly behind him. He slowed his pace, not wanting to draw attention. He needed a quiet corner. A shielded spot. Somewhere to breathe— somewhere to look.

Then he spotted it.

Chapter 42

The Message

The red phone box stood hunched against the side of a post office, its glass smeared with age and traffic grime. It backed onto a stone wall—tight against . Three sides exposed to the street. Not ideal. But cover enough. He crossed quickly and slipped inside—the door creaking on worn hinges. The stifling smell of damp paper and cigarette ash that permeated the space, the floor covered with discarded paper cups. He groaned as he bent to pick them up—a message screamed from the advert – The Sailor's Comfort Good les.

Good Meals

Good Times.

Dockside Road East End.

One last cautious sweep—the street was clear—His gaze flickered from the book to the street; a man rode by on a bicycle—a knot tightening in Maxwell's stomach— the cyclist rounded the corner. *What now? Dump the book—rip the page.* He curled his fingers around the spine of the book, his thumb brushing the worn edges. The thought of ripping a page, destroying the evidence, kept flashing through his mind, and then vanished, leaving him with the same frustrating indecision.

None seemed right—he rejected the idea. The book was rammed deep into his pocket—its weight seemed heavier now. A sense of fleeting relief washed over him as the weight of it pressed securely against his ribs. The marker—the thin strip of card stained with age, lingered in his fingers. He let it drop. It floated down, landing among the cigarette butts and flattened cups. Unnoticed, it settled among the refuse of forgotten dreams clinging to the floor of the phone box. A final sweep. He paused, his eyes moving deliberately across the empty street, before stepping out of the box. His stride deliberate. No rush. No hesitation. Unhurried, his hands tucked into his coat pockets. Just a man, indistinguishable from any other, melting into the shadows of the deserted street.

Maxwell didn't head straight for the Tube. He walked—not aimlessly, but without leaving a pattern behind him—ordinary behaviors. He cut through side streets, crossed and re-crossed the same junction twice, paused at shop windows to check the reflections. The book in his pocket tapped lightly against his coat— a constant reminder he wished he could ignore.

He ducked into a small café near Goodge Street and ordered a tea he didn't want. Sat with his back to the wall, eyes on the door. People drifted in and out—a man in overalls, a young mother soothing her baby, two students whose bright chatter grated more than it should. No one lingered. No one looked twice at him. Still, the paranoia stayed.

By the time he left, the light had shifted; afternoon shadows stretched long across the pavement. He checked his watch— nearly four. Too long to stay put. Too early to go home. He set off again, heading toward Tottenham Court Road, his pulse steady but high.   Maxwell's shoulders, which had been tension-bound, finally relaxed—for now, breathed a long, slow breath as he set a calm pace towards the Tube station at Tottenham Court Road. Sweating nervously, he blended in with commuters, eyeing each one suspiciously. With furtive eyes he lingered at a news rack before a wary move toward the Victoria line to Walthamstow.

The Victoria tube was crowded with the evening exodus. A quick glance at his watch—5:10. The whiff and crush of bodies was claustrophobic. The book felt flattened—the spine ramming his ribs. The transfer to the bus to Highams Park brought no relief. An oversized woman with a large bag of vegetables squeezed her way into the seat—too late to move. Maxwell fought the urge to retch, the foul stench of Brussels sprouts and body odor making his eyes water. A man behind exhaled a stream of blue that curled toward the ceiling..

The bus hissed to a stop outside Highams Park Station. Maxwell stayed frozen in his seat, eyes locked on the dim street beyond the doors. Beside him, the overweight woman shifted uneasily, the heavy scent of body odor mixed with the sharp tang of Brussels sprouts washing over him. She was pinned in tight, no space to slip past. He cleared his throat softly. She glanced over, eyes shrinking.

"You're gettin' off, then?" Maxwell nodded, keeping his voice low. "Yeah." With a grunt, she heaved herself up, the sour scent intensifying as she stood flush against him.

Maxwell tensed, careful not to touch her as he squeezed past, the book pressing warm and heavy against his side.

He paused. And then—it struck. A shiver—sharp and electric, rippled down his legs. His body tensed without control.
Shoulders tight, breath shallow. A primal alert. Fight or flight. Something had shifted— not in the air, but in him— a movement, a flicker— something his conscious mind hadn't yet grasped. He turned, slowly, eyes scanning the street. Empty. Just the distant whistle of a kettle boiling somewhere. Still—his hand slipped instinctively to the inside of his coat, brushing the edge of the book. *A foolish talisman.* He stayed motionless. Listening. His own heartbeat too loud. He waited— regained his composure—his jaw muscles relaxed. One more cautious lap of the block— all clear. He stepped backward until his spine

pressed against his own door. The key turned fast, the door swung open, and he was inside. But he didn't relax until the door closed behind him and the bolt clicked. Only then did he exhale.

Inside, he breathed a sigh of relief.

The warmth and security of the house—home. Safe. A kettle jangled franticly on the hob. The muffled throb of the Telly in the next room—weird but comforting. Ashling was still home, about to leave for night duty at the hospital. It was Tuesday – Friday, The Sailor's Comfort—three days. The kettle whistled. As he reached for the well-worn wooden handle a barb prodded his ribs—the book.

A swift reaction and there it lay on the table— The

Broken Compass

Footsteps—panic—the book was shoved into a draw. Ashling moved to the bathroom. He exhaled— *What will I tell her? A mate's book—yes.* He retrieved the book, throwing it casually on the table. Maxwell sat at the kitchen table; the book opened again in front of him. It didn't look like much now. Just a dull old novel about a man in crisis—an ex-cop haunted by the past. He flipped through a few Chapters. There were moments that felt… familiar.

Parallels. Shadows of things he'd lived or buried

Coincidence? He closed the cover slowly. Maybe the address was the only message. But maybe it wasn't.

CHAPTER 43

Nightmares

A piping hot mug of tea sat waiting for Aisling.

She entered like an early spring morning. He gulped—regret for years that now were nowhere to be found. The crisp blue fabric of her scrubs, still warm from the dryer, hung easily over her slim body, the untied drawstring dangling. "Good evening," she chirped like someone who had slept peacefully.

"You sound cheerful," he forced himself to say.

"Last day on nights for a while—how did the office go— the wrapping up?"

"Good for now," he muttered, reaching for his mug. Aisling glanced in the mirror that hung beside the sink, a faint line of worry creasing her forehead. "Your tea will be cold," he added, a feeble effort to change the subject. He watched her as she continued her routine. She meticulously braided her long hair, securing it with a simple elastic band, and fastened the drawstring with a practiced hand, accentuating her well-molded figure. "What's the book?" she asked as she sat down. "Strange title— someone lost?"

His fist tightened. "I don't know—a mate at the station loaned it— said it was a good read—something about a retired cop with regrets."

"Don't we all," she muttered, a small sigh escaping her lips. He caught the look. *I should have dumped the fecking book.* She finished her tea in silence.

Her sensible white shoes, already scuffed despite their newness, made a soft shuffle as she slipped them on. A small, faded charm bracelet peeked out from beneath her sleeve. A flicker of a confident smile touched her lips as she slung her bag over her shoulder and grabbed her coat from the hook. She smiled, ready to face the night ahead, knowing the dreaded night duty was coming to a temporary end. "Have a good one," she mouthed inaudibly. The door clicked shut, leaving only silence in her wake.

For the next nerve-wracking three days, Maxwell paced in irrational, obsessive mistrust. Every knock at the door stopped him cold—glances on the street raised suspicion and overanalyzing. Aisling's shift to day duty gave her more daylight, but less of Maxwell. Her questions, even casual, were answered with jittery, defensive replies. Her absence left him alone with thought. On infrequent walks, he moved with the calm of a man rehearsing lies—feet steady, stomach in knots.

The book lay where Aisling left it, haunting—beckoning. Whiskey had lost its appeal; cigarettes were king. One morning Aisling breezed out, leaving a fresh citrusy fragrance in her wake. Maxwell nursed his coffee; his hand moved involuntarily to the book. Fidgety fingers flicked the pages. Page 250 stared back— the missing marker, gone. He hurried on, read a few pages.

"He thought he was the hunter," Maxwell muttered once, staring at a passage, "but he'd been walking in circles, dragging his past behind him like a dead weight." The ironic words hit home.
He closed the book, struggling to delete the toxic message.
Aisling was on day duty now, gone by dawn and home by dusk, always too tired to notice how much he'd unraveled. He said

little. Watched too much. Every knock at the door, every slowmoving car outside the window turned his head. Nothing happened. But it could. He walked once, just to burn off the shake in his hands. A man in a brown coat passed him twice outside the chemist. Coincidence? Maxwell followed at a distance, but the man vanished at a corner, like smoke.

At home, the pages blurred together. *The Broken Compass* moved from room to room, open to a chapter on loyalty and the wreckage it leaves behind. He read the same paragraph three times.

Nothing stuck. *Is there a missed message?*

He couldn't reach anyone—who could be trusted? Not old friends. Not former contacts. Even the silence felt predetermined. Once, he found a letter from years ago. Read it. Burned it. Watched the ash curl in the sink and wondered what else he should have destroyed.

Aisling was awakened again, incoherent mutterings of Maxwell's recurring nightmares filling the quiet room. He thrashed beside her, soaked with sweat, wrestling with unwelcome demons. He always rejected her worries and pleas for explanation, building a wall she had long ago learned not to breach, but she noted the shift in his demeanor.

The burden of boredom and stress wore heavy. The third cup and fifth cigarette stumped his appetite. Cold water cleared his eyes. The eyes in the mirror stared back—gaunt—empty. The habitual routine of the shoe-shine— the glitter of the toe cap and familiar smell of the polish—all in a mind fog. *The Sailor's Comfort* emerged.

Should I bring a piece? He placed the polished Oxfords in the corner and went to his room.

He returned within minutes and placed the towel on the table. The Walther PPK sat lightly in his palm—cold, compact, almost elegant. It rested there—weightless—dependable. He wiped the slide clean with a lint-free cloth, the faint hint of solvent dallying in his nose. The bore gleamed silver-blue under the kitchen light. He dabbed a trace of oil on the rails—not too much— racked the slide—cocking one up the spout. Safety on.

For now.

In the blink of an eye the momentous day was at hand. Friday. Maxwell's nerves were stretched to the limit—raw. The waiting unyielding. *The Sailor's Comfort* loomed. He slept little.

Thought too much.

In the kitchen, Maxwell moved disconnected—longing for an impossible escape. His exhaustion went beyond tiredness—it was a profound weariness that dulled every thought—a shroudlike blanket that overwhelmed his spirit and blunted his thinking. His vacant eyes stared nowhere in particular. The hand that held the cup shook involuntarily. The smoldering cigarette between two nicotine-stained fingers.

Aisling's early departure was a relief—the growing mountain of delusional lies had distorted his mind. Maxwell took a deep, shivering breath. He needed comfort—a whiskey. No. Another strong cup of tea. Must keep vigilant.

Slumped at the kitchen table he reached for the book. His eyes felt jagged around the edges. He read a few fuzzy pages— eyes heavy. His head nodded. The book dropped—crashed to the linoleum floor with a clatter. An abrupt jolt of his head— chaos— not knowing where he was or what happened. The weighted eyelids, the blurred vision, the difficulty concentrating— insides pleading for rest.

The tea failed to push back the exhaustion threatening to swallow him whole. Maxwell forced himself to his feet— dragged himself upstairs and grabbed a quick shower—cold.

Stepping into the icy gush, he gasped for breath—muscles tightening involuntarily as a wave of shock flooded his system. For a moment the first instinct—to escape—crushed any other thought. The initial shock felt painful as the cold water seemed to pierce through his resistance. He gasped for deeper, controlled breaths, slowly acclimatizing to the cold. The initial panic subsided—replaced by a newfound logic—the coldness acting as a sharp jolt to his distrusting, paranoiac mind, forcing him into present awareness. Tense muscles relaxed, the anxiety that had engulfed him ebbing away. A strange calm settled. By embracing the discomfort, he found a quiet strength emerging—a feeling of having faced a challenge and come out stronger. *I can handle this.*

CHAPTER 44

The Sailor's Comfort

The Sailor's Comfort crouched by the docks like it was waiting to be condemned. Maxwell stepped in, letting the door swing shut behind him. He didn't belong here and didn't pretend otherwise. Inside, the air was thick with hairspray and cheap perfume, fighting through the stench of stale beer and the sweet, skunky trace of pot.

He was careful but acted cavalier as he scanned the bar. Not his first rodeo; he had numerous operations under his belt. Some were humdrum, but many were bizarre and reprehensible. He had become impervious to the moralities involved. He had signed up for this and was adept at his trade. All thoughts of Derry or his loyalties were long faded. Sure, there was dirty work, but he relished it. Guilt or innocence was irrelevant. Orders received; orders carried out.

Maxwell arrived early out of habit. The bar was on neutral ground, as ever. *These guys plan every detail.* The Friday night bar was crowded and loud, with too many faces to matter. He ordered a pint of bitter, picked up a discarded newspaper, pretending to read, and waited. The worn linoleum squelched faintly underfoot—his shoes sticking to something—he hoped, chewing gum. Mirrors lined the walls, greasy with fingerprints and age. The bar glittered in places where the light caught false nails and sequins.

The jukebox vibrated to life, thumping out Nancy Sinatra's

"These Boots Are Made for Walkin'"—her voice raucous and insolent, cutting through the low murmur of forced laughter and slurred flirtation. The women were already swaying to the music—heads held high and shoulders back. Seventeen-year-olds dressed like twenty-five-year-old *Charlie's Angels*, and fortysomethings who hadn't let go of their inner Brigitte Bardot— hot pants, halter tops, fishnets, and kinky boots with too much heel and not enough comfort.

A "Charlie's Angel" left with her "uncle." Maxwell sniffed as he slid into the empty booth, the floral fragrance of lily of the valley and sandalwood still lingering—cracked red vinyl, sticky table, just enough shadow to watch without being watched. The landlord clocked him with a glance—a new face. Maxwell marked him—a barrel-chested man in a sleeveless wool vest, arms like knotted rope, unmoved by newcomers. A cricket bat leaned casually beside the till.

One of the "Bardots" broke from the bar. Bleach blonde, tired eyes, gold tank top stretched tight across her chest—a tear in the fishnet just above her right knee. She gave Maxwell a onceover, decided he might be interesting. She stopped at his table, leaning in just enough to suggest experience. "You waiting for someone, luv?"

His eyes swung to the brawn behind the bar—he squashed his cigarette and for the first time glared hard-eyed at the woman. She met his glare with an indignant curl of her lips— with a shrug of a naked shoulder she swaggered off with a slight smirk—back to the blur of mirrors and laughter that didn't sound real.

Five minutes passed and he wondered if it was a no-show. A man, too old for the regular patrons, entered the swinging doors. He squinted around the bar until he caught the barman's eye and signaled a double scotch. There was something about him that held Maxwell's attention. He was rough around the edges, his face blotched, showing signs of too much whiskey. The face was older, the general appearance on the downturn, but something in Maxwell's recall stirred.

The man approached the table and sat down uninvited. Casual, but too casual. Maxwell stiffened. The man took a stiff drink, wiped his greasy coat sleeve across his mouth and slyly said, "Well, well. If it isn't young Maxwell. You've filled out nice—I remember you. Marriage agrees with you." With a wily tilt of his eyes toward the bar, "Getting a slice on the side then.   Are we?"

"Pot's strong tonight," he muttered, voice flat. "Not our problem."

He took a slow sip of his whiskey, eyes already scrutinizing Maxwell like he was a file waiting to be opened. Maxwell was completely caught off guard. *Who is this, and why is he here?* There was something about the way he moved—a twitch of the shoulder, a twist of the mouth—and recognition slithered back into Maxwell's mind. Scott. Malcolm Scott.

The name evoked something devious and cunning. A drunk even then, but he had been around a few corners. It was all trickling back. There were rumors about stepping over the line. Was it money or a discipline issue? A cover-up, and then he disappeared. *So how, why is he here? A handler? Surely not.*

Scott took another swallow and licked his lips as though he was savoring every drop. "Is this one of your drinking holes?" he asked, voice flat but carrying a tone Maxwell recognized. That quiet, echoing note of a good-cop calculation. The kind of voice you heard in interrogation rooms, just before the mask came off and the real work began.

Maxwell's demeanor, usually boastful and arrogant, tightened at the corners, with a faint sheen of sweat appearing on his forehead, knowing he was putty in this bloke's hands. He swallowed, his gaze darting toward the door. Then back to Scott, whose hand clamped hard and unyielding—like a manacle around Maxwell's wrist.

"No, I was just passing," Maxwell said, his voice a little too loud, a little too forced, "And now I have another appointment." He shifted, a nervous tremor running through him, but the vice tightened—a silent warning.

"No rush, lad." Scott's voice rumbled, a low hum of power. "We have things to talk about."

"There's a thing coming down the pipe. And someone, somewhere, thinks you're the man for it." It was Scott talking in a low monotone.

Maxwell's mind was scrambled. "What are you talking about? Who said what? What pipe?" Maxwell blurted. His voice had become too shrill.

Scott lowered his head and growled, "Cut the shit, Max, we both know the game."

Maxwell could feel it now. That old familiar itch. The one that says this wasn't a coincidence. Still trying to get the higher ground, he pushed, "Who sent you and whose orders?"

Scott looked him squarely in the eyes and smirked, "You know how it works—no names, no need to know. I'm here with your briefing." It was confirmed. This is the handler—an unsavory one, but this was the world he had bought into.

Scott continued, "As I said, there's been chatter. A new cell—maybe a splinter group who couldn't take orders. We're not sure, but we know they're for real. They're led by a man— only name we have is 'Hawk.'"

Something stirred in Maxwell's memory bank—a shiver in his shoulders screamed alert. "Hawk? Heard the name. Didn't think he was still active."

Scott smirked, his lip twisting. "Active enough. These cowboys are as devious as us. They spread all sorts of rumors about their operations—men being shot or missing. We've got reports they're planning something big. Something to shake the foundations—bombs, ambushes—the usual bloody mess. But this time it's personal. They have specific targets."

Maxwell's heart skipped a beat. He struggled for a breath. "So, what's the play? When do I get my briefing?"

Scott downed the whiskey and scowled, "God damn it, man, are you listening? This is the fucking briefing. That's why I'm here. They want you involved."

Maxwell's jaw tightened; something didn't sound right. Every instinct screamed, *Don't trust this*. He had heard whispers about this type of setup—either to test loyalty or to remove a no longer needed agent. *Remember that yarn about the bloke in Northern Ireland who was told to prepare for an undercover job in Dublin? He died three days later—head cracked open on a gym floor. Official line was a slip. No one believed it.*

Maxwell shifted, the red vinyl sticking to his trouser leg. "Do you think it's a setup?"

Scott signaled a buxom barmaid—another round—before turning to Maxwell. "Does it matter? Would you believe me? You won't be riding solo on this one. A special squad's been assigned—handpicked, tight, and by people who don't like surprises. You'll meet them tomorrow at the Harrow. It's further down the docks. Nine sharp. No mistakes." The orders landed in a single breath, steamrolling any protest.

With undaunted pretense, Maxwell mustered enough courage. "Wait. I always pick my own squad," he stressed emphatically.

His words fell on deaf ears.

"Not this time, mate. If it's real—you're in deep. If it's a sting—you'll spot it soon enough. Just don't tug too hard, okay?" Scott stood, adjusted his coat and with a cynical smile, "This is a real shit-stick business we're in, but slithery bastards like us survive." He swigged the whiskey in one gulp and slithered back to whatever sewer he came from.

Maxwell felt a cold knot tighten somewhere in his gut—a shiver in his hand as he reached for his drink. His gaze darted around the crowded bar, every face a suspect. Every instinct screamed to run. Cracks in the seat held him like a trap. His instincts warned him to flee, but old loyalties, old fears of isolation gnawed at him. The amber glow of the beer seemed to mock him, the taste of stale tobacco suddenly pungent in his throat. The boisterous laughter from a nearby table grated on his nerves.

He wanted to go home to Aisling—but first, a stiff drink. He clenched and unclenched his fist, his gaze unfocused on the untouched pint. He considered a double shot, a quick escape into numb oblivion. But no—he needed a clear head, a chance to dissect Scott's succinct words. A slow pint would grant him the illusion of control while his mind raced through the ramifications.

The fact that he was not briefed on the details of the mission was disconcerting but not unusual until a final date had been established. The words "special squad" echoed in his skull, each reverberation bringing a fresh wave of unease. He saw himself trapped, surrounded by unseen faces, pawns in a game he didn't understand. Who is the pawn? A setup? It has to be. London wouldn't just... not like this. Unless... unless they wanted him cornered—exposed—neutralized.

Either way, it spelled trouble.

"Not this time, mate." The words hung there like a noose. Orders like that came from high up—or not at all. Who were these men, who were they loyal to? The people who picked them? Scott? London? Or their own agendas? He wasn't worried about amateurs. He was worried about professionals with instructions of their own.

Where did he fit into the plan? He had no answers.

All he could do was be alert.

He finished his pint and headed home.

CHAPTER 45

Shadows at Home

By the time he reached the house, his mood had darkened. He was in a foul state, his face drawn tight, eyes shadowed with something between rage and fear. The door closed with a dull thud behind him.

Aisling greeted him in her usual cheery way. "You're back," she said with a smile, pretending not to notice the two nights of nightmares. She told herself it was the job—the odd hours that came with his new promotion.

He gave a grunt in reply, barely sparing her a glance as he yanked off his coat and slung it on the peg.

"I kept your supper warm," she offered, forcing lightness into her voice. "Wasn't sure when you'd be in."

"I'm not hungry," he mumbled. The words landed between them like a barrier. She felt them settle in her chest, heavier than they ought to have been.

Aisling watched him, noting again how the sharp edge in his eyes hadn't dulled in months. It had started after the promotion— three years ago now—when he'd come home one night with a stiff smile and the news. She'd been proud, of course. Told him it was about time they saw what he was worth. But he hadn't wanted to talk about it then. Not that night, nor any night since. And slowly, the man she married had begun to slip away.

"I'm going to bed—rough day," he said.

"Alright," she said quietly.

Maxwell didn't delay. He moved past her, his footsteps heavy on the stairs. Aisling stood in the hallway, listening as the bedroom door closed. She let out a sigh of resignation. The house was silent again. She turned back to the kitchen, setting the untouched supper aside. Whatever darkness the job had wrapped around him, it was getting harder to pretend it hadn't made its way into their home. Into her heart. But for now, at least, he was home.

Maxwell sat on the side of the bed, unlacing his shoes. The words kept pounding in his head: *"You won't be riding solo on this one."*

CHAPTER 46
The Harrow

Maxwell spotted the pub half a block before he reached it—a squat brick building hunched at the bend where the dock wall curled in on itself. Its windows were smeared with grime, its painted sign so weathered only *H A R O* remained legible.

A place forgotten by time, and safest for that very reason. He paused just outside, taking in the lay of the street. The roofline opposite drooped and sagged. A second-floor window blinked behind threadbare curtains. Greedy pigeons shuffled along the ledge, grabbing scraps of gutted fish. Uncaring. The air reeked— salt, diesel, rotting fish, and seaweed—thick enough to taste.

A quick sweep—no obvious tails. No parked cars idling too long. Still, the hairs on his neck stayed bristled. He knew it wasn't the rotting fish.

Maxwell stepped inside.

The light changed immediately—low and jaded, oozing through stained-glass panels that hadn't been cleaned since Adam was a boy. The bar curved like a spine—dark wood along the left wall. Beneath a mounted marlin, an old man stared too long at the cribbage board; his opponent grimaced impatiently. A framed photo of the Queen, gathering dust, hung haphazardly behind the bar.

A casual eye sweep checked the exits. Two—front door and a rear hallway near the toilets. A third, maybe, through the kitchen hatch behind the bar. The two booths were dark— empty.

Maxwell chose the far booth. Back against the wall, facing the door—always. They'd know where to find him. His coat was folded neatly next to him—the bulge in the pocket within reach.

He ordered a pint, hoping the glass was clean. The tired, overweight woman behind the bar wheezed as she waddled over with the pint. He checked his watch. 08:51.

Too early. But better that way. The beer was flat—it wasn't important.

08:59.

The door opened with a groan. Rain gusted in. A woman walked in. Her smooth skin contrasted sharply with the weathered faces around her, a stark difference in age that was almost jarring— too young for the regulars, but no one heeded her. A vigilant antenna was alerted; Maxwell zeroed in on the redhead— his hand unconsciously tightened on the Walther in his pocket.

Her hair, damp at the edges, was pulled back in a tight twist. She wore a dark coat; boots made for walking and watching. She didn't hesitate—just swept the pub with one sharp look, then beelined for the booth. No smile. No words.

She slid in opposite him, nodded once, and sat still. Not nervous—just coiled. Like a spring waiting for its moment.

"Hartley."
Maxwell nodded back. "Maxwell." "I know." Curt
and clipped.

Maxwell fidgeted slightly. *Tough bitch—be careful.* Her gaze pinned him, unwavering, daring him to challenge her.

09:02.

The next to arrive was an easy read—jet-black hair, back erect—trench coat buttoned, belt tight, briefcase in hand. He didn't bother with the bar. He spotted them and strode with a confident, measured pace, his shoulders back and his head held high, personifying a distinct military bearing. He gave a curt nod to Hartley before looking directly at Maxwell—eyes piercing. "Murch."

Maxwell sensed introductions were superfluous. *Dyed hair— Oxford—prick.* He smirked. Ironic.

09:05.

Maxwell recognized the next type immediately—flawless hair, trim suit, soft shoes, the faintest trace of aftershave not meant for this part of town. He smiled too easily. *Lightweight? Maybe.* A quick second look—message boy? Reporter?

"Nice place. Has a real... rustic charm," the newcomer quipped, sliding in beside Hartley without waiting for an invitation—lemonade in hand. "I'm Russell, sorry I'm late."

He was met with silence. Maxwell watched him but said nothing. *Casual. Too off the cuff.*

09:07.

The door strained again. Maxwell gauged him. Thickset. Balding. Worn coat, scuffed boots. Smelled faintly of something— maybe a hangover. He barked a drink order to the bar, then plodded over with a gin and a half-grin.

"Bloody lovely meeting place. A cut in the budget, is there?" he muttered, easing himself into the last seat with a breathless wheeze, casting a jaded eye over the group. He was late but seemed unworried by it—as though he had witnessed all there was to see and felt all there was to feel. He swallowed half his gin in one gulp.

"Cowan, if anyone gives a shit."

Maxwell studied him hesitantly. A shiver went through his shoulders—it came to him in a lightning bolt. *Scott. Cut from the same cloth.*

Now they were all here. Five strangers. One squad. Maxwell didn't like it. Not the timing. Not the faces. And especially not that he wasn't in charge. He glanced at the briefcase, then at Murch.

"Let's have it," Maxwell ordered.

Murch glanced dismissively at him, then at the others. He didn't reach for the briefcase immediately. Instead, he looked around the room. Still, he kept his voice low. "We don't fan things open in places like this."

He unlatched the briefcase carefully and withdrew a plain brown envelope—thick, creased at the edges. He placed it gently on the table, his voice remaining low—toneless, cutting through the silence. "Inside are four map fragments. Keep them close. Memorize the details. Burn them if you need to."

Hartley raised an eyebrow. "Fragments?"

Murch nodded stonily. "Same area. Two scenarios. We've got a rumor suggesting two possible targets—no confirmation on which, or if either is real. Could be deliberate misdirection. Each of you gets one copy. Same content. Don't swap. Don't mark them. Study them tonight. You'll find two red circles."

Cowan reached for the envelope. Murch stopped him with a firm hand. "Distribute them properly."

Maxwell took the envelope and opened it just enough to peek inside—four neatly folded maps, no markings beyond the red circles. He slipped one out and passed it silently to Hartley. Then one each to Cowan and Russell. He kept the last for himself. Murch watched the handoff like a tigress protecting her young.

"Two targets. Same general zone. One's a rail warehouse. The other's a riverside compound. Both have seen recent foot traffic; both were flagged in chatter. No guarantee either's the real play."

Russell gave a low whistle. "What are we expecting—a bang, a body, or a ghost?"

Maxwell's jaw tightened. He pounded the table impatiently. "We cover every angle."

Murch ignored Russell. He looked at Maxwell—held the stare. "You're used to giving orders, Max. Not this time." The words weren't spoken—but they were written in the cold weight of his eyes. No anger. Just a quiet, surgical reminder.
Maxwell didn't blink. But he felt the shift again—that tilt in the balance. He wasn't driving this car. He was in the backseat, with no idea who had the wheel.

Murch turned to the rest—a momentary flash of narrowed eyes, or a sharp, unblinking stare. He took a deep breath and exhaled slowly. His finger tapped once on the table before sliding the envelope into his briefcase. "This place is too exposed." His flat baritone voice was tight, a scratchy octave higher than usual.

"Tomorrow. 9:30 AM sharp. Greenhouse Café, Battersea Park. Rear conservatory. Don't wander. Don't improvise."
He slowly slid out of the booth. Coat adjusted. Briefcase clicked shut. He exited with exaggerated strides. The others sat in

silence before fading into the night. Maxwell held his face in his hands—exhaling unconsciously. *"Just don't tug too hard, okay?"* Scott's voice echoed in his head.

CHAPTER 47
Greenhouse Café

The café sat at the edge of the park, glass-paneled and sundrenched. Birds chirped in the trees outside, joggers passed along the gravel path, and the place smelled faintly of espresso and toffee.

Inside the rear conservatory, Maxwell was already seated. The strong, steaming coffee, with its tart bite, jolted him awake, clearing the lingering haze of sleep. It had been another sleepless night, but now he needed a clear head.

The low buzz of background babble and the clinking of ceramic cups and saucers was disrupted by the soft jingle of a bell as she pushed open the heavy wooden door.

Hartley entered. Her red hair was loose today; her jacket zipped halfway over a white silk blouse. She gave him a nod— more acknowledgment than greeting—and sat across from him. The light scratch of a ballpoint pen as she made a guarded note in a small notebook worried Maxwell.

Russell arrived next, holding two caffè lattes like some eager intern. He passed one to Hartley with a half-smile, then took the seat at the head of the table.

Maxwell studied him with new, suspicious interest. The hair— moderately short, neatly parted, subtly brushed back— and a well-maintained appearance that hinted at Ivy League polish.

Preppy. Military or law-enforcement background, for sure.

Maxwell's jaw tightened. He chewed the inside of his cheek. It hadn't gone unnoticed where Russell sat.

Cowan puffed his way to the table, coffee in both hands. "Bloody maze of a park," he grumbled, sinking into the seat closest to the wall. Hands shaking slightly, he lit a cigarette.

The apparent misfits gathered at a long wooden table tucked behind ferns and potted fig trees. Casual at a glance— four people sipping coffee, chatting lightly. Except nobody was chatting.

Murch entered last. Hair freshly brill-creamed, he strutted into the room with a confident, deliberate gait—no apologies, no explanations for his lateness. He moved toward the head of the table, ignoring everyone, but stopped short when he saw the seat already taken. He cleared his throat, shuffled a few unnecessary papers, and chose a chair with his back to the wall.

"This location is secure," Murch said, his voice crisp. "Far better than that dockside tavern dump. No prying eyes here."

His rudeness hung in the air. A hush fell over the group; the only sound was the soft whirr of the coffee machine. Maxwell sat opposite him, arms folded, resisting the urge to light a cigarette. Murch's presence grated—too polished, too controlling.

Russell, already scribbling in a notepad, glanced up. "Let's get to it," he said, his voice low but firm. "Targets are narrowed to two. Both in the river district. One's a transport warehouse— rail link. The other, a riverside compound.

Possibly a VIP visit pending."
Murch leaned back in his chair, arms crossed, exuding an air of superiority and disinterest. Maxwell raised an analytical eyebrow. Russell hadn't waited for Murch's nod. Murch stiffened but said nothing—just unlocked the briefcase and pulled out four small maps, sliding them across the table.

"You've each got one," Murch said. "Study it. Memorize it. Burn it after."

Hartley leaned forward, already scanning the map. Her pen tapped against the table rhythmically. "Intel confirms movement in both locations?" she asked.

Russell, quick as a clay launcher, answered first. "Yes. Intel flagged both. No confirmation on Hawk's position. But—" He slid a grainy black-and-white photo onto the table. "We believe this was him. Taken two nights ago—riverfront."

The figure in the photo was hooded, mid-stride, face obscured. Just a shadow.

Murch, like a counter-puncher, stepped in quickly. "No confirmation. The image is inconclusive. We're treating it as unverified. No assumptions."

Maxwell, with an inward smile, looked impartially between them. *Power shift—subtle but clear.* Russell was pushing the briefing; Murch, the counter-puncher, was reasserting control but falling behind on points.

Russell turned to Maxwell, his gaze penetrating, pinning him in place. "You'll assign the tail. Hawk needs eyes on him— discreetly. Who do you trust?"

A pause. All eyes on Maxwell. He hesitated—the old roles were gone. This wasn't his squad anymore. Was it a test or a sign of trust?

"Hartley," he said at last, assertively. "She's quick. Quiet. No mistakes."

Hartley gave a curt nod of acceptance. Murch said nothing— perhaps expecting some form of recognition. The group sat silently finishing their coffees, each with their own thoughts. Russell's smooth voice delivered the dismissing orders.

"Right. That's it for now—keep alert. Hartley will be in touch."

Chairs scraped roughly against the floor. Papers were scooped, cups gathered, movements efficient but wordless. Cowan was first to leave—muttering something about needing fresh air, though the nearest bar was likely his destination. Murch followed, polished shoes clicking in measured rhythm down the path. Russell lingered just long enough to pocket his notes before stepping out behind him.

Hartley folded her map neatly, tucking it into her coat. Maxwell remained seated for a moment longer. The air still held the weight of their silence—and something else, heavier: the sense that none of them fully trusted one another. He gave the room one last once-over, straightened his tie, and walked out. Maxwell was halfway through his coffee when Hartley appeared, sliding into the seat opposite without a word. No pleasantries— just a small manila envelope placed on the table between them.

Maxwell didn't touch the envelope right away. His eyes scanned the café—a small place near Highams Park, not far from his house. Familiar. Quiet. Not too quiet.

She spoke in a tone no louder than a whisper. "He was at the riverside compound. Brief stop. No sign of a meet. No security detail. In and out in under ten."

Maxwell kept his gaze on her. "And?"

She leaned in slightly. "The arms dump is active. Foot traffic last night—three figures, all masked. One carrying a case, military style."

Maxwell exhaled through his nose, finally reaching for the envelope, but she stopped him with a slight shake of her head. "Already briefed the others."

Maxwell raised an eyebrow. "You did what?"

Hartley didn't flinch. "Russell wanted it tight. I had eyes, I moved fast. We meet again at eleven to set final positions."

Maxwell sighed in reluctant acceptance. "I'll be there."

Hartley met his eyes, poker-faced. "Not your brief."

Maxwell felt the shift—subtle but definitive. The tempo had changed, and he wasn't invited to the dance. "You're taking the dump?" he asked, voice neutral.

She nodded. "Me, Murch, and Russell will cover the warehouse perimeter. We think they'll move arms out tomorrow—maybe a transfer."

Maxwell's fingers drummed on the tabletop in a pensive rhythm, his jaw tense. "And me?"

Her eyes held his. "The riverside compound. The less likely target. Cowan will cover you. But if Hawk shows up again, you'll be the only one in range."

Silence settled. Outside, a bus hissed to a stop. Maxwell stared past her, then back again, lips tightening. He shifted—the paranoia resurfaced.

Hartley stood, adjusting her coat. "You'll be solo. I'll send comms to your secure location."

Maxwell stiffened, mind rushing. This is an MI5 job—eyes only. No outside interference. No uniforms, no marked cars. Backup on standby—only in an emergency. And even then, help might come too late.

Maxwell had more questions, but she was gone before he could ask them. The envelope lay untouched. He stared at it, then at his reflection in the coffee's surface.

The unspoken truth followed him like a shadow: if things went sideways, he'd be on his own. And maybe—maybe that was the plan all along.

Alone. Again. Less likely, my arse.

CHAPTER48

TheAmbush

The target was audacious—even for Gallagher.

After weeks of surveillance, he'd chosen his mark: a government minister. Two more weeks went into planning the hit. He hand-picked five of his most trusted men—his elite. The small number didn't dissuade him; it hardened his resolve.

Gallagher had grown self-reliant to a fault—isolating himself, refusing help even when the task turned desperate. He felt no hatred toward the English people—only a relentless need to strike back for the wrongs done to his own. Somewhere along the line, he'd lost sight of the Movement's aims. What drove him now wasn't politics but obsession—a personal reckoning disguised as revolution.

His men never saw it that way. To them, he was the model of courage and command. They trusted how he moved—calm, deliberate, never asking from them what he wouldn't do himself. He didn't bark orders or wave flags. He was authority—always at the front when things got hairy, always watching their backs.

Gallagher carried the weight differently. Every operation etched strain into him: the tight focus in his eyes, the surge of adrenaline mixed with dread—excitement sharpened by fear. He hid it well, but it never left him. The risk wasn't just his; it was theirs. That knowledge and responsibility gnawed at him more than any enemy could.

He imposed his own code: no contact outside the job.

Separate flats. No shared routines. In and out—clean and silent. Before any move, he walked the terrain himself, noted exits, blind spots, the rhythm of the street. Every role was mapped, every maneuver timed to the second. For a long time it worked— flawless execution, clean retreats.

At times he felt pangs of guilt that he had not fully committed to the cause. Increasingly he realized he had no cause. He craved the adulation of his team and felt a duty to protect them. Each operation was an internal struggle between the thrill of danger and the anxiety of keeping them safe. Out of that duty he demanded strict adherence to security.

The morning of the attack, his team was in position. A pub frequented by off-duty soldiers had gone up in flames—a diversion. Two police officers had been shot in the pandemonium as they retreated. Whether anyone had died in the explosion, they didn't know.

Gallagher stood at his vantage point, eyes sweeping the quiet street, the weight of inevitability pressing against his chest. The minister's group would arrive any second. A strange stillness hung in the lane opposite. A curtain twitched— barely—too controlled. Too timed.

Gallagher's stomach sank. Something was wrong. His gut turned—a trap.

A crack of gunfire tore through the stillness—sharp, sudden. Gallagher didn't hesitate. Muscle memory kicked in and he hit the ground hard, rolling toward cover. This wasn't part of the plan.

He yelled, "Pull back, abort," but it was a second too late. The ambush was already being ambushed. Heavy gunfire erupted—deafening in the constricted street. Shattered glass rained down. Gallagher's men scattered, returning fire. Chaos. Screams. A car jerked to a halt; its driver slumped over the wheel.

One of his men was shot trying to escape through a back yard, leaving a crimson trail to the garden steps. Gallagher groaned, guilt ripping at him. He had led his team into an impossible fallback. They had trusted him—their leader, their protector. There was no easy escape.

Gallagher moved like a ghost through the smoke, trying to regain control. Why? A missed tail? How had it been compromised? The ambush had fallen apart in under a minute. Sirens howled in the distance. "Go!" he yelled, knowing they'd follow his orders.

Gunfire cracked down the constricted street as the team scattered, slipping toward the mews—a cobbled alley behind the old Georgian terraces, their escape route. Gallagher fired twice; the Browning 9mm bucked in his hand. A figure dropped. Another dove behind a parked car. He turned to see his men vanish into the mews. The wounded assailant lay moaning— blood mixed with saliva at his mouth. He looked too old to be here.

Gallagher stayed behind, crouched against a rain-slick wall, breathing heavily. This was his job now—buy them time. He counted rounds: thirteen, one magazine—enough. Options tumbled through his head. None seemed workable.

Finally—surrender. He'd claim he'd forced his two remaining comrades at gunpoint to let him into their flat. It was a calculation—survival and a chance to live to fight another day.

As he stepped from the building with arms raised, he shouted, "I'm here, I'm here." His hands rose, the Browning dangling from a finger. Then he saw him.

Across the chaos, framed by smoke and gunfire, a man moved with terrifying precision. No hesitation. Calculated. A face stirred in Gallagher's memory—the one he hadn't seen in years, not since they were boys on football fields and school benches. Maxwell.

A split-second recognition condensed a lifetime into a heartbeat. Maxwell's eyes flickered as he saw Gallagher—an instant of something unshakable: perhaps regret, perhaps relief.
No one would ever know.

Time slowed. A curtain of rain separated them. Two men, old ghosts in each other's eyes.
Maxwell raised his hand, signaling the others to hold fire— Gallagher saw—there were no others. "Gallagher," he said. No rancor, no insult. Just the name.

Gallagher's jaw tightened. "Didn't expect you here."
"Should've. You always were predictable."

The gun in Maxwell's hand didn't waver. Neither did Gallagher's.

Two shots rang out, almost as one.
Maxwell staggered back, eyes wide with surprise—a red stain spreading across his chest. For a moment he stood upright, staring

at Gallagher with something like sorrow in his gaze, then crumpled.

Gallagher grimaced as the bullet tore through his left arm—he didn't move. Couldn't. The pounding of boots on wet cobbles filled the air—sirens wailing. The rest of his men were gone—scattered into the London streets.

He stood over Maxwell, still clutching his weapon. "You shouldn't have been here," Gallagher whispered through a quivering lip.

Maxwell's lips moved—a word Gallagher didn't catch. Maybe regret. Maybe finality. Maybe nothing.

Then Maxwell was gone.

Gallagher moved slowly, heart sapped—yet his heart hammered in his chest. The thudding feet were louder now—*Escape*.

He knew what came next. No safehouse this time. No quiet debrief. Only the long road back through alleys and memories. The ghost of Maxwell would walk beside him every step.

No one called. No orders. Just silence. He was no longer needed, no longer trusted, no longer wanted.

The war had moved on. Gallagher would move on too. There was always another front. Another fight. Bogotá.

CHAPTER 49

The Funeral

Aisling's lunch was a hurried tomato sandwich and half a cup of tea. The washer's swish and the dryer's hum had become the morning's soundtrack, drowning out the soft music that once promised calm.

Aisling, her hair an unkempt mess, wrestled with the stubborn creases of Maxwell's blue shirt. Her shoulders ached, and a dull pain throbbed behind her eyes. The mountain of clothes grew taller every minute, mocking the idea of three days off.

The demanding knock startled her—too firm, too deliberate.

She opened the door, startled to find Inspector Callan, his face grave, his coat speckled by the morning drizzle. "Tom?" Her voice cracked. "Is it Max?" she blurted instinctively. Callan removed his hat and lowered his head. "May I come in?"

Aisling sat distraught, hands crushing the blue shirt. Her thoughts swirled—words reeling, refusing to settle. A strange numbness settled over her; a single, unwavering reflex propelled her hand forward. A soft, almost unnoticeable click broke the sound, plunging the room into an unsettling silence.

The kitchen felt too quiet, too normal. Callan stood stiffly, smoothing the rim of his hat, eyes fixed on the floor.

"There was… an incident," he began. "This afternoon. A raid. Max was involved. He didn't make it."

Aisling's hands shook. "I thought he wasn't even on duty. What was he doing at a raid?"

Callan hesitated, visibly struggling for an answer. Then he delivered the line, flat and rehearsed. "I'm sorry, Aisling. He wasn't acting in any official capacity. As far as the force is concerned…

Max was on leave. That's all I'm authorized to say."

Her breath caught. "That's all you're authorized to say Tom, what the hell does that mean?" Her voice rose with every word.

He looked at her, pain in his eyes. But he only repeated, softer, "I'm sorry."

Aisling sat, knuckles white, fingers gripping the table, her breath shallow and uneven as she stared blankly at nothing. She didn't remember Callan leaving. "All I'm authorized to say" kept echoing in her head.

The doorbell rang once—almost apologetically. Aisling exhaled, a deep, weary sigh, before dragging herself to answer. She swallowed hard—it was Fr. O'Kane. He stood ashen-faced. "I am so sorry for your loss, Ash." Her hand went unthinking to her hair. He stepped dutifully into the hallway.

"I'm still in shock," she whispered with a slow inhale.
"Come in—please."
They sat in deferential silence, a quiet, unspoken understanding passing between them. The priest fingered imaginary beads with twinges of guilt and remorse. "When is the funeral?" he muttered delicately. His words were a reality jolt to Aisling—a shiver went down her back.

The church was cold. A deep, profound cold, as if death itself lingered there.   Aisling sat in the front row—alone, stiff-backed, her hands clenched in her lap. O'Kane's voice rose from the altar—steady, measured, almost too calm. His words jumbled in her ears. She hadn't cried yet. She didn't know when she would.

O'Kane's well-meaning homily was a blur. Halfway through the Mass, she turned unconsciously to see the mourners. There was no fanfare—just a regular, quiet police funeral—a few colleagues in uniform looking solemn. With his broad shoulders, Callan stood vigilant in his dress uniform.

Something—someone—caught her eye. A woman at the back, standing alone. Her face was hidden beneath a black veil, but a shock of red hair escaped—vivid against the lace.

Aisling frowned. The woman wasn't local—not one of Maxwell's colleagues, not a neighbor. She stood still, head slightly bowed, never glancing up. The church emptied slowly, but the figure lingered—slim, composed, silent beneath the veil. Aisling watched her, heart tight. There was something intimate in the woman's stillness, the way she stood apart, not with the police, not with the neighbors. Aisling's stomach churned— heartache or distrust, she couldn't tell.

At the graveside, she was there again—the same veil, the same red hair, watching from under the yew tree. Not with the mourners, not with the police.

Aisling whispered to Callan, "Do you know her?"
He turned slowly, eyed the woman under the tree, then shook his head. "Never seen her before."

Aisling said nothing more. But a thought gnawed at her— was this who he spent his nights with? The phone calls? The lies?

A tortured impulse compelled Aisling. She turned to look again, heart pounding, but said nothing. The woman's gaze never faltered. For the first time, Aisling inhaled deeply and exhaled slowly, her throat tightened. Was this Maxwell's secret? All those late nights, the silences? She would never know. And no one would tell her.

Then, as quietly as she had appeared, the woman turned and walked away—swallowed by the mist. Aisling stared into the gap; the woman was gone. Was she real—or just another secret buried with Maxwell?

O'Kane saw her too—during the homily—and wondered.

The final graveside prayers were said. The mourners dispersed in low whispers, coats pulled tight against the biting wind. It was the kind of chill that settled deep in the bones—a cold unique to graveyards.

Aisling stood desolate by the grave, her vacant eyes fixed on the wreaths, her lips pressed tight. She felt O'Kane's presence beside her, but he said nothing. She glanced at him once—
O'Kane's shoulders bent; his gaze lost on the lonely horizon.

Inspector Callan's sharp-eyed glance caught the priest and Aisling in hushed conversation—nothing untoward, just a caring priest and a grieving woman.

His understated cough alerted them to his presence.
"Ready when you are, Mrs. Maxwell."

Aisling's nervous cough perplexed him. "Thank you, Inspector." As she broke away, she muttered something inaudible

CHAPTER 50

Breakdown

The house had grown quiet—too
quiet. The murmurs of the mourners had faded; the last car door
slammed shut an hour ago.

The half-drunk cups of tea sat cold. The tray of sandwiches,
untouched now, mushy at the edges.

O'Kane stood near the curtained window, jacket off, sleeves
rolled up, watching dusk settle over the garden.
Behind him, Aisling cleared a

plate for the third time—placed it on the table, then lifted
it again. Her fingers trembled.

"Those lilies... the ones from the hospital..." she said,
voice barely above a whisper. "They were beautiful, weren't
they?"

O'Kane nodded, though she wasn't looking at him. She was
staring past the flowers, past the clock, into some grey, vacant
distance. Her hand hovered overa teacup, then dropped to her
side.

"I should thank Mrs. Williams for the tray," she said.
"And... someone said the neighbors pooled for the wreath.
Wasn't that kind?"

He opened his mouth to agree—but her shoulders gave a
sudden shift. It was slight. Just a breath caught in the wrong place.
Then she folded.

A plate clattered to the floor, rolled on its rim before settling.

Aisling slumped into his arms—like a puppet doll whose strings had been cut. Her face buried in his chest, her sobs escaping in gagging bursts. He staggered slightly at first— caught off guard— then steadied her, his arms folding around her instinctively.

"It's alright, it's alright," he whispered, though he knew it wasn't.

Her anguish came unabated—a low, guttural sound in his ear. Her fingers locked around his—vice-like. Her forehead pressed against his shoulder. The scent of her hair, warm and haunting, filled his lungs.

He held her—tenderly at first, tenderly then tighter as her whole body convulsed in sorrow. His hands moved without thinking, one cradled her lower back, the other pressed gently to the nape of her neck. She clung to him like grim death.

And something inside him cracked. A feeling he had buried deep surged up like floodwater. He closed his eyes. God forgive me for even thinking it.

Her breath was hot on his neck. He felt her heart—frantic, thudding against his ribs. His collar felt like a noose. A warm ache curled in his gut—guilt and yearning woven so tightly he couldn't separate one from the other.
She lifted her face, eyes red-rimmed and raw.

"I don't know how I'll go on, Liam," she whispered. "I don't know why I feel so guilty —will God forgive me?" He blinked. Her body was so warm against his. The room seemed to tilt. He gulped for air, his head swirling.

"Aisling," he said, his voice steadier than he felt, "of course,
He will. Of course. You loved him—in your way. It's natural to
feel," —He searched for words—conflicted.
She nodded slowly, eyes cast downward, lashes wet.

He reached for her hand, gave it a light squeeze. Not too
much. Just enough.

"Time will calm you," he said. "And I'll be here… as long as
you need."
The words lingered in the space between them—tender, true— but
shaded with a truth they both felt and couldn't name.
Forbidden.
And in his heart, he knew: Not like this. Not for long.

Another wave came. She shook in his grasp—not ladylike
weeping but broken, childlike sobs that came from some place
deeper than words. Her grief gushed out, and he stood firm
beneath the surge, letting her unravel.

"It's alright… let it out," he said sympathetically, his hand
resting between her shoulder blades. But even as he held her,
something stirred in him—a warmth, a yearning, a memory of
longing.

No. Not now. Not ever.
He shut it down like closing a insubordinate door. His grip shifted,
becoming less a hold, more an anchor. He took a breath—deep,
grounding. Then, gently, he eased her back just enough to see her
face.

"Aisling," he said, calm and low, "I know this is too much right now. But you don't have to carry it all alone. I'll help in whatever way I can. That's a promise."
She blinked at him, her cheeks tear-streaked and weary.

"I feel so lost," she whispered. "And guilty. Will God forgive me?"
He reached for a handkerchief and gently placed it in her hand. "Yes," he said. "He will. He sees the whole of you—your grief, your doubts, your love. He understands more than we ever will."

She gave the slightest nod, clinging to his words as if they were a lifeline.

"Sit down," he said quietly, guiding her to the sofa. "Let's slow everything down. Just for now."
He poured a glass of water and pressed it into her hand. He sat beside her—not touching, just near. He took a deep controlled breath.

No longer the man wrestling with temptation—now, just the priest she needed.

She sipped, breath wheezing less with each passing moment. And slowly, the storm inside her began to settle.

O'Kane stood to go, his stomach still tight. Aisling's outburst soothed, the handkerchief dabbing the corner of her eyes.

"You saw her, didn't you?" The question trapped O'Kane— one arm already in his jacket. He slowly shrugged into it, each movement deliberate, buying precious seconds before answering. "Yes, I saw her, Aisling. I'm sure it was something harmless." The silence screamed for answers. O'Kane shuffled his feet.

There was nothing right to say.

"I should be going," his hand already clutching his umbrella. His words unheeded, Aisling's expressionless eyes drifted aimlessly.

"I used to hate when he was away at night. The silence… it was like the walls leaned in." She paused, glancing at O'Kane's back.

"But now, it's worse. The silence feels final." O'Kane's grip tightened on his coat.

"You're not alone, Aisling. You're not alone, while I'm here." The words of comfort lingered dubiously in the air.

Aisling turned, her hand touching his shoulder. Her voice barely above a whisper, "Sometimes I wish…"
He turned, meeting her gaze. A long pause. Her breath caught. She looked away. O'Kane's head reeled. "You need to
rest. I should go."
Aisling's face flushed, stuttered tenderly to his back, "Liam… thank you. I'm sorry."

He paused at the door, turned slightly—flustered. "I'll always be here for you, if I can."

He hesitated a moment longer. "If you ever need anything, anything at all, the parish is here for you. I am here." Aisling stared. O'Kane opened his mouth to speak—stopped.

She clutched his hand again—brief, desperate—and for a moment, O'Kane felt both the mercy and the cruelty of fate.
He left quietly, closing the door quietly behind him.

Aisling stood alone in the soft light, the unspoken words still hanging in the room.

CHAPTER 51

The Letter Unsent

O'Kane's unrelenting anguish continued unabated. His nights were haunted by the phantom feel of her in his arms. His days were tormented by the scent of her hair, the warmth of her grief—and he hated himself for it. At the altar, during Mass, her face appeared in his mind. He paced in his room, fingering beads, his thoughts in bedlam. His body and soul pulled in opposite directions.

The rain had eased as O'Kane finished his supper. His jaw, for now, was stress-free as he walked to the nearby church. The hushed stillness of the empty nave was filled with a sense of reflective peace, punctuated only by the fading light filtering through the stained-glass windows. The prayers did not come easily—he listened instead. Finally, he rose from his knees, a quiet resolve settling on his features. As he exhaled slowly, the tension in his shoulders began to ease. He headed back to the rectory; the smell of wet grass felt comforting.

A single lamp cast a warm pool of light on the desk; the incessant drumming of his fingers finally rested. His thoughts— at last—found shape. O'Kane sat, his jacket hung on the back of the chair, his collar on the desk, pen in hand. He paused, then wrote— slow, deliberate strokes—a long delay between each line. The clock ticked, building suspense for what was to come. The parish outside slept. As he finished the final line, he set the pen down. His eyes lingered on the letter, the name *Aisling* carefully written. He read it once more, lips moving silently.

He folded it slowly, precisely, as if performing a ceremony. Then—a long pause. He rubbed his thumb along the crease of the letter, pondering its contents. He sat in silence—brooding. Finally, he reached for a matchbox. The letter trembled slightly between his fingers as the flame inched close to the edge of the paper. He hesitated. The match burned too low—he dropped it, extinguishing it under his shoe.

"No. Not like this," he whispered aloud.

With shaking hands, he slipped the letter into a worn, leatherbound prayer book. He closed the drawer, knowing that Aisling would never receive it.

CHAPTER 52

Aisling's Farewell

The house, once a warm companion, had become a stranger—leaving only a frigid, hollow shudder behind.

O'Kane's sudden departure had left a stillness, as if something sacred had quietly wandered away. The loss felt sharper—more immediate. The tea mug he used was still sitting in the back of the cupboard, and for some reason, she didn't move it. She was startled. Hurt, perhaps. But mostly, she was left wondering: *Was it too much for him, too?*

There was the armchair in the corner—where he once sat, hands folded, listening to her stumble through her grief. It was silly, she told herself, but she avoided sitting there. After all, he barely— never really—said goodbye. Perhaps he couldn't.

She never did get a goodbye. Not a word. Not a note. It hurt—why should it?

Just the news, passed on in a murmured aside at the back of the church: transferred back to Ireland—a small parish somewhere west. Or was it Derry or Belfast? There were rumors. Strange there was no statement, no farewell party. The shock was brief, replaced quickly by a dull ache she didn't know how to name. She told herself it was unexpected, nothing more.

Still, for days after, she caught herself listening for his knock. Sensing his presence.

She still attended Mass, but it felt different now. No qualms of conscience. No trace of the man who once looked up and caught her eye, only to look away too quickly. The man whose hold she found so comforting and shamefully satisfying.

She found herself looking for his face during Sunday Mass, even weeks later. Her eyes drifted up to the altar as if longing might summon him. But it was the new curate now. He was kind— younger—but he read his homilies like a weather forecast— too cultured, too aloof. And when the choir began their final hymn, she felt the absence like the loss of the child she never had.

She resumed her routines—work, parish charities, groceries, tea with neighbors. But something was different— empty. It wasn't heartbreak, not exactly. More like the abrupt closing of an unfinished act of a play where she played a part.

The real surprise was how rarely Maxwell entered her thoughts. He came in flashes. Few happy memories. She opened the wardrobe one evening. The scent of his cologne still lingered. She took out a suit coat, folded it, then stopped. Stared for a moment—nothing. She placed it back—forgetting why.

Eventually, she brought a few things to the church charity shop, but not all. Not his police dress uniform—he never did wear it. An off-hand rummage through the chest of drawers on his side of the bed—socks, underwear, cigarette lighter—all assigned to the bin.

In the bottom drawer was an old answering machine. Aisling's hand trembled as she reached for it. She had to listen. It was his voice—nothing significant—maybe code. The voice was neutral—no feeling—no emotion or weight behind it. Aisling listened again. No surge of grief. No tears. No guilt, either. Her face was deadpan. She turned it off. The drawer screeched as she stretched to close it. A stark black piece of paper caught her eye— a photo from Brighton. A deep sigh— she framed it but placed it in the hallway, not the bedroom.

Every Monday, Marie Williams came by with biscuits and small talk. They sat at the table and talked about anything but Maxwell. Then, too suddenly, for no apparent reason, Marie said, "Have you thought of selling?"

Aisling hesitated. "Sometimes," she answered thoughtfully. Then an afterthought: "But I'd miss the garden."

Marie nodded in agreement. "You always keep it beautiful."

Later that night, Aisling stood at the back window, staring at the flowerbeds. Everything was overgrown now. She pondered Marie Williams's words. *"Have you thought of selling?" I wonder why she never mentions Fr. O'Kane.*

It wasn't a solution that needed an answer; the idea came in the quiet reflections of a morning cup of tea as Aisling looked out at gray rain. She recalled her mother's whitewashed cottage in Mayo, the open hearth, and the warm welcome. She reminisced about the hills and the lakes.

The decision came like a spring sunrise—clear, bright. Just... right. It was time.

The for-sale sign went up one Monday morning. From the window, Aisling saw the man drive the stake into the damp earth, the hammer's crack inviting a new owner. The new owner came faster than Aisling thought. The "Sold" sign announced a new era—a new beginning.

Time to pack. Her mind flashed back to the morning after Brighton. Where to start? Upstairs—two bedrooms empty— never used.

She returned to the half-packed boxes of books, but the house already felt strange, as if the sign outside stated closure.

CHAPTER 53

Homecoming

Aisling stood in the doorway, suitcase in hand. The house was nearly bare now—walls stripped; rooms hollow with silence. The laughter, the fights, the long silences, the late nights. The dinners, O'Kane's visits—all reduced to echoes.

She took a final breath inside and stepped out. No backward glance. The new owners would arrive tomorrow. Let them fill it with their own noise. Wish them luck.

She lovingly held a single framed photo. Not of Maxwell. It was of her—sun-drenched, windblown hair, smiling on a cliff path somewhere in the West of Ireland. Long ago. Before London. Before everything.

She locked the door. Walked away. Not toward answers. Toward herself.

Liam—Fr. O'Kane's quiet departure clung to her like an unfinished statement. No goodbye. No explanation. Just want.

Maxwell's death—once unimaginable—now felt like a chapter closed long before the final page. She searched herself for grief and found only a dull ache, part guilt, part relief. And yet, rising above it all, was something steadier—a calm anticipation.

Twenty years. That's how long it had been since she'd seen the green fields of Mayo.

Aisling sat, knuckles white, as the plane took off from Heathrow. The flight was short, but her restless mind wouldn't settle. Her tense jaw relaxed once the plane reached cruising height.

She rummaged through her handbag; her fingers found a crumpled note at the bottom—Declan's scrawled handwriting.
She read it for the third time.

"You'll take a taxi from Dublin Airport to Heuston Station—take the Galway train and transfer at Galway to reach Claremorris. I'll be there to meet you in the new car."

Outside the train window, Dublin's sprawl gave way to fields, stone walls, and winding country lanes. The soft greens of home.

She transferred at Galway without thinking much—her body moved, but her heart was still catching up. The train meandered west, cutting through misty green hills.

Aisling sat alone at a window seat, watching the landscape blur past as Galway's coastal sprawl gave way to quilt-patch fields, mosaic stone walls, bogland, and distant lakes—Lough Corrib, then Lough Mask—framed by misty hills and scattered cottages. The land grew quieter, greener, as the train neared Claremorris. Her reflection in the window—another face, Liam's—flickered for a moment and was gone.

Beside her, a worn leather-bound book—not hers, but a gift from her mother, tucked away years ago. She opened it absentmindedly; a pressed wildflower fell out. She smiled at the memory. By the time the train pulled into Claremorris, a quiet certainty had settled in her chest.

The rumble of the engine, the screech of the brakes as it slowed down—a welcome home to Aisling's happy ears. She wasn't returning to the past. She was going back to where she had begun.

Aisling's breath caught—a warmth spread through her when she saw Declan standing alone on the platform, his tie askew. He never did learn to tie a knot. A wave of affection washed over her—a feeling that instinctively made her want to reach out and hug him. Her hand moved, but she slipped it into her pocket for a handkerchief instead. A small smile of understanding—the unspoken affection that had always flowed between them— passed between them.

"You cut yourself?" she asked.

A rough finger went instinctively to the sticking plaster on his chin. "Ah, new blade. Happens every bloody time."

"How's Mother?"

"You know Ma. She's grand—she's grand." The suitcase looked smaller in his hand.

In the distance, the sun dipped behind the hills—Mayo— the future open, the past no longer chasing her. Somewhere, not far across the hills, a church bell tolled. But for now, Aisling heard only the wind and the soft rhythm of the tires.   Who knows what lies ahead.

CHAPTER 54

O'Kane in Belfast

Belfast still wore its wounds openly. Whole streets bore the marks of old blasts—scorched brick, mismatched patches where new stone met old. Some buildings stood wrapped in scaffolding; others were gone entirely, replaced by gravel lots behind chain-linked fences, waiting for resurrection.

O'Kane moved through the drabness anonymously, collar turned up against a persistent drizzle. Saint Patrick's parish, on the city's edge, was smaller than his last but busy in its own way— weddings, baptisms, funerals, a steady stream of confessions. Life pushed forward, even among the disturbances.

In the evenings, he walked past the center, where rebuilt shopfronts sat shoulder-to-shoulder with boarded-up remnants, the smell of chip vans mixing with the cold river air. He told himself he was settling in—and in some ways, he was.

But some wants travel with you.

Aisling's face surfaced unbidden: in a bus-stop reflection, in a shop-window flicker, in the turn of a young woman's hair. He had left without a word, without a goodbye—the only choice he could live with—yet it had cost him more than he expected. Did Aisling notice? Did she care?

When the parish priest suggested he take on hospital chaplain duties alongside parish work, O'Kane agreed. More work meant less room for thought.

The rain had eased to a mist by the time he reached the hospital gates. Umbrella open, pace measured—not slow, not hurried—as if speed might alter what waited inside. Today would not be the last visit; he sensed that already.

Crossing the parking lot, he caught himself thinking back to his first trip six months earlier, when the ward was still unfamiliar and Gallagher was only a name on a clipboard. The disinfectant smell clung to the corridor air above the faint clang of a tea trolley. He had signed in at the chaplain's desk, still learning the nurses' names.

Nurse McCracken greeted him with her usual easy warmth.

"Father, there's a new patient in room six—Mr. Gallagher. Poor man's having a rough time." Her eyes had crinkled at the corners. "Quite a character when he's alert." The name stopped him mid-step.

"Gallagher?" he repeated, as if shaping a half-forgotten word.

"Aye," she said, glancing at her chart. "He's in and out some days. Headaches, disorientation. Might not remember you've been in at all. Best keep it light."

He followed her down the corridor, each step heavier than the last, until she pushed open the door. Gallagher lay propped in bed, soup cooling on the tray.

"It's Liam—Liam O'Kane," he said quietly.

Gallagher blinked. "O'Kane? Don't know an O'Kane."

Nurse McCracken gave him that look that said don't press, then slipped out, leaving the two men alone.

Even now, the memory of that first meeting settled on O'Kane's shoulders like a weight. He had stayed by the bed, unsure

whether it was Gallagher's forgetfulness, the emaciated face, or the ghosts the name had stirred that unsettled him most.

CHAPTER 55

Last Confession

The ward had settled into its night noises: distant wheels moaning, a cough swallowed behind a curtain, the soft prolonged beep of a monitor. O'Kane paused at the door of room six, fingers worrying the knot of the purple stole in his pocket.

Nurse McCracken looked up from the chart. "He's been in and out all evening," she whispered. "Sharper now than he was at supper." A small smile. "He asked for you by name, Father. Then he asked who you were. So… both."

O'Kane nodded and stepped towards the bed and whispered, "I'll be careful."

She squeezed Gallagher's wrist, gently.

"You've a visitor, Mr. Gallagher."

Gallagher lay on his side, jaw rough with grey stubble, eyes half-closed. The harsh white of the pillow made the hollows of his face deeper, like a hill after the wind has stripped it bare. His right hand searched blindly across the blanket, found the bedrail, held it for security.

McCracken patted the chart closed and slipped out. The door shut with a murmur.

O'Kane leaned in at the bedside. "How're you feeling?"

Gallagher shifted, wheezing. "Like there's a bloody Orangeman drumming in my head and he's no rhythm." Gallagher leaned forward to ease the labored breathing. "You've the look of a man about to announce a second collection." He chuckled hoarsely.

O'Kane placed his hand on Gallagher's shoulder, sighed, a long, weary whimper. "I came to keep a promise."

"Ah." A quizzical smile flickered. "A promise?" he questioned.

O'Kane dragged a chair closer and sat. He rested his hands on his knees to keep them from fidgeting. "Do you remember it? The fight in the schoolyard. Maxwell picking on me and you stepping in?"

"You stepped between us. You told him to leave me alone or you'd… what was it?"

"Break his nose with the hand of peace."

Gallagher chuckled, a strained rattling laugh, then winced at the ache. "It's coming back through the fog—very poetic, wasn't I?" "Brother O'Connor gave me a week of extra homework and a clap on the back for that one."

"You saved me." O'Kane's voice steady, skilful, but something raw sat just under it. "I owed you then. I owe you now."

"You don't owe me a damn thing," Gallagher murmured, gasping for breath. "I wasn't protectin' your soul. I was protectin' any wee fella. I always did that. Ah. It made me feel bigger standing in front of trouble."

The silence clung between them—stopped for a breath, then not.

O'Kane pulled his scratching chair closer. "I brought you something." He sat a rosary on the blanket. The beads, brown and plain, worn smooth. O'Kane ignored the priest, but his hand moved to finger the beads.

"Still wear the collar?" O'Kane took no offence.

"It fits, most days."

Gallagher's throat struggled. "You came to ask if I'm sorry."

"I came to sit with you," O'Kane said. "And… yes. If

there's a door you'd like to open, I can help."

"Doors," Gallagher coughed, trying to laugh. "Some open, some shut. Some are bricked up and painted to look like they never were." He rubbed his forehead with two fingers, as if the words were trapped there. "I lost it, you know." Eyes blurred. "The faith—it slid out of my clutch. One day I was holdin' it like a lifeline—the next." A deep sigh. "The rope… the rope just slipped through my fingers, no matter how tight I try to hold on."

Thoughts wandered too long—forgotten times, a memory so distant he could no longer place the year. He closed his eyes, inhaling and exhaling slowly through his nose, a well-practiced routine to steady himself against the surge of regret.

Was it the day he placed a bomb beneath a young soldier's car? He could still clearly see the young man emerge, his little daughter laughing on his shoulders. The deep thunderous boom— the dark cloud of dust and debris filling the air. It was an image that haunted his sleep. Maybe the day he heard a confession in a safe house. He stopped himself—smiled wryly. "No, not a confession.
An admission. We all had our lists. Names to blame in case the walls listened."

O'Kane leaned forward. "I did Maxwell's funeral," he said, the words careful. "You should know that. It was simple. There was rain. There were flowers. A woman in a black veil stood at the back and never came forward."

Gallagher's jaw tightened. He swallowed. "I wondered." "Was it a dream?" "Did you say that before?"

"I say this not to needle you," O'Kane added. "Only to say I stood there, and I thought of the schoolyard, and I thought: if we'd all turned left instead of right—" He let it trail off.

Gallagher's eyes closed. "Left or right, the road still ran through Derry." He opened them. "You buried him? I shot him."

"Did you know that? Do you hate me for it?"

"No." O'Kane's anguished voice whispered.

Aisling's questioning face flashed on the white wall— only visible to O'Kane, God forgive me.

"Do you forgive me?" two voices in unison.

From the silence O'Kane answered. "I'm not the one you need forgiveness from."

Gallagher nodded in expectation. He grasped the rosary and released it like it burned; his fingers restless—bony. "I did some bad things, Liam. I thought the good might cancel out the bad. That's how arithmetic works in dreams."

O'Kane's head bowed low—an agonized mutter.

"You kept men alive. And others died."

"Others died." Gallagher's stare drifted to the rosary again. "What would you have me say?"

"The truth," O'Kane said. "Whatever it is."

"The truth." Gallagher's lips quivered. "I wanted to hurt the ones who hurt us, the poor people. I wanted to feel stronger than the boot on my neck. I wanted… I wanted to be the boy forever, stepping in. As if I could fix the whole world by raising my hand." He crumpled—exhausted. "And sometimes I enjoyed   the fear in their eyes. There. I said it."

O'Kane didn't flinch. "Thank you."

"Is that how confession works now? I say the ugly part, and you say thank you?"

"It's a start."

"Faith without the dressing, you mean."

"Truth without the dressing." The words ping-ponged.

Gallagher considered that. The drummer in his skull seemed to tire; his face eased a fraction. "And you?" he said, suddenly. "You, with your collar too tight. What ugly part do you say?"

O'Kane took a breath and let it out slow. The room waited. "That I have been a coward in softer ways," he muttered. "That I held my tongue when I should have spoken out. That I clung to the safety of a parish bulletin when a friend needed—" he stopped, corrected himself, "when a city needed a spine."

"You were never a coward," Gallagher mumbled, more gently.

"I have loved things I could not have," O'Kane said, flat. "And I let the shape of that love govern me more than the shape of God. That's ugly enough."

Gallagher studied him. Something like pity passed over his face—gone like a fleeting shadow. "We're a fine pair," he smirked. "The bully's shield and the schoolboy priest, both with hands we're ashamed to show."

His breathing hitched, a sudden unfamiliar weight pressing in his chest. A gooey lump formed in his throat, thick as clay. He desperately gulped. He shook uncontrollably.

He turned his head to ride it out. O'Kane steadied the water cup; Gallagher sipped, grimaced, and fell back.

"Listen," O'Kane said delicately. "All my life I've said words for other men. I believe they're more than words. I believe grace is not a treat for the good, it's a rope thrown into dark water. You don't have to swim. You just have to grab."

Gallagher's eyes glistened, though his face didn't change much. "And if my hands won't close?" "I'll hold on with you." Somewhere down the hall a TV blared—then quiet.

"Do you want the prayers?" O'Kane asked. "Not because I am pushing. Because I'm here."

Gallagher was silent long enough that O'Kane thought the words had been repelled. Then Gallagher nodded once—a gasp.

"I don't know if I can mean them."

"Meaning grows in the saying sometimes," O'Kane said.

"Like a tune you don't remember until your ear finds it." Gallagher's laugh was a sickly gasp. "You always did have the words."

"I have a few," O'Kane said. "Not enough. But a few."

He took Gallagher's hand. The fingers cold, the gnarled knuckles protruding. He began quietly; his voice lowered to a whisper. "It's something. Let us try together."

"Do your part then," Gallagher told him through labored breathing. "You always did your part."

O'Kane leaned forward; his voice dropped lower, familiar words threaded with plain speech.

"God, who knows this man from boyhood, who saw him stand in yards and alleys and rooms with no windows—" His voice caught, and he steadied it. "—have mercy on what's tainted in him and bless what was brave. For all he has done and failed to do, for all he loved and broke, be a Father to him now."

Gallagher watched him, eyes heavy—not blinking.

"If you are sorry even a sliver," O'Kane said, "if you wish you had done less harm, if you wish you had held back your hand sometimes, if you wish you had knelt before something better—
God is not small. He can work with that."

Gallagher's mouth twitched. "A sliver," he said. "A thin, calloused sliver."

"It's enough."

O'Kane marked the sign of the cross slowly on his

iend's forehead.

"Through the ministry of the Church," he whispered, and by the grace given me, I absolve you…" He finished the prayer in a low voice, each word careful, as if preparing a way across a river.

When it was done, neither of them spoke. Silence filled the room. The radiator ticked.

Gallagher looked at the rosary again. "Don't leave that," he said.

"It's yours."

Gallagher shook his head in refusal. "You'll need a new one for your rounds."

"I'll manage." O'Kane smiled, small.

O'Kane stood, stretched his back, and then sat again. Neither man wanted the visit to end.

"You know," Gallagher said, voice distant now, "when I shoved Maxwell against the wall that day, I thought: if I did that right, you would learn to fight back. That was the plan. That was the whole grand plan." He turned his head on the pillow to face O'Kane fully, eyes vacant. "You didn't learn it, did you?"

O'Kane held his gaze. "Some days I learned it," he admitted. "Today? —maybe a little."

"Good," Gallagher smiled. His eyes glistening, not from pain. "Then maybe it wasn't all wasted."

His face tired, he fell back. O'Kane reached and adjusted the blanket, tucked it under an elbow the way a mother might. He felt foolish doing it and did it anyway.

"Will you come tomorrow?" Gallagher asked, eyes half- lidded. Maybe I'll confess tomorrow." "I'll come," O'Kane said. "Tell me a story then," Gallagher whispered, already drifting. "About the time we dropped the chalice and Father Connolly said we'd shake hands with the devil before we'd shake with him again."   "You dropped it," O'Kane said, a smile audible.

"Details," Gallagher breathed heavily.

O'Kane watched him a moment longer. He placed two fingers on the rosary and pressed it into the fold of Gallagher's palm. Gallagher bowed his head in acceptance. No words now. Just breath. The heavy emotional burden lifted, he drifted into a peaceful sleep.

O'Kane rose noiselessly, leaned in to make the sign of the cross on his friend's forehead, and slipped quietly from the room.

CHAPTER 56

Go in Peace

Within an hour, O'Kane was back. Night drew the ward in close: a lift chimed far off, the soft tick of the clock marking time that no one could bargain with. O'Kane removed a folded stole from his pocket. Gallagher lay on his side, eyes thin, mouth set, the jaw he used to brace for fights now braced against pain. He saw the collar and tried a smile that didn't last.

"Save your breath, Liam," he wheezed. "Keep the tricks for the willing."

"I brought no tricks," O'Kane answered, taking the chair and angling it so Gallagher wouldn't have to turn. "Only what we used to know."

"What we used to know," Gallagher echoed, and let his gaze slide to the window's black glass. "We were boys. We didn't know anything."

"We knew some things." O'Kane kept his hands in sight, resting on the blanket's edge. "Like where the cruets lived and how to keep the bells from clattering."

Gallagher's mouth twitched in a half-smile. "You were heavyhanded with the bells."

"You were always trying to ring them early," O'Kane said, and waited for the answer that didn't come. He tried again. "I can hear your confession if you like."

Gallagher raised his hands in self-protection. "Don't start again," he muttered. "I'll not be dying on your terms."   "Then not on mine," O'Kane said quietly. "On yours."

A silence settled. Gallagher's breathing struggled. The clock ticked on—relentless. O'Kane looked down at his hands and, without lifting his eyes, said it as if he were speaking into an echo:

"*Introibo ad altare Dei…*"

Gallagher's lids flickered. A seam opened in the stubbornness.

The reply arrived, hoarse but steady from somewhere unexplained:

"*Ad Deum qui laetificat juventutem meam.*"

They both breathed, surprised by the sound it made as it ricocheted through the room. For a few heartbeats, they were two boys again, thoughts gliding through the years.

The next few minutes were spent discussing Gallagher's health, and gradually O'Kane piloted the conversation back toward redemption. "You remember that you were the one who convinced me that I should become an altar boy?"

It was a fact that Gallagher was an altar boy when they first became acquainted, and he had urged O'Kane to join him. The conversation was a welcome distraction for Gallagher as they recalled the various comical incidents that happened. But when the priest broached the subject of confession, Gallagher recoiled and complained of fatigue. The conversation came to an end, but O'Kane asserted that he should return within a few days. Gallagher had become too weak to resist; besides, he was glad for any display of warmth or friendship.

O'Kane touched the stole, then let it lie across his knee. He took Gallagher one step further, careful as a man leading someone across slick crossing stones. "*Confiteor Deo omnipotenti…*"

Gallagher stared at the ceiling, as if searching for the words that were written there—faint. His lips shaped the old rhythm, returning like a river through a ditch. "*…et vobis, fratres…*" His voice thinned; he paused, sucking breath. His right hand lifted, two inches off the sheet, and tapped his chest once, then again, a third time—weak strikes—

"*…mea culpa—mea maxima…*"

The last word tattered. He swallowed, jaw tight, eyes shining with something that could have been pain or could have been memory.

O'Kane leaned in. "Brendan," he said, not a priest now but the boy who once held the communion plate while the other rang the bells, "are you sorry before God for what ought not to have been done?"

Gallagher blinked slowly. The monitor kept up its small rhythm. He looked at O'Kane, and for a moment all the conviction of a cause and code and hardened explanations wasn't there; only faces—those he had shielded, those he had sent away forever.

"I'm—" He stopped. A deep swallow. "I'm tired of carrying them," he said. "The faces. All of them." He shut his eyes. "If that's not the word you want, it's the only one I have."

O'Kane let the air out of his lungs as if setting down a weight. He slid the stole over his shoulders and straightened it with a fingertip. "I think God will read it as the right word." He placed his hand lightly on Gallagher's forehead, another over the back of his hand. A long inhale. He murmured the words of absolution, his voice low and steady. His hands trembling in excitement, he took the oil and anointed the brow and the hands with small crosses, the scent rising clean and sharp above disinfectant.

"Through this holy anointing," he murmured, "may the Lord in his love and mercy help you with the grace of the Holy Spirit."

Gallagher's fingers tightened around his once, the last of the old grip surfacing, then fading.

"And by the authority which the Apostolic See has given," O'Kane whispered, head bowed, cheeks wet, "I grant you a full forgiveness and the remission of all your sins." He paused, the words still hanging between them— a final nod of agreement.

"Go in peace."

The room held its breath. The silence stretched, taut and charged. Rain streaked the window, then stopped. Somewhere a bell rang.

Gallagher opened his eyes. "We used to race the bells," he whispered, his breathing light and fading.

"You always won," O'Kane said.

"That was because you let me," Gallagher sucked for air, and a ghost of a grin crossed his mouth. It faded. "Will they… stop coming?"

"Maybe not," O'Kane said. He didn't offer a lie. "But maybe they'll come different."

Gallagher turned his head a fraction, measuring the truth of that. His gaze dipped, found O'Kane's face once more, and stayed there. A breath in. A breath out. The lines of his hand loosened under O'Kane's palm.

When the nurse checked in, O'Kane raised a finger without looking away. She nodded and closed them back into quiet.

He prayed the prayers for the dying in a voice barely above the clock's tick: a word for mercy, a word for rest, a word for the boy who once stepped between another boy, and a word for the other boy. When the prayers were finished, he didn't move. He watched until the breaths grew shallow and were gone into a shape that was almost sleep.

Only when the monitor ceased its beep did he lift his hand. He made a small cross on Gallagher's forehead with a thumb that trembled, then slowly folded the stole and slid it into his pocket.

In the corridor, the world resumed. Footsteps, a trolley wheel groaned to a stop, the smell of coffee that had been left too long on a hot plate. O'Kane stood a moment, listening to ordinary life carry on past the open door—an end of an era.

Had Gallagher confessed? The words were there; a child's answers pulled om somewhere deep. The strikes to the breast. The faces. The *mea culpas*. Was at contrition or only the liturgy speaking through tired bones? He had given hat he could give.

e had believed as far as he dared, and then a step further.

He turned down the corridor, and Aisling rose in his mind— not as she as at the graveside, not as she folded herself into his arms and shook, but at a tchen window in Mayo, early light on her hair, hands on a mug she didn't ink from. The letter lay where he'd left it, in the cracked spine of his eviary— unopened. He knew he would burn it—soon. He also knew he ould think of her when he struck the match.

He walked on, in the rain

www.ingramcontent.com/pod-product-compliance
Lightning Source LLC
Chambersburg PA
CBHW061422150726

47987CB00001B/66